ZANE PR

A NOVEL

THE SECRETS *of* SILK

Dear Reader:

All I can say is wow… I've already said that Allison Hobbs is "the only one on the planet freakier than me." Well, the prolific author, known for her over-the-top erotica, has outdone herself with her twenty-fourth novel, *Secrets of Silk.*

This time she spins a tale in the 1960s about Silk Moreaux, a woman who throws no punches and whose best friend is a switchblade. Raised by Big Mama, a voodoo queen in the backwoods of Louisiana, Silk ventures away to the city of Chester, Pennsylvania where she continues to attract men at every turn. They fall for her Creole looks and Southern "charm," providing her whatever she seeks.

Find out what happens when she lures Richard "Buddy" Dixon, a recent widower and father, and moves into the family household. Chester will never be the same once this vixen follows her wretched path of evil and deception.

I appreciate the love and support shown to Strebor Books, myself, and our efforts to bring you cutting-edge stories.

Blessings,

Zane

Publisher
Strebor Books
www.simonandschuster.com

ZANE PRESENTS

ALLISON HOBBS

A NOVEL

THE SECRETS *of* SILK

SBI

STREBOR BOOKS

NEW YORK LONDON TORONTO SYDNEY

Strebor Books
P.O. Box 6505
Largo, MD 20792
http://www.streborbooks.com

This book is a work of fiction. Names, characters, places and incidents are
products of the author's imagination or are used fictitiously. Any resemblance
to actual events or locales or persons, living or dead, is entirely coincidental.

© 2014 by Allison Hobbs

All rights reserved. No part of this book may be reproduced in any form or by
any means whatsoever. For information address Strebor Books, P.O. Box 6505,
Largo, MD 20792.

ISBN 978-1-59309-576-5
ISBN 978-1-4767-5910-4 (ebook)
LCCN 2014935326

First Strebor Books trade paperback edition October 2014

Cover design: www.mariondesigns.com
Cover photograph: © Keith Saunders/Keith Saunders Photos

10 9 8 7 6 5 4 3 2 1

Manufactured in the United States of America

For information regarding special discounts for bulk purchases,
please contact Simon & Schuster Special Sales at 1-866-506-1949
or business@simonandschuster.com

The Simon & Schuster Speakers Bureau can bring authors to your live event.
For more information or to book an event, contact the Simon & Schuster Speakers
Bureau at 1-866-248-3049 or visit our website at www.simonspeakers.com.

FOR STEPHANIE S. FITCHETTE
My Favorite Cousin
Marathon conversations. So much love and laughter.
It's wonderful beyond words.

ACKNOWLEDGMENTS

What would I do without the support of my loyal readers? There's not enough space to list everyone who has touched my heart in a special way, but I'll do my best to get to all of you eventually. Special thanks to: Ivella Dennis, Darlene Mai Roberts, Letitia Evans, Brady Townes Ingram, Morgin Mansfield, Keisha Gray-Seltz, Detina Watts, Sonya Lee, Chevy Johnson, Sharon Bandy, Natasha Potts, Carnetha Leech, Tara Goodman-Baruwa, Shannon SG Gregory, Sharney Batts-Thomas, Gary Shumlai, and special thanks to the Juice Lovas Review.

I also want to acknowledge my fellow authors whose friendships over the years have meant the world to me. Thank you to my sexy boo, Erotica author, Cairo, and to my baby girl, the Drama Queen, Daaimah S. Poole.

God Bless the day I met Charmaine Parker and Zane. Saying thank you will never be enough.

Deb Schuler, I'm convinced that you're a saint. Thank you for your kindness and all the fast turnarounds.

Karen Dempsey Hammond, what can I say except you can't choose your family but sure can choose your friends, and I'm so freakin' lucky that I chose you!

Carlos Bautista, welcome back!

CHAPTER 1

How the infant found its way into the backwoods Louisiana shack of Mattie Moreaux was as much of a mystery as the ingredients in the potions Mattie sold to white folks who lived on the right side of the tracks. Some of the residents of Devil's Swamp said the baby was the unwanted offspring of some hot-to-trot white gal with a penchant for colored boys.

More imaginative gossipers said the child was one of many discarded fetuses that old Mattie had helped desperate women purge from their wombs.

But there was one secret that the townsfolk only dared to whisper. According to legend, when the old voodoo woman put one particular fetus in the ground, as she had with all the others that fertilized her unnaturally bountiful garden, the tiny, dead baby came to life, howling and screaming in fury. And the resurrected baby girl that she named Silk on account of her straight, blue-black hair, had been raising hell ever since.

The Low Moon, a honky-tonk in Devil's Swamp, had seen better days and more illustrious entertainment than was currently available on the weekends. Old-timers enjoyed reminiscing about the time Bessie Smith had put on a bawdy show that raised the roof from eight o'clock Saturday night until it was time for Sunday morning sermon. The glory days of the Low Moon spanned the Depression Era through the early 1950s when Big Mama Thornton charged onto the stage singing her hit record, "Hound Dog," the same song that catapulted Elvis Presley into an international celebrity when he recorded it a few years later.

By 1962, The Low Moon was nothing more than a dilapidated, wood-frame structure that leaned a bit to the right side. The dimly lit, one-room establishment with its uneven, wood-plank floor, littered with cigarette butts, housed an untuned piano as a testament to the days when Fats Waller came through, tinkling the ivories, and had the joint jumping. Nowadays, a dusty, old juke box that was filled with mostly out-of-date music was the only source of entertainment, but that didn't deter the locals from filling the place to the rafters every Friday and Saturday night.

Wearing a low-cut, tight, pink dress and a pair of black, spike heels, Silk Moreaux looked gloriously scandalous as she came wiggling into the honky-tonk around ten o'clock when the place was in full swing. She brusquely pushed past dancing couples as she made her way to the bar.

Pudgy Hales, who was as drunk as a skunk on a combination of beer purchased from the bar and the homemade corn liquor he had stashed inside his seersucker jacket, took the liberty of grabbing Silk by the wrist. "Come on, gal; let's shake a tail feather," he slurred, his eyes bucking as his plump body shook comically from his shoulders down to his feet as he invited Silk to join him in a lewd, fast-moving dance.

The average woman would have rebuffed Pudgy in a more courteous manner, but not Silk. "Keep your filthy fucking hands off me or I'll cut you too short to shit."

Becoming instantly sober, Pudgy backed up, both palms held up in surrender. "I ain't mean no harm, Silk. The way you all dolled-up, I thought you was looking for a good time tonight."

"Not with your fat ass," Silk scoffed, giving Pudgy a searing look of disgust.

As she continued her tantalizing sashay across the bar room, couples that had momentarily paused to observe the fireworks now scrambled to get out of her way. Silk was known to use her switchblade for lesser offenses than being asked to dance, and if she didn't get you first, the all-seeing eyes of her blind-as-a-bat, voodoo mama would locate you no matter how cleverly you hid. If you messed with her baby girl, Mattie would put some roots on you that the most experienced voodoo priestess was hard-pressed to remove.

Only a few months ago, Darcy Nesbit developed severe facial spasms and started walking with a terrible limp after she began spreading the rumor that Silk was carrying on with the husband of one of the white women she delivered Mattie's passion potion to once a month.

At that very moment, there were at least two of Silk's victims inside The Low Moon, women who bore physical evidence of the sharp, slicing stroke of Silk's knife.

Silk sat atop the ripped, plastic seat of the barstool and smiled at the bartender. "I'd like a rum and Coke, please," she said in a honey-laced voice that was guaranteed to earn her free drinks with a generous shot of liquor added to each Dixie cup.

Drink in hand, Silk swiveled around on her stool, crossed her legs and leaned back against the bar. Slowly sipping her strong cocktail, she scanned the room, weighing her options among the men whom she felt were all at her disposal.

The mood in the place changed when the first few beats of a slow song poured from the jukebox. On cue, the space closed up between couples who moments earlier had been frenziedly dancing to a driving upbeat tempo. As if hypnotized, they reached out and clung to each other, their eyes filled with a primal longing. Their bodies were pressed together as they rhythmically dry-humped and grinded. In the midst of this public display of unbridled passion, tight skirts inched upward, while groping male hands palmed and squeezed the plump derriere of their partners.

During these intimate moments at The Low Moon, when the room became muggy with body heat, there was bound to be an unwelcome tap on the male partner's shoulder by a fellow who found himself deprived of a female dance partner, and who desperately wanted to get in on the erotic action. The intrusion was handled in various ways. Some men bowed out gracefully, reluctantly handing over his dance partner and others flat out refused to allow another man to cut in, growling in objection. On rare occasions, a fistfight would break out.

It was unheard of for a female to do the shoulder tapping and cut in on another woman's slow dance.

Warmed by the effects of the alcohol, Silk started off innocently enough, moving sensually to the music while sitting atop the barstool, her black hair swaying back and forth like a satin curtain blowing in the night breeze.

But when she slid off the stool, and sauntered in the direction of her old beau, Duke Durnell, who was thoroughly engaged in a slow grind with Gwen Withers, a hush fell over the room. Silk didn't merely tap Gwen on the shoulder; she gave her a harsh and impatient smack on the back, and when Gwen didn't let go of Duke fast enough, Silk bunched up the fabric of Gwen's yellow blouse into her fist and roughly snatched Gwen out of Duke's tight embrace.

Several expressions crossed Gwen's face: surprise, annoyance, embarrassment, and finally acceptance as she skulked away to join Brenda and Fayette, two lonely wallflowers who sat at a table in the back, sour-faced and bordering on drunk. Gwen flopped down on a wooden chair and without asking permission, she picked up Brenda's drink and guzzled it down.

The record was coming to an end when Duke welcomed Silk into his arms with an inviting smile. Another slow song immediately followed, and Silk and Duke launched into a lustful dance that was so provocative, tongues quickly began wagging.

"Looks like they need the privacy of a rented room," Fayette groused, noticing how Duke's hands freely roamed over Silk's body as he hunched over, kissing and sucking the side of her neck.

"Duke ain't nothing but a fool when it comes to Silk," Brenda added. "She treats him any way she wants and all he does is take it with a big, ol' stupid smile plastered on his face."

"Mmm-hmm," Fayette agreed with her lips twisted to the side. "He could have at least told her to wait for the next record instead of letting her embarrass Gwen in front of everybody."

Gwen nodded in agreement as she finished off Brenda's drink and now reached for Fayette's half-filled cup of gin, hoping to numb the pain of humiliation.

While Silk and Duke were carrying on as if they had the place to themselves, the door burst open and trouble entered in the form of a well-dressed, scowling white man, whose fierce eyes scanned the semi-darkened room. A few people recognized Nathan Lee Willard as a city-slick politician, but since none of the coloreds ventured into the city much, nor did any of them have the legal right to show up at the polls and vote, most had never set eyes on the man.

Figuring an innocent colored man was about to be accused of some petty crime or perceived misconduct, male patrons attempted to make themselves scarce…or even invisible. Bunny Carter kept his face obscured by lowering his head as he studied the repertoire of music in the jukebox, Aaron Joseph made a beeline to the john, and Tad Pritchard scanned the packs of smokes inside the cigarette machine as if considering changing his regular brand. Those who were left without cover, mopped nervous perspiration from their brow and quickly downed stiff drinks.

The shift in atmosphere went unnoticed by Silk and Duke, who were enthralled in their wanton display of passion and lust. The white man stalked across the dusty floor, and yanked Silk by the wrist, pulling her out of Duke's arms. "What the hell do you think you're doing?" he shouted.

"What's it look like," Silk answered, snatching her wrist out of his grasp. She turned back to Duke, but he backed away without uttering a single word, relinquishing her to the white man.

"Come on here, gal. We're gonna talk this thing out in private." Nathan Lee took hold of Silk again. She laughed derisively, stumbling over her high-heels as he jostled her out of the honky-tonk and down the dirt path that led to the small parking area in the rear.

"Get in," he demanded, pointing to his flashy, brand-new Plymouth. Silk got in and slammed the door. Nathan Lee got into the driver's seat, and he too, slammed the door. "I waited under the bridge for two solid hours. What do you have to say for yourself?" he demanded, his face turning red with anger.

"I ain't got nothing to say." Silk examined her fingernails briefly and then turned her head and looked out the window.

"You can't treat me like I'm one of those jiggaboos you got wrapped around your finger."

"And you can't treat me like I'm nothing more than a good-time girl. I'm tired of meeting you under the bridge and by the lake. When are we gonna run away up North like you promised?" Silk had an image of her and Nathan Lee living together in a place like New York or Chicago where interracial couples could cohabitate without anyone batting an eye. In her fantasy, Nathan Lee bought her a shiny Chevrolet like the one his wife had. She daydreamed about him keeping her jewelry box overflowing with trinkets, and providing her with plenty of help around a house that was much too large for her to even consider cleaning.

"We're gonna run away together as soon as I get some things straightened out." Nathan Lee's tone softened as he placed a gentle hand on her shoulder, his fingers meandering upward, caressing the soft hairs at the nape of her neck, and then moving around to the side and lightly stroking.

Silk flinched as his fingers touched bruised skin. With the glint of moonlight shining into the car, Nathan Lee detected the bluish-purple, passion mark that Duke had left on Silk's fair skin. Enraged, he grabbed her by both shoulders and shook her. "How'd you get that love bite on your neck? You been two-timing me, you dirty tramp!" he accused and then slapped her soundly.

Silk laughed tauntingly and offered him her other cheek. "Go ahead and smack me around if that's what it takes to make you feel like a big, strong man. Maybe if you'd hit me enough times in the past, you would've felt virile enough to get your wife knocked up without the help of Big Mama's potions!"

A stunned look appeared on his face. "How you'd know about Dolly's pregnancy?"

"Not much gets past Big Mama's all-seeing eyes. She has a special way of knowing when her remedies take hold."

Nathan Lee reached inside his shirt pocket and pulled out a pack of filter-tipped menthols. He shook one out of the pack and fired it up, using a lighter that was engraved with his initials. "I'm sorry for losing my temper, honey." Looking remorseful, he extended a hand, but Silk leaned out of his reach.

"Now that the missus is carrying your baby, I suppose that puts the brakes on our plans." She waited for him to respond, but he puffed away at his cigarette without speaking. "When were you planning on telling me, Nathan Lee?"

He shrugged.

"Did you change your mind about our big plans?" she persisted.

He looked down guiltily. "No, but we'll have to postpone things for at least nine months."

Silk made a scoffing sound. "That's a mighty long time to wait when I done already been waiting for over a year. What happens after nine months have passed? Oh, let me guess...you're gonna tell me we have to wait for your little crumb-snatcher to start school. And after that, you'll try to keep me on standby, doing nothing but twiddling my thumbs until he finishes college."

"You're exaggerating the circumstances; it's not going to take that long."

"I'm not exaggerating a damn thing. Every word I spoke is the truth, and you know it. What kind of fool do you take me for?" Silk asked bitterly.

"All I'm asking for is a little more patience, sugar plum."

"Don't try to sweet-talk me 'cause I done ran clean out of patience." Silk glanced out the window to keep from having to look at his puppy-dog expression, which enraged her rather than softening her heart.

"I can't leave Dolly high and dry with a new baby on the way. I need some time to figure things out," he said softly as his hand wandered beneath her dress and then lightly caressed her firm thigh. "I miss you, Silk. Let's take a drive over to the lake, and look at the moonlight together."

Silk chortled. "I done lay on my back and watched enough moonlight to last me a lifetime. What I'd like to watch is a picture show or even a little bit of television every once in a while."

"I'd buy you a TV set if your mama had some electricity in that ramshackle hut y'all live in."

"You're a politician; why can't you get some electricity to run through our place?"

"That area's not wired for it."

"And that's one of the reasons why I want to leave this godforsaken town."

"I know, I know," he murmured in a placating tone, while his fingers took more liberties, rubbing on the crotch of her panties.

Silk jerked his hand out from under her dress. "I'm going back inside the honky-tonk and finish having me some fun."

"No, the hell you're not," he said brusquely, roughing her up as she reached for the door handle. "I didn't buy that dress and those snazzy shoes on your feet for you to prance around, enticing a bunch of black bucks." He put a vise-like grip around her forearm and spoke through clenched teeth. "You try to step foot out of this here car and I swear for God, I'll break your neck. Now get your ass in the backseat and take those drawers off. I'm not gonna waste any more time fooling around with your uppity nigger-ass tonight."

"Fuck you, cracker!" Silk looked him dead in the eyes, staring so defiantly, she didn't see the hand coming that flew up and backhanded her hard across the face, splitting her bottom lip.

The metallic taste of blood that filled her mouth sent her into a blind rage. But she didn't kick, bite, or scratch as was common among most women who found themselves in the sudden position of having to defend themselves.

Silk stuck her hand down in her bosom and pulled out her switchblade, and quick as lightning, Nathan Lee's throat was slashed from ear to ear, presenting a deep, crescent-shaped gash that flowed dark red. Staring at Silk in horror and disbelief, he clutched his neck, attempting to staunch the gush of blood that squirted through his fingers, splashing the insides of the car. The interior of the new Plymouth suddenly looked as if it had been spray-painted carmine red.

There were also blood splotches on Silk's arms, her face, her dress, and her shoes. She sat paralyzed for a moment or two. But when Nathan Lee's body fell heavily against hers, she let out a little shriek and scrambled out of the car.

She looked right and left, searching for prying eyes, but there was no one to be seen in the desolate back lot. The only other car was an old beat-up Ford that belonged to Mr. Roland, the elderly owner of the honky-tonk. And by the time Mr. Roland or anyone else discovered Nathan Lee's dead body, Silk would be long gone.

CHAPTER 2

S ilk took her heels off and ran barefoot through a dark field of damp, muddy grass and wild flowers with thorns and bristles. Running for her life, she darted past low-hanging trees with moss-covered branches that seemed to reach down and grab her, trying to slow her down so the law could catch up with her and dispense justice.

Night creatures made sounds that she should have been accustomed to, but the sudden noisy squawks and whistling sounds of large-winged birds were as startling as a police siren. Adrenaline kept her legs pumping and prevented her from reacting to the scrape of sharp-edged stones and the prick of knotty twigs that lacerated her bare feet.

Silk had drawn blood from plenty of people who had provoked her, but it was only the second time she'd killed a man. It was an unnerving sensation, yet thrilling at the same time. But there was no time to bask in her excitement. In about three hours, The Low Moon would shut down for the night, and when old man Roland came outside to get in his car, he'd discover the bloody murder scene she'd left behind. She ran faster, rushing to get home and pack her things. A pretty gal like her wouldn't have any trouble hitching a ride to Baton Rouge, and from there, she'd hop on the first thing smoking, and get the hell out of the state of Louisiana.

Silk was counting on the fact that witnesses to the spat she'd had with Nathan Lee would be too afraid of Big Mama's wrath to accuse her of harming the white politician. They'd have no choice but to suggest that her old beau, Duke Durnell, had gone into a jealous rage and murdered Nathan Lee. Duke would be lucky if Sheriff Thompson got to him and locked him behind bars before an angry mob of Klansmen came calling to string him up, vigilante style.

If and when somebody put two and two together, and figured out that Silk had committed the crime, she'd be somewhere up North, living the good life.

She glanced up at the sky and squinted at the bright half-moon. She was in luck. Big Mama always went out on the nights of the half-moon to do a little night hunting and to dig around in the ground until dawn. Although blinded by cataracts, Big Mama could see amazingly well in the moonlight, when she went out to hunt down the mysterious assortment of small critters, worms, insects, and vegetation required to prepare her occult remedies.

At last Silk reached the shack in the woods she shared with the peculiar old woman who had loved her as mightily as any natural mother would…in her own way.

She crept into the darkened place, feeling her way around as she searched for Big Mama's battered old suitcase. The scrapes and cuts on her feet left a trail of smeared blood as she roamed the wood cabin. She pulled the suitcase out of a closet and dumped the contents: yellowed documents, old invoices, and faded black-and-white photographs of Big Mama's relatives—people Silk had never known. After stuffing her fanciest clothes into the suitcase, Silk stripped out of the bloodied pink dress and stuffed it under the mattress. She would have burned it if she had more time.

She hastily washed her face, neck, and arms with water from a bowl on a table near the sturdy bed with its iron headboard and footboard, the same bed Silk had shared with Big Mama since the day she was born.

Wearing only underwear, she tiptoed to the area of the shack where Big Mama cooked up her remedies in a pot-bellied stove. She hated stealing from Big Mama, but had no choice. Silk fumbled in the dark, looking for the tin breadbox that was Big Mama's money vault. To hasten her mission, she was tempted to, but dared not light the kerosene lamp or a candle. A mere flicker of light would draw Big Mama back to the house with her shotgun cocked, ready to mow down an intruder.

Feeling her way around in the dark, she touched items near at hand. Her fingers skimmed across pots and pans, straw baskets, and other objects. Finally, she tapped against the smooth surface of the breadbox. With a sigh of relief, she opened the lid, reached inside and grabbed handfuls of paper money, but her heart dropped in disappointment. Though she was holding what seemed to be a lot of cash, it wasn't anywhere close to the piles of money Big Mama had been squirreling away over the years. Where could that money be? Big Mama loved to brag about the ten thousand dollars she'd been saving up and planned to share with Silk on her twenty-first birthday.

Silk figured that since it was technically her own money, Big Mama wouldn't have too much to complain about when she discovered her savings were gone. But where was the bulk of the money? With no time to search any further, Silk smoothed out the crumpled bills from the breadbox, and concluded that she'd have to make do with whatever amount she'd scrounged from the tin money vault.

She dressed hurriedly in a navy-and-white, polka dot swing dress with a sailor collar. It was a decent-looking garment with a full skirt and a tight bodice that showed off her trim waistline. It was pretty enough to travel in, but not so provocative that it would draw unwanted attention to Silk. She didn't feel the pain of her cut feet until she slipped her feet halfway into a pair of navy patent leather shoes that were tucked beneath the bed. No time to give in to discomfort, she pushed her right foot and then the left into the glossy, flat shoes.

Next, she doused her hands in the bowl of water and applied her wet hands to her hair, slicking it back and twisting it into a hastily styled bun. Unable to see her reflection in the dark, she imagined she looked as innocent as a schoolteacher.

Ready to go, she picked up the suitcase. But before she made it out of the cabin, the door burst open and the shimmering moonlight lit up the place. With her shotgun pointed at Silk, Big Mama's wide body filled the doorframe. The snow-white, coarse, little beads of hair that covered her dark-brown head seemed to glow ethereally in the darkness.

Silk gasped in alarm. "Big Mama!"

Big Mama sniffed at the air. "I can smell your blood on the floor and someone else's is on that dress you hid under the mattress. What have you done, chile?"

"I ain't done nothing," Silk protested in a quavering voice.

Big Mama lowered the shotgun and came inside, slowly closing the door behind her. Wearing a man's shirt, a long, wide skirt, and a pair of black brogan boots, she lifted the skirt and sat down heavily on a wooden chair.

"Don't lie to me, Silk. You know Big Mama's got eyes in the back of her head. I had a vision about you," Big Mama said in an ominous tone and then nudged her head toward the bedroom area. "These blind eyes saw the vision right there in that basin of water that's now red with blood." She shook her head. "Stealing my money and running up North ain't gonna solve your problems. From what I seen, it ain't likely that you'll ever find the easy living you're hoping for. If you could be faithful to one man, you could live like a queen. But you ain't nothing but a tramp. You'll spread your legs for any man who got hisself a shiny car and some folding money in his pocket. I tried to keep your nature down with my potions and the womanly attention I gave you. But you're jest like that white-trash woman who borned you—headed for disaster."

Despite her blindness, Big Mama was always several steps ahead of Silk. No matter how hard she tried, Silk had never been able to outslick Big Mama, and it was frustrating.

"I'm sorry, Big Mama, but I ain't got time to go back and forth with you. I gots to get out of town before the sheriff and his men come looking for me."

"Don't sass me, gal. Sit yo' yella tail down before I go outside and pull up some switches or better yet, I'll grab my leather strap to tan your ornery hide," Big Mama said menacingly.

Intimidated, Silk immediately sat on a crude wooden chair that was identical to the one Big Mama sat upon. Although Silk was close to twenty years old, Big Mama didn't think twice about turning the young woman over her knee, pulling her panties down, and giving her a sound whipping when she felt Silk needed discipline.

"The sheriff ain't looking for you, not yet. He ain't coming for you until morning. Now, tell me, something…" Big Mama looked at Silk intently as if she could actually see her.

"What do you want to know, Big Mama?"

"Do I have to interrupt my hunting to go drag another dead

body out of the woods and bury it on my property to keep you out of the hands of the law?"

"No, ma'am," Silk said respectfully. "I didn't leave him in the woods. He's in his car with his throat slit…in the parking lot behind The Low Moon. Old man Roland won't find him for a few more hours."

"Who's *him?* Who'd you kill this time?" Big Mama inquired as she reached in her shirt pocket and pulled out a pinch of snuff, which she promptly tucked in between her bottom lip and gums.

"I killed Nathan Lee Willard, but I didn't mean to, Big Mama. It was an accident; I loved him."

Big Mama snorted and then spat out excess, brown-colored saliva into a rusty bucket. "That's hogwash. You was born bad, and you don't have it in your heart to love nobody except yourself."

"That's not true. I loved me some Nathan Lee, with all my heart."

"Hush up and let me think." Big Mama closed her eyes, screwed up her lips, and rocked forward and backward as she contemplated Silk's dilemma. From deep in her throat, she made a discordant humming sound. A few minutes later, she opened her eyes and pronounced, "This ain't gonna be easy to cover up like that other one. Nathan Lee Willard is a big-time politician with a pregnant wife. White folks will want you to hang for what you done did."

"I know; that's why I'm trying to get out of Devil's Swamp and make it to the bus depot in Baton Rouge," Silk said, her eyes darting around nervously as she stood up, prepared to hightail it out of the cabin.

"Not so fast. We got business to handle. How much of my cash did you steal?"

"I don't know, I didn't have time to count it. But don't worry, Big Mama, I'm going to pay you back every dollar…I promise."

Big Mama got up and shook the tin breadbox, rattling around the small change that Silk had left behind.

Accurately estimating the amount of money Silk had taken, she said, "Your promises ain't worth spit. You owe me a hunnid and sixty-two dollars...plus interest."

"I'll send you the money as soon as I get settled up North."

"There you go, telling falsehoods. You don't intend to pay me back one red cent. After all these years of raising you up, you jest gonna steal my money and try to make fast tracks outta here."

"I'm sorry, Big Mama. I really am."

"You ain't sorry about nothing, except for the fact that you got caught. I reckon I need to collect on the interest while I still got you here," Big Mama said, hitching up her wide skirt.

"Please, Big Mama; not tonight," Silk whined.

"Hush up and get your yella tail in that bed and spread your legs for me. I don't see you closing your legs to none of the menfolk you like to entice, so don't try to close your legs to me."

"I don't have time, Big Mama. I gotta get going before the sheriff catches up with me."

Big Mama stroked her shotgun threateningly. "All that sass coming out yo' mouth is gon' be your ruination. Now, go get in that bed and gimme some poontang! Don't make me do Sheriff Thompson a favor by putting a bullet hole through your thieving hide."

Resignedly, Silk felt along the walls as she moved in the dark, making her way to the big iron bed. She took off her traveling dress to keep from wrinkling it. And then she took off her panties, uncovering her privates for Big Mama's pleasure.

The heavy weight of Big Mama's plump body on top of her was as normal to Silk as getting her butt tanned, and as normal as breathing. For as long as she could remember, she'd been giving

Big Mama poontang whenever she wanted it—before she went to bed at night and oftentimes, Big Mama wanted more poontang first thing in the morning.

But tonight was the first time Silk felt inconvenienced and violated. There could be a lynch mob heading her way while Big Mama was writhing on top of her and dripping tobacco down Silk's neck.

It seemed like Big Mama was taking an extra-long time to get her thrills. Trying to speed her along, Silk reached under her manly shirt and squeezed her floppy, big tits. This action resulted in Big Mama groaning louder and drooling more dark saliva on Silk's neck.

"Come on, Big Mama, don't hold back; let it go," Silk purred in a coaxing voice.

"Stop trying to rush me, gal!" Frustrated, Big Mama rolled off of Silk and lay on her back, huffing and puffing. "The half-moon and the smell of that dead man's blood on your hands is messing with my nature. I think I'ma need me some special treatment tonight."

Silk was appalled. She didn't have time to give Big Mama the special treatment, but she dared not refuse the irritable woman who ruled with an iron fist. With her brogan boots on, Big Mama propped her legs up and spread them wide. Silk shimmed downward to the middle of the bed, but instead of giving Big Mama the special treatment she desired, Silk slipped out her switchblade and shoved the blade into the large flap of flesh that was Big Mama's lower abdomen.

"Here's your special treatment," Silk said through clenched teeth. Enraged, she yanked the impaled knife upward and then downward, trying her best to gut Big Mama like a pig. But Big

Mama's excess flesh prevented Silk from getting the job done. Big Mama flailed around on the bed for a moment or two and then attempted to pull the knife out of her gut.

Frustrated, Silk wrenched the knife free and promptly plunged it into Big Mama's neck. With her eyes wide open in surprise, Big Mama lay choking on a mouthful of blood and tobacco. Using her index finger, she circled the air and made zigzag motions, putting a hex on Silk before taking her last breath.

CHAPTER 3

Using the red-tinted water in the basin, Silk washed the blood off her hands and her knife, mixing Big Mama's blood in with Nathan Lee's. Although she couldn't bring herself to look at Big Mama's sprawled-out, dead body, she felt oddly exhilarated by the same mixture of fear and adrenaline she'd felt immediately after killing Nathan Lee.

She quickly threw on the polka dot dress and shoved her feet into the patent leather shoes. Without bothering to spruce up her hair, she picked up the suitcase that had a big dent in the front and hurried out of the shack. Guided by the light of the half-moon, she found her way to Highway 61. She stuck out her thumb when she saw approaching headlights.

A light-colored station wagon screeched to a halt. "Where you heading, Missy?" a white man with a toothy smile asked. The words "Jimbo's Exterminating" were painted on the side of the station wagon.

"I'm going to Baton Rouge, sir."

"You're in luck; that's where I'm going, so hop on in." Being helpful, the driver got out and relieved Silk of her suitcase, putting it on the floor of the back of the car that was crowded with exterminating equipment, large paper bags, boxes, and all manner of junk.

Silk rushed around to the passenger's side and climbed into the station wagon that stank of roach spray and cigarettes.

"You sho' is a pretty lil' gal," he observed, acknowledging her good looks in a tone that sounded more fatherly than flirtatious.

"Thank you for the compliment, sir."

"It's mighty peculiar for you to be hitching a ride in the middle of the night, but I shouldn't be surprised. I done seen many a strange thing while driving through Devil's Swamp at night. So, who are you running from this hour of the night? You got a no-good husband chasing after you?"

"I'm not running from anyone. I got me a teaching job up North and if I don't get there on time, I'm likely to lose the position," Silk said, reinventing herself on the fly.

"Ain't that something—a hitchhiking, mulatto schoolteacher." He laughed uproariously.

As the station wagon sped along the asphalt road, Silk, relieved to be putting distance between her and the murders she'd committed, smiled broadly.

The driver introduced himself as Floyd.

"Oh, I thought your name was Jimbo," Silk said cheerily, looking out the window as they swiftly left Devil's Swamp behind. She became practically giddy with the knowledge that Sheriff Thompson would come up empty-handed when he came looking for her with a pack of hound dogs and a pair of handcuffs.

"No, I work for Jimbo. I cover hundreds of miles of territory, exterminating restaurants and diners all over Louisiana. You'd be shocked at the amount of cockroaches and vermin that food establishments have crawling all over the meals they serve to customers. I remind my wife of that fact every time she tries to get me to take her out to dinner." Floyd gave another hearty burst of laughter.

"Cockroaches in the food…that's awful."

Floyd turned his mouth down in disgust. "I done seen worse than cockroaches. Eateries are the worst when it comes to breaking all sorts of health codes. They don't bother to call for Jimbo's Exterminating until the Board of Health is about to shut them down. And that's when I make my side money."

Silk's ears perked up. "What do you mean?"

"I tell the customers they're gonna need an extra-strong mixture to get rid of their infestation of bugs and vermin, and then I charge 'em an extra twenty bucks. That's my side money that goes right inside my pocket," he boasted, holding the steering wheel with one hand and smacking his bulging left pocket with the other.

"Does the stronger mixture get rid of the bugs?" Silk asked, feigning interest in the exterminating business, when her mind was actually focused on his left pocket that was filled up with cash.

"Nah, I spray those restaurants with the same basic, pest control spray that I use for all commercial businesses. But you know what they say: What the customers don't know won't hurt 'em." He chuckled and gave Silk a conspiratorial wink.

"Anyways," Floyd continued, "aside from the filth that I find in the kitchens of restaurants, my wife is such a heck of a good cook; I don't want to eat anyone else's cooking."

"What's your wife's specialty?" Silk asked, faking a smile while her brain was at work trying to figure out a way to sweet-talk Floyd out of some of the money he'd collected from the restaurants. Maybe he'd fall for a hard-luck story about a sick old mother who was depending on her. The cash she'd taken out of the bread box would only last but so long, and she suddenly wanted Floyd's money so badly, it became difficult for her to breathe.

"My wife, Shirley's baked ham is one of her best dishes, but everything she cooks is mouthwatering." He patted his protrusive belly, and said, "This here ain't no beer belly—it's from Shirley's good, home cooking. She packs me up enough food to feed an army when I have to drive long distances out on the road. I got some fried chicken in a Tupperware container in a brown sack, back there." He turned slightly, nudging his chin toward the backseat. "If you're hungry, reach back there and get yourself a leg or a wing. I'm a thigh and breast man, so you won't find none of those parts left." Again, Floyd erupted in laughter.

"I'm not hungry, but thanks for your hospitality," Silk said politely. Looking out the window, she noticed a sign indicating Baton Rouge was only eight miles ahead. Floyd was tearing up the road, driving fast. With time ticking away, she didn't have a lot of time to come up with a believable sob story.

"So, where are you gonna be teaching school, Missy?"

"I'll be teaching at a private school, uh, for Christian children."

Floyd chuckled. "A teacher with your good looks is gonna give those little Christian boys a head full of impure thoughts."

Silk lowered her eyes demurely.

"I ain't never been up North and can't say I want to. What city is the school located in?"

Silk was planning on putting down roots in either New York or Chicago, and willing to go wherever the next bus that pulled out the station was headed to, but she didn't want to give Floyd the full truth about her intended destination, in case he was ever questioned by Sheriff Thompson. "I'll be teaching in Boston, Massachusetts."

"Oh, that's where President Kennedy hails from. I'm Irish like the president and I was happy to give him my vote. But I'm not too pleased with the way he supports those radicals that want to change the segregation laws here in the South. I consider myself to be a reasonable person, and as long as you coloreds stay in your place, I treat you with decency. I don't like the way those high-minded Negroes are starting to insist that their little pickaninnies be allowed to go to the same schools as white children. It's unnatural and goes against God's plan." Floyd gazed at Silk curiously. "Is that school you're gonna be teaching at, a school for coloreds-only or are the races all mixed together?"

"It's all colored, sir," Silk replied.

Floyd nodded in satisfaction. "That's good."

They rode along with Floyd jabbering a mile a minute, his conversation shifting back and forth from pest control to race relations. They were only five miles from Baton Rouge when Silk turned to Floyd with her face flustered in embarrassment. "I hate to trouble you, but I need a restroom something terrible. I tried, but I can't hold it any longer. Would you mind pulling over so I can relieve myself in those bushes?" She pointed to the forest area on the right side of the darkened road.

"I reckon it'll be all right if I stop for a few minutes," Floyd said, pumping the brakes.

"Did your wife put any napkins in with your food?" Silk lowered her eyes demurely.

"I forgot…you females can't piss and shake your snake like men can." He twisted around in his seat, reaching inside a large paper bag, scrounging around for napkins.

While his back was turned, Silk reached into her bosom and pulled out her knife. When Floyd turned to hand her a napkin, she plunged the knife in his chest.

"What did you do that for?" Floyd stared at Silk and then grimaced down at the knife that was sticking out of his chest. Dying pain fully, Floyd beseeched her in a croaking voice, "Don't let me die. Help me." Not only did Silk ignore his plea, she gripped the protruding handle of the knife and twisted it cruelly. With Floyd now silent and still in death, she rifled through both pockets, relieving him of the thick wad of money he'd collected from the restaurants.

Using Floyd's pant leg, Silk wiped her knife clean and returned it to her bosom, and then calmly counted out four hundred and eighteen dollars. *Woo wee. I hit the jackpot!*

"Thanks for the ride," she said to the dead man. She retrieved her suitcase, opened it up, adding Mr. Floyd's money to the pile she'd stolen from Big Mama. Humming one of the songs she'd heard playing from the jukebox in The Low Moon tonight, she began the trek to Baton Rouge.

CHAPTER 4

The only bus going up north was headed for Pittsburgh, Pennsylvania, but it wouldn't be pulling out of the station until six in the morning. Half-expecting Sheriff Thompson to burst inside with his hounds, Silk ambled over to the colored waiting room, steadily glancing over her shoulder. There wasn't any point in trying to blend in with the straggling few late-night travelers. With her fair skin and straight hair, she stood out like a sore thumb. She considered hiding out in the restroom, but that was futile. The other colored travelers would only point the sheriff in that direction after he described her.

Hoping her luck would hold out until sunrise, Silk sat on a bench and tried to relax herself. Three killings in one night had given her a sort of high unlike anything she'd ever experienced. It seemed like her whole body was tingling and buzzing with excitement.

Clutching the handle of her suitcase that was filled with cash, Silk closed her eyes and began to reminisce about her childhood.

"Miss Mattie ain't your real mama," Ozella Scott said to six-year-old Silk.

"Yes, she is," Silk shot back.

"I heard that some trampy white woman left you in Miss Mattie's backyard."

"That's a lie."

"It's the truth," Ozella insisted, giving Silk a hard shove that knocked her down and resulted in a scraped knee.

When Silk went home, crying to big Mama, the old woman frowned in disapproval. "If you don't stick up for yourself, those ornery churren jest gon' keep on taunting you."

"But Ozella is bigger than me; she's a fifth-grader."

"The bigger they are, the harder they fall," Big Mama stated, whipping a switchblade out of her ample bosom. "You take this here knife and I want you to use it on that blubber-lipped gal the next time she starts deviling you. If you give her a deep slash across the arm and if you draw a good amount of blood, I guarantee you won't have any more trouble out of the little heifer."

The next day, Big Mama lured Ozella to their shack under the pretext of wanting her to run a quick errand with the promise of paying her fifteen cents for her time and trouble. When Ozella arrived, she knocked on the creaky wood door and yelled through the wire screen, "I'm here, Miss Mattie."

In the shadows of the darkened shack, Big Mama put the switchblade in Silk's hand. "Go on out there and cut her. Make her blood flow like a river; do you hear me?"

"Yes, ma'am," Silk said in a shaky voice.

"All right, then. Get to it, gal." Big Mama gave Silk an encouraging shove.

With the switchblade hidden behind her back, Silk went outside.

"Hi, Silk," Ozella said in a friendly tone, as if she hadn't taunted and pushed Silk the day before.

"Hi, Ozella," Silk said shyly.

"Where's Miss Mattie?"

"She'll be out in a minute."

"Okay." Ozella stomped her foot, scaring off a chicken that had come snooping around her shoes. That sudden movement prompted

Silk to take action. In two swift movements, she slashed Ozella across her arm and put another gash across her back. Ozella shrieked to high heavens, which was a signal for Big Mama to come outside.

"What's all the fuss about?" Big Mama asked. "Goodness, gracious, where'd all that blood come from?"

"Silk cut me for no reason at all. She just hauled off and cut me," Ozella cried as Big Mama examined her wounds, clucking her tongue.

Big Mama shook her head. "Looks like you need stiches, so I guess I'm gon' have to sew you up." She turned to Silk. "Go clean that knife you cut her with before it turns rusty."

Silk scampered off, skipping happily as she went to clean and polish the switchblade.

Ozella howled in pain as Big Mama doctored on her. After she finished, she patted Ozella on the head and said, "You're too messed up to run my errand, so go on home. Tell your mama that she owes me a dollar for doctoring you up. And tell her to bring my money around here by Friday...or else."

"Yes, ma'am; I'll tell her," Ozella responded. Bent over in pain, the girl slowly made her way back home.

It took several more knife slashings for kids to realize if you messed with Silk, you'd end up requiring stitches. Since the closest physician was eleven miles away, it was Mattie Moreau who tended to the wounded. Parents who complained about Silk found themselves hexed: their chickens refused to lay eggs, fresh milk suddenly turned sour, and alligators began crawling out of the swamp and hanging around their property.

As the years progressed, Silk didn't have to be provoked to cut someone. If she so much as suspected a girl had eyes for her current boyfriend, she'd cut her on the spot and ask questions later.

Big Mama accused Silk of being hot-in-the-butt and boy-crazy.

She tried her best to dissuade Silk's interest in the opposite sex by climbing on top of her numerous times throughout the day. Sometimes she kept Silk in bed for hours on end, but even her best efforts failed to calm down Silk's unnaturally high nature and her desire for sex with members of the opposite sex. As a last resort, Big Mama made up a potion for Silk to drink. "You gon' wind up with a gut-full of responsibility if you don't calm your hot butt down. And if you get pregnant, you're on your own. I'd be a fool to take on another screaming baby with a big ol' mouth to feed," Big Mama had grumbled.

Early one morning when Big Mama was out fishing, Silk opened the door for Mr. Perry, who made a weekly delivery of a big, cinder-block-sized chunk of ice. He carried the block of ice with a pair of sharp, pointy-ended tongs, dripping water as he made his way to the antiquated, wooden ice box against the wall, a few feet away from the outdated stove.

"You're growing like a weed," he commented, looking Silk over with a slow, caressing gaze. She was fourteen years old at the time, and her body had ripened into womanly maturity.

"Did Mattie leave me any money for this ice?"

"No, sir, Mr. Perry, but she'll have your money for you next week."

Mr. Perry mopped sweat from his brow with a large, pink hand. "I had to leave my truck back there on the side of the road and travel on foot through the forest to get to this out-of-the-way shack and bring y'all this here block of ice. I need something for my trouble," he said in a voice that oozed with a sexual overtone as his eyes roamed Silk's curves that were visible in a tight pair of orange pedal pushers. Braless, her pert, young breasts pushed at the cotton fabric of her sleeveless blouse.

"You sho' look tempting, Silk. Looky here," he said, advancing toward her with a leering expression. "You take care of me and I'll forget about Mattie's ice bill."

Silk backed away. "If you come back tomorrow, Big Mama will have the money for you," Silk lied, trying to get rid of Mr. Perry.

"I won't be anywhere near these parts tomorrow." Mr. Perry shook his head regretfully. "Now, you keep what goes on between me and you to yourself. Don't go running your mouth to Mattie. You hear me?" He yanked Silk toward him.

She yelped in fear.

"Shh. Shh. I just wanna feel you up a little bit." He squeezed her breasts, ran his hands over her backside, and then roughly dug his fingers between her legs, stroking on the thick seam of fabric in the crotch of her pants. "Take them pants off so I can get me some." He tore at the side of her pants, popping off the button and ripping open the zipper.

Silk looked around in desperation, wishing she could defend herself with the knife Big Mama had given her for protection. But in the safety of her home, she rarely kept her weapon on her.

Mr. Perry backed her across the room, threatening her with each step. "You'd better be nice to me, nigga bitch, or I'll beat the living daylights out of you." Soon, he had her stretched out on the iron bed. His physical frame, comprised of mostly bulky muscle, was much heavier than Big Mama's loose, fleshy body. Feeling as if she were being crushed, Silk could barely breathe. She didn't possess the strength or the courage to try and fight him off.

She wasn't a virgin and it didn't physically hurt when he pushed himself inside her. But each thrust was an intrusion, a violation of her personhood. She hadn't felt this helpless since she was a six-year-old being taunted and bullied by Ozella Scott. Only this felt a hundred times worse.

After ten excruciating minutes elapsed, he gave a harsh groan and a violent shudder before rolling off her. Lying on his back, he stared at the moldy, exposed-beam ceiling, smiling in satisfaction. Finally, he stood, pulling up his pants and straightening out his shirt.

Afraid that even the most subtle movement might entice Mr. Perry into wanting to start up again, Silk lay still and dared not move a muscle.

"Tell Mattie the ice is free of charge this week," Mr. Perry said, giving Silk a head nod and a wink.

Silk didn't move until she heard the screen door slam behind Mr. Perry. The rage that overcame her seemed to vibrate through her system. She shot up from the bed and pulled up her pedal pushers, which were loose around her waist due to the ripped zipper and missing button. In a blind fury, she felt beneath the mattress and retrieved her switchblade. Knife in hand, she moved purposefully across the room, and when she reached the cabin door, she noticed that Mr. Perry had left his tongs behind.

"Mr. Perry! Mr. Perry!" Silk yelled, running through the forest in the direction that led to the road where Mr. Perry always parked his truck. She spotted him in the distance, moving swiftly through the thicket of trees and bramble bushes. "Mr. Perry!"

Hearing his name, Mr. Perry stopped walking and turned around. Silk waved her hand through the air. Realizing that Silk wanted to tell him something, he sighed as he waited for her to catch up.

"You forgot your ice tongs," she said, breathless, when she caught up to him.

"Girl, what's wrong with you…are you simple-minded or something? I have extra pairs of tongs. Why you come running out here in the woods, slowing me down when I'm already behind schedule from fooling with you?"

"I'm sorry. I thought you needed these," she said, extending her arm, offering him the tongs. But before he could accept them, she swung the heavy, metal object upward, knocking him upside the head. Mr. Perry let out a sound of pain and stumbled backward. Silk whacked him again. Only harder. And this time, a big knot appeared on the side of his head, and his knees buckled. He tried to get away from her, but disoriented, he stumbled around with no idea of which way to turn.

Silk had him at her mercy, and with a deadly look in her eyes, she approached him, waving the ice tongs menacingly. "I don't think you're in any shape to drive that ice truck, Mr. Perry," she said with an amused smile.

"You…you're crazy; get away from me." His voice shook and so did the hand that he held up defensively, but to no avail. Silk had him at her mercy. With a malicious glint in her eyes, she swung at his head with the ice tongs until blood seeped and his legs gave out.

The burly man hit the ground hard, like a fallen tree. As he lay on his side, balled up and with his hands pressed against his battered head, Silk struck again. Knocked unconscious, his arms fell to his sides. He was lying on his back now, exposed and vulnerable. Silk dropped the switchblade that she'd been hiding behind her back. Using both hands, she opened the tongs, aiming the pointy ends at Mr. Perry's closed eyes. She widened the handles and then tightened them together, using the sharp, curved ends to gouge out his eyes.

Howling like a trapped animal, Mr. Perry's screams echoed through the forest. With bloody eyeballs hanging on both cheeks, he scrambled around, trying to sit up. Silk dropped down, picked up her knife from the ground, and straddled him. Using her switchblade, she slashed him up, causing the flesh of his face and arms to hang like ribbons. Barely alive from blood loss, he softly whimpered, emitting a whoosh of air when she plunged the knife into his privates.

Back at the cabin, when Silk told Big Mama what Mr. Perry had done to her and how she'd left his bloodied body for the buzzards to eat, Big Mama insisted on going out to the woods and dragging the dead body back to her property. Burying him in the ground would fertilize her garden and also keep the iceman's remains undetected by Sherriff Thompson and his lawmen.

CHAPTER 5

S
ilk boarded the bus for Pittsburgh, Pennsylvania not knowing much about the place she was heading. She wondered if
Pittsburgh was a fast-paced town like New York City with
plenty of nightclubs and twinkling neon lights.

After traveling a few hours, the bus stopped in Biloxi, Mississippi.
Silk hadn't banked on stopping until they arrived at her destination in Pittsburgh. Biloxi was too close to Louisiana for comfort,
and Silk looked left and right, holding her breath in fear that
Sheriff Thompson and his lawmen would bum-rush the bus and
arrest her.

She didn't relax until every passenger had boarded and the bus
pulled away. A woman with smooth, root-beer-colored skin boarded
the bus, carrying a baby. Her suitcase was stored in the luggage
compartment, but she was still laden down with several cloth sacks
as well as paper sacks with handles. She moved awkwardly down
the aisle, passing empty seats that were reserved for white folks.
When she reached the back of the bus, she and her fussy baby sat
next to Silk.

"Boy or girl?" Silk asked.

"A little boy. His name is Vernon…after his daddy."

"He's a plump little muffin," Silk commented. "By the way, are
you headed to Pittsburgh?" She hoped the new passenger could

give her the lowdown on the city she was considering settling down in.

"Yes, I am."

"Me, too. You got family up north?"

"My brother. And my nieces and nephews." A troubled look appeared in the woman's eyes. "My sister-in-law...her name was Ernestine. She was killed in an accident, and I'm going up north for her funeral."

"Oh, I'm sorry for your loss."

"She was only in her twenties, and she left behind five mother-less children, including newborn twins."

"Twins! Now, that's a sin and a shame for those poor babies to lose their mama before they even got to know her."

"It's so sad," she agreed, shaking her head. "My brother, Buddy... Well, his name is Richard, but we call him Buddy. He went up north eleven years ago and met Ernestine at church. They married right away. I never had the pleasure of meeting my sister-in-law, but that doesn't stop me from mourning her loss. She was killed when a truck ran into the taxi cab she was riding in. The doctors had to cut those twins out of her. It's a miracle they survived."

"What a pity. Are you gonna stay up north and help raise them?"

"No, I can't stay. I have a husband and two more little ones at home to look after. I'm going to stay until my brother finds a babysitter to take care of the children."

"Woo-wee. That babysitter is going to have a lot on her hands with three children and a set of infant twins."

"That's another sad part of the story. The twins were born pre-maturely and they're still in the hospital—in incubators. They may not make it."

"I'm gonna keep those little Pittsburgh twins in my prayers,"

Silk said, practicing the name of the city she would soon call home. However, if Pittsburgh didn't have the fast life she was looking for, she'd get out of there in a hurry and go to New York or Chicago.

"Oh, my brother and his family don't live in Pittsburgh; they're in a city outside of Philadelphia—a small town called Chester. I have to transfer to another bus headed for Philadelphia when we arrive in Pittsburgh."

Silk hadn't considered Philadelphia as one of her options, but it was a big city and most likely offered the bright lights and nightlife she yearned for. Perhaps Silk would also transfer to that bus going to Philadelphia.

"By the way, my name is Clara; what's yours?"

Not having a fake name handy, and highly doubting if Sheriff Thompson would ever travel to Philadelphia to hunt her down, Silk went on ahead and divulged her real name. "My name is Silk."

"That's an unusual name. It's pretty, too. Nice to meet you, Silk," Clara said, smiling as she rocked her baby.

"Losing a wife suddenly must be rough on your brother."

"It is. And having so much to deal with while he's grieving makes it extra hard. He has to make funeral arrangements and he also has to deal with all sorts of paperwork for the insurance claim. You see, Buddy stands to get double the money of Ernestine's insurance policy due to her accidental death." Clara readjusted the baby's blanket and then peered at Silk. "So, where are you traveling to?"

Double insurance money! Hot damn! Silk would be a fool not to get tight with the grieving widower and get a piece of that windfall. She took a deep breath and smiled. "It's such a coincidence that we're traveling in the exact same direction. I have a teaching job lined up in the same, small town—Chester, Pennsylvania."

"Are you kidding me?" Clara said, surprised.

"I'll be teaching at a private, Christian school for colored kids."

"My goodness! This is too good to be true."

Silk nodded enthusiastically and smiled back at Clara. "I've never been there before and I don't know a soul. I hope I can count on you to be a friend."

"You certainly can. The long trip won't be so lonely now that I have someone to talk to. I've never been up north before and it'll be comforting to have a new friend along. The two of us country girls might have to lean on each other amongst all those city-slickers." Clara laughed gaily and then covered her mouth. "Oh, Lord. I feel terribly guilty. My sister-in-law is not even in the ground yet, and I'm sitting here laughing like a fool."

Silk patted Clara's arm. "You didn't mean any harm by it. My mama always told me to rejoice for the dearly departed for their suffering on earth is finally over."

Clara nodded solemnly.

"I'm sure those grief-stricken, little motherless children could use a little bit of sunshine in their lives, right about now. Wearing a long face isn't gonna help anyone. It's not gonna be easy, but if you can pretend to be cheerful, the better off those children will be."

"I think you're right." Clara looked Silk over. "I suppose being a Christian school teacher has taught you a lot about children and a lot about faith."

"It surely has."

"I would have never guessed you were a schoolteacher. To be honest, when I sat next to you, I thought you were an actress, on your way to the Big Apple or Hollywood to become a movie star."

"Me—a movie star? Imagine that!" Silk laughed and Clara joined in.

After several more hours into the bus ride, Silk finally relaxed and stopped expecting Sheriff Thompson and his lawmen to flag down the bus and order her to get off at gunpoint. The ride to Pittsburgh was unending, but Silk used the time to find out everything she could about Clara's brother. Clara loved to talk and eagerly shared the information. According to Clara, Buddy was a devoted, hardworking, family man who was soft-spoken and easygoing. He migrated to Chester back in '51 when his uncle got him a job at a shipbuilding company. As a master welder and the supervisor of his department at the factory, Buddy had earned a good living and received excellent company benefits.

It turned out that the paper sack that Clara had lugged onto the bus contained an assortment of food for the journey: Vienna sausages, Saltine crackers, canned sardines, thick slices of corn bread, and fried chicken wrapped in aluminum foil. She generously shared her food with Silk, who repaid the kindness by buying Clara soft drinks from beverage machines at the various rest stops along the way.

"Do you have a boyfriend?" Clara inquired.

Silk started to tell Clara that she was footloose and fancy free, but thought better of it. "Yes, my sweetheart's name is Duke. He's in medical school...you know, training to be a doctor. We're going to get married when Duke starts his practice, and at that point, I'll give up my teaching career to raise our children and be a good wife."

"You have your life all planned out, don't you?"

"Uh-huh. My mama gave me a big ol' hope chest and it's already filled to the brim with all sorts of household items that Duke and I will use in our future home."

"Are you planning a big wedding?"

"Yes, indeed. Five bridesmaids and two flower girls."

"That's wonderful; you're a lucky girl. I wish I'd had me a big wedding, but I was already in the family way when I got married," Clara said in a lowered tone of voice.

"Oh, you had a shotgun wedding?" Silk teased. She could tell she'd struck a nerve by the way Clara flinched and began to fiddle with her wedding band.

"My husband, Big Vernon, didn't have to be forced to the altar. He wanted to make an honest woman out of me. But we didn't have enough money for anything fancy, so we got hitched by the justice of the peace."

"Well, you're a happily married woman, and that's all that matters," Silk said soothingly. Though it was in her nature to needle a person once she'd located their weak spot, it was in Silk's best interest to keep Clara as a loyal friend, and so she let her be.

As the bus drew closer to their destination, Silk stared out the window, observing the mountains, the muddy skies, the smoky air, and the sickly-looking trees. The effects of the coal-mining industry had left the city of Pittsburgh dark and depressing. Thanks to Clara, Silk wouldn't be pitching her tent in such a dreary town.

CHAPTER 6

With the numerous rest stops and layovers, the bus ride to Pittsburgh had lasted almost twenty-four hours. Silk dreaded the additional five hours it would take to get to Philly. But motivated by the idea of putting even more distance between her and the lawmen of Louisiana, she purchased a ticket to Philadelphia and climbed on board the bus.

The last leg of the trip was pure hell. Silk was hungry, but Clara's food had run out. Making matters worse, Clara's baby was fussy and starting to irritate Silk. Each time Clara asked Silk to hold the child for a few moments, Silk would close her eyes and pretend to snore. The only good thing about the bus ride from Pittsburgh to Philadelphia was that there weren't any Jim Crow laws that forced them to sit in the back of the bus.

At last they arrived in Philadelphia, and when Clara announced they had to catch a local train to get to her brother's house in Chester, Silk was ready to haul off and slap Clara for giving her such bad news.

In downtown Philadelphia, Silk was intrigued by the tall buildings and the many business establishments that were lit by neon signs in broad daylight. She was fascinated by the hordes of people walking at a fast pace like they were all in a big hurry to get somewhere. And she was particularly interested in a couple of colored sailors who had begun to give her the eye the moment she had stepped outside the bus terminal. Eager to explore the big city for a while, Silk decided that Clara and that big-headed baby of hers had suddenly become more of a liability than an asset.

"I'm sorry, but I can't ride any further—not today. My backside is sore and I'm gonna pass out for sure if I don't get myself something to eat," Silk said with her lips poked out.

"What are you saying?" Clara asked nervously.

"I'm saying…you go on ahead to Chester and get started with that funeral business; I'll catch up with you in a day or so." Distracted by the handsome men in uniform, Silk no longer had any interest in Clara's brother or the insurance money he had coming. Continuing on to Chester was out of the question when Philadelphia seemed to have so much to offer.

Clara's eyes grew large with alarm. "I can't leave you in this big city all alone. It's too dangerous. If something happens to you, I'll never forgive myself."

"Don't worry about me; I'll be fine," Silk said, cutting her eyes at the sailors who were hanging around waiting for her to ditch Clara and her baby. "Listen, I'm gonna find me a room to relax in. I need a quiet place to study for the teacher's exam at that private Christian school. So you go on, now. I'll catch you later."

"How?"

"How, what?" Silk wrinkled her brow in irritation. There was a lot of fun to be had and Clara was holding her up.

"How are you going to catch up with me when you don't even have my brother's phone number?"

"Oh, silly me! Give me the number and I'll call you later."

Silk was forced to hold the squirming baby while Clara jotted down the phone number on the back of an old receipt.

Carrying a suitcase, a diaper bag, and her baby, Clara ambled along. Wearing a fearful expression, she stopped and looked over at Silk several times. Impatiently, Silk motioned for Clara to move along. Finally, mixing in with the throng of people on Market Street, Clara disappeared in the crowd.

With Clara out of her hair, Silk whirled around and flashed a smile at the two sailors who were waiting for her. "Hey, sailor boys," she greeted boldly. "How would you two like to give me a tour of the city?"

Taken aback by Silk's brazenness, the sailors blushed and bashfully agreed to show her the area.

"Feels like I've been traveling for a month of Sundays, and I'm nearly dying of starvation. I hope you boys plan on feeding me before you take me on a walking tour."

"Uh, sure. There's a steak house a couple blocks from here," said the cuter of the two. He was medium height, lean and muscular with mahogany skin that was complemented by jet-black eyebrows and bright, brown eyes. His pal was several inches taller and had broader shoulders, but he wasn't nearly as good-looking as his bright-eyed friend.

"Here you go; be a doll and carry my luggage," she said, handing her beat-up suitcase to the less attractive sailor.

"What's your name?" asked the cute one.

"Why don't you try and guess," Silk said with a devilish smile.

He studied her with squinted eyes. "You look like you'd have a sweet name—something like Cookie or Honey," he ventured.

Laughing and enjoying the attention, Silk shook her head, swinging her bun loose, and causing her hair to fall past her shoulders. "Nope, it's not Cookie or Honey."

"Give us a clue," said the sailor who was awkwardly holding her suitcase.

"My name begins with the letter 'S,' and while you're trying to guess, why don't you fellows tell me your names."

The cute sailor made the introduction. "I'm Julius and this is my buddy, Hank."

"Before we go to the steak house, why don't you put your suitcase away in one of the lockers inside the bus station," Hank suggested, looking embarrassed to be holding the battered piece of luggage.

"Good idea," Julius agreed.

Silk frowned. "I don't want to be separated from my possessions. This here is my piggy bank," Silk said, lovingly stroking the dented suitcase.

Julius and Hank exchanged puzzled looks when Silk referred to her suitcase as a piggy bank.

"It'll be safe inside the locker. I don't want to be toting anything around when we take you out to eat and give you a tour," Julius said, trying to convince Silk to ditch her embarrassingly shabby travel bag.

"All right," Silk relented. She and the two sailors went inside the bus terminal, and like a perfect gentleman, Hank paid the twenty-five cents fee to rent the locker. He handed Silk the key to locker 105. She deposited the key inside her pocketbook.

With one arm linked in Hank's arm and the other linked in Julius's, Silk was escorted to the steak house with both men trying to guess her name.

"Sybil…Sharon…Sallie," Julius suggested.

"Wrong answers! Listen, boys, I'll give a kiss to the first one who gets my name right," Silk said, sweetening the pot.

"Stephanie!" Hank blurted, trying hard to win a kiss.

"Nope." Shaking her head adamantly, Silk swung her hair back and forth, tempting Hank to briefly unlock his arm and stroke her luxurious mane.

By the time they reached the steak house, both young men had gone through every "S" name imaginable from Sapphire to Suzie. Silk was falling over giggling at some of the silly names the two sailors had come up with.

"My name is Silk," she finally divulged when the waiter arrived with the menus.

"That name suits you," Julius said, and Hank nodded in agreement.

Silk quickly scanned the selections and ordered a strip steak, salad, baked potato, and large Coca-Cola. Julius and Hank only ordered soft drinks, commenting that they'd already eaten.

While Silk chowed down, her dates admired her looks and tried to outdo each other with the compliments they bestowed upon her.

"I love the sound of your Southern accent," Julius said. "Where're you from?"

"Biloxi, Mississippi," she lied.

"Your skin is so smooth and flawless, I bet you wash your face with nothing but Noxzema," Hank offered, gazing at her adoringly.

"Nope. I pamper my skin with a mixture my mama makes out of special herbs and castile soap. I follow that up with a mud mask made from Louisiana soil."

"Louisiana?" Hank questioned. "Didn't you say you're from Mississippi?"

"The soil comes in the mail," Silk responded quickly. She grew solemn, missing Big Mama suddenly. If Big Mama hadn't tried to slow her down by asking for the special treatment, she wouldn't have had to kill her. *I'm sho' gonna miss my mama, and I hope my beautiful skin can survive without her preparations.*

"You look sad all of a sudden," Julius observed.

Silk shrugged. "I'm feeling homesick, I guess." She ignored the salad, but quickly polished off her steak and baked potato, and then stabbed through the chunks of ice with her straw, tilting her glass, and loudly sipping the last drops of cola. "Y'all ready to give me a tour of the city?"

Julius and Hank scrambled to their feet, reaching in their pockets and tossing dollar bills on the table, both eager to pay for Silk's meal.

Outside on busy Market Street, Silk took in the sites. The marquee of the Fox Theater advertised the movie *Gypsy* starring Natalie Wood. She was mesmerized by the beautiful images of film clips that were displayed outside the movie house. Each time the door to the theater opened, she was struck by the delicious aroma of popcorn.

"Do you want to catch this flick?" Hank asked her.

Silk had never been inside a movie theater, and she nodded enthusiastically. Hank checked with the ticket attendant and then announced that the next show wasn't scheduled until five p.m. and the next one after that would begin at seven.

With time to kill, Silk accompanied the sailors to a nearby arcade. Inside, Hank asked her to take a picture that he could have as a keepsake. She eagerly obliged, striking a glamorous pose next to a gigantic, inflatable whiskey bottle prop that the photographer provided. The photograph was placed inside a cardboard frame with the words: *Thinking of You, Always* imprinted at the bottom.

While Hank admired Silk's picture, Julius stole a kiss. Silk wrapped her arms around his neck, inviting him to kiss her long and deeply.

Hank gazed at Silk's picture. "I guess I have to settle for kissing your picture since I can't get any sugar from you."

Julius's lips were soft and the taste of his sweet kiss had an unsettling effect on her nature, causing her to squirm with desire. Being in a public place, there wasn't much Silk could do about her discomfort, but she did manage to subtly rub her groin against Julius's, letting him know that she wanted more than a kiss.

"Hank and I have a room a few blocks away on Arch Street. I'll tell Hank to give us some privacy. Later, we can go and catch the seven o'clock show at the Fox Theater."

"Sounds good to me." Silk waited by the door while Julius delivered the news to Hank. Left holding Silk's picture, a dejected Hank watched as his buddy and the girl he desired walked out of the arcade.

CHAPTER 7

On the way to the hotel on Arch Street, Julius made a detour at a liquor store and bought a bottle of Wild Turkey. Hugged up as they walked along Arch Street, Julius and Silk alternately kissed and drank from the bottle of bourbon.

When they arrived at a flea bag hotel, Julius apologized for the condition of the place. Silk walked inside without batting an eye; she felt frisky enough to raise her dress in a back-alley to get the thrills she yearned for.

Images of the dead bodies she'd left back home filled her mind, exciting her. She reached a hand behind her back and began un-zipping her dress before Julius could get the key in the lock.

The room stank of dirty socks and armpits, but that didn't deter Silk. She had stripped down to her panties before Julius had even taken off his shoes. She pushed him on the bed and climbed on top of him, gyrating, while her tongue traveled from his neck to his ear. With her lips cupped around his earlobe, she used the tip of her tongue to sensually probe the small orifice. Heated up, Julius moaned as he caressed Silk's tummy and breasts.

"You want some poontang?" she whispered.

"Some what?" Julius's voice was hoarse with lust.

She reached for his hand and steered it down to her crotch. "Poontang," she repeated.

"Oh, yeah, I definitely want some of that."

"I wanna give it to you, but I can't…" She tugged at his crisp, white uniform. "You can't get to this poontang with those sailor pants on." She rolled off him and sat back on her haunches, rubbing her crotch circularly. Smiling alluringly, she slowly pulled her knee caps apart, welcoming him into the space between her opened thighs.

Tripping over his pant legs, Julius hurriedly removed his uniform. Easing Silk down until she was flat on her back, he positioned himself on top of her and awkwardly attempted to get his dick inside her.

"I like to be on top," Silk said, gently nudging him with the palms of her hands. "I'm the driver and you're the car."

"I'll be the car, as long as I'm a Cadillac," Julius said with a chuckle. They switched places, and as Silk expertly guided his stiffened member into her moist warmth, she began bucking and humping desperately.

"Whew! I didn't figure you'd be such a wild cat." Julius smiled in wonder and appreciation of his good luck.

"Fuck me, fuck me," she moaned. "So much blood, so much blood," she murmured, replaying the murders of Nathan Lee and the exterminator in her mind. She blocked out the imagery of what she'd done to Big Mama.

"What're you saying about blood?" Julius asked worriedly, halting his thrust. "It's not that time of the month, is it?"

"Naw. Keep fucking me, boy; don't stop 'til I tell you to!" she demanded, riding him savagely until they both collapsed and lay panting, trying to catch their breath.

Julius pulled himself up, sat on the edge of the bed, and lit up a Chesterfield cigarette. Silk swigged down more bourbon, trying to rid herself of the memory of Big Mama grunting in determination as she struggled to use her last bit of strength to hex her. She wondered what kind of curse Big Mama had put on her. Whatever it was, it had to be mighty powerful being that it was done while in the act dying.

Feeling the afterglow of good sex, Silk smiled as she chugged down more liquor. One thing was for sure: Big Mama's curse hadn't messed with her nature.

"You want some more?" Silk offered the half-filled bottle of Wild Turkey to Julius.

He waved his hand, declining. "Girl, you're something else. You can eat and drink a man under the table."

"And I got a nature that's stronger than most men," she said with a smirk.

"Are you trying to say that you can fuck me under the bed, too?" Julius said with humor.

"I'm ready to go again, what about you?" Silk said challengingly.

"Let me take a quick nap. Fifteen minutes is all I need to get my engine revved up."

"I'm gon' hold you to it," she said, glancing at the alarm clock next to the bed. Julius dozed off quickly and Silk was left with her thoughts.

Why'd you try to delay me by asking for the special treatment when you knew I needed to make fast tracks? Why, Big Mama? Silk wiped away the tears that slid down her face and straightened her shoulders.

She turned the bottle up to her lips again and took big swallows of the burning liquid. Every time she thought about Big Mama, she took another sip, drinking herself into oblivion. Sprawled on the bed next to Julius, she was barely conscious when someone knocked softly and then used a key to enter the shabby hotel room.

In that shadowy state between wakefulness and sleep, she imag-ined Big Mama was on top of her getting some thrills, but when someone jammed a hard dick inside her, she remembered that Big Mama was dead. Silk cracked an eye open and glanced at Julius, who was still asleep beside her. Though confused as to who was fucking her, that bewilderment didn't prevent her from accom-modating her mystery lover with widened thighs and energetic pelvic thrusts.

At some point she heard angry male voices. She sat up a little and drunkenly observed Julius and his sailor buddy throwing punches at each other.

"What are you boys fighting about?" she inquired in a slurred voice.

"I caught him raping you," Julius said in a voice full of indignation.

"I didn't rape her; she gave it to me willingly," Hank retorted.

"No need to be at each other's throats. There's more than enough poontang for y'all to share," Silk offered with a drunken smile.

"See! I told you she gave it up on her own free will." Hank glared at Julius.

"She doesn't mean it; that's the liquor talking." Julius covered Silk's nude body with the sheet.

She flung the sheet off. "Who's next?"

"Ain't gotta ask me twice." Hank dove on top of her. Silk wel-comed him by wrapping her legs around Hank's waist.

"I can't watch this," Julius uttered in disgust. "I'll wait in the bathroom…call me when it's my turn."

The fact that Silk drifted in and out of consciousness didn't bother Hank. He didn't require her awareness or active participa-tion to have a good time. Proving to have more stamina than Julius, Hank went quite a few rounds with Silk before collapsing next to her prone body in exhaustion.

"We better start packing up and head back to the naval base," Hank said, breathing heavily.

"What about her? We can't leave her in this condition," Julius said worriedly.

"She needs to sleep it off. She'll be all right in the morning... isn't that right, Sweet Cakes?" Hank patted Silk's derriere.

"Mm-hmm. I need to sleep it off," she mumbled drunkenly, and snuggled beneath the covers.

CHAPTER 8

Sunlight invaded the hotel room and cut across Silk's face. She grimaced and muttered profanities as she placed a forearm over her eyes, trying to block out the unwanted light. Flopping onto her belly, she pulled the covers over her head and attempted to go back to sleep, but the sunrays were strong and relentless, forcing her to sit up and face the new day.

Disoriented, her blurry eyes bounced around the unfamiliar room, landing on an ashtray overflowing with cigarette butts and an empty pack of Chesterfields. Next, she zoomed in on a nearly empty bottle of Wild Turkey, which jogged her memory. That sailor boy had brought her here. She jerked her head back and forth, wondering where the hell he'd gone. Her mouth was dry and her breath smelled like pig guts. She picked up the bottle of liquor and used the last dregs of bourbon as a mouthwash, swishing it around in her mouth, and then spitting it back into the bottle.

She wondered if that sailor boy, whose name she couldn't recall, was in the bathroom. "Hey, sailor? Are you in there taking a crap?" There was no answer, and her full bladder demanded relief, so she swung her legs off the bed. At home she would have simply reached for the chamber pot, but that wasn't an option this morning.

The bathroom could have used a good scrubbing down, but she'd seen worse. She squatted down on the toilet seat and relaxed her muscles, releasing an everlasting stream of urine. In the midst of pissing, there was a thunderous pounding on the hotel-room door.

"Who is it?" She figured that sailor fella had probably gone out to get her some coffee and breakfast and had most likely left his key behind. "Hold your horses," she called out in irritation.

"Check-out time," yelled a surly voice.

She came out of the bathroom and pulled the threadbare blanket off the bed and covered herself with it before opening the door. "Say, what?" she questioned the beer-bellied white man standing outside the door.

"Check out time was at ten. If you're staying another day, you have to pay in advance." He held a receipt book in his hand, and a pen was tucked behind his ear.

"This ain't my room; I'm visiting that sailor boy…you know, whatshisname." That damn sailor hadn't been as good-mannered as he'd appeared, cutting out on her without so much as a good-bye.

"Pay up or hit the road," the man said, speaking to Silk as if she were a derelict.

It was on the tip of her tongue to tell the honky that he could kiss her ass and keep his funky ol' room, but then she remembered that she needed a place to stay. "How much does this room cost?"

"Two dollars a day, the weekly rate is twelve bucks."

Silk pondered the options and decided to pay for only one day. As soon as she found a night spot where highfalutin' Negroes frequented, she'd find herself a Cadillac-driving sugar daddy who'd set her up in style. Meanwhile, she'd use the money that was stacked inside her luggage very sparingly, in case she ever fell on hard times.

"So, what's it gonna be?" the beefy white man inquired irritably.

"I'll pay for a day. Hang on; I got two dollars in my purse." Silk scanned the room, wondering what she'd done with her patent leather clutch. She scowled when she located it on the floor with the clasp open. She'd obviously had a wild night, and hoped she didn't have to get down on her knees and scrounge underneath the bed, searching for the scattered contents of her purse.

"Dammit," she muttered when she picked up her purse and discovered it contained only a comb, a tube of lipstick, a few scraps of paper, and a stick of chewing gum. Although alarm bells were sounding in her head, she chose to ignore them. Down on her knees, she lifted the tangled bed covers and peeked beneath the bed. Unwilling to accept what her eyes could clearly see, she stretched out her arm and felt around the dusty floor, grasping nothing but cobwebs.

She stood up, and with a burst of strength brought on by desperation, she shoved the bed several feet across the room. She swiped a hand across her face. The money that had been tucked inside her purse hadn't fallen under the bed, nor had the key to the locker. In a panic, she yanked the sheets off the bed. Frantic, Silk's eyes swept the room, but the key was nowhere to be found. Her eyes glistened, but she stubbornly refused to allow them to fill with tears. Crying meant she'd given up, and she hadn't. The key to that locker had to be somewhere in the room.

She overturned a waste bin and poked around in the rubbish.

The man with the receipt book stepped inside. "What're you doing, Miss? Cut it out before I charge you extra for trashing the place."

Arriving at the terrible conclusion that she'd been robbed of all her worldly goods, Silk wrung her hands and said in a distressed tone, "Listen, mister. Those two sailors who rented this room robbed me. Can you give me their full names and addresses? I need to locate those fellas."

"No one who checks in here gives out their true identity," he said, slightly amused by Silk's dilemma. "You can go to the nearest police precinct and fill out a theft report if that'll make you feel better, but I'm going to have to ask you to clear out of this room in the next five minutes."

Her heart began to pound. She was penniless and without shelter in a strange city filled with smooth-talking wolves in sheep's clothing.

Unwilling to give up easily, Silk found her way back to the bus terminal. She searched the banks of lockers, looking for number 105. Her heart jumped when she saw it. The door was closed with the key jutting outward. Mistaking that as a good sign, she yanked the locker door open, but her shoulders sagged when she found it empty. Those damned sailors had made off like bandits with her windfall of money.

Hit with a burst of enlightenment, she came to the conclusion that Big Mama had put a money-loss curse on her. Folks from Devil's Swamp preferred a harsh illness or the love-gone spell over the dreaded money-loss curse. Silk covered her face with both hands and shook her head in regret. Somewhat dazed by her tragic predicament, her knees were about to give out. She took a seat on a bench and sat amongst the travelers in the bus terminal.

Having nowhere to go, she stared into space as if entranced. The aggravating sound of a baby crying snapped her out of the altered state, and she was suddenly reminded of Clara and her cranky baby.

Like a dog digging for a bone, Silk plowed through the various slips of paper in her purse until she found the receipt with Clara's brother's telephone number.

Silk gave a quick sob story to an old woman sitting next to her and asked if she could bum a dime to make a phone call. Even though the woman agreed with a sympathetic smile, Silk wanted to backhand her for taking so long to give her the coin that jangled along with others inside a handkerchief that was tied in a million tight, little knots. *You'd think that in a big city like Philadelphia, folks would be modern enough to keep their small change in a coin purse instead of a wrinkled, old, knotted-up handkerchief.*

The woman finally handed over the dime and Silk hurried to the pay phone without bothering to thank her. She stood at the end of the short line to the pay phone, but too impatient to wait her turn, she moved to the front of the line, excusing herself and mumbling that she'd had a death in her family and needed to make an emergency phone call.

With a shaking finger, she dialed the number and could have cried tears of joy when she heard Clara's familiar voice on the other end of the line. "Hello, Clara? Is that you?"

"Yes, this is Clara. Who's this?"

"It's Silk, your friend from Louisiana."

Clara made a little sound of excitement. "My Lord, I was worried to death about you. Are you all right?"

Deeming it an appropriate time to release the tears that were building up inside of her, Silk wailed into the phone, "No, Clara, I'm not all right. I'm ashamed to tell you, but I've been robbed of all my possessions. I had to borrow a dime to call you."

"Where are you?"

"I'm sitting in the bus terminal in Philadelphia, surrounding by thieving, city slickers."

"There are a lot of people here at the house, paying their respect for my sister-in-law, and quite a few of them have cars. I'm going to ask Deacon Whiteside if he'd be willing to drive to Philadelphia and bring you back to Chester. Hold on for a second."

"Okay," Silk said in a weak voice followed by pitiful sniffling.

Clara placed her hand over the receiver and Silk couldn't make out what she was saying to the deacon, but she crossed her fingers, hoping for a favorable outcome.

"Okay, Deacon Whiteside is coming to pick you up and I'll be riding with him. Now, sit tight, you poor little lamb. We'll be there as soon as possible."

CHAPTER 9

In the presence of Clara and Deacon Whiteside, Silk did her best to speak in a manner that was becoming of a teacher.

"How'd you happen to lose your suitcase and all your belongings?" the deacon inquired.

"Well," she said, dabbing her eyes with a tissue that Clara had offered her. "I had my luggage secured in a locker while I walked around the city searching for a quiet place to study for my teacher's exam. I'd heard that the Young Women's Christian Association was a good place for decent, young ladies to reside, and so I tried to hunt that place down."

"Did you have any luck?" Clara asked.

"Yes, I found it and after I paid for boarding for a single night, I immediately returned to the bus terminal to get my suitcase, which contained my study papers, money, and clothes. But when I walked up to my locker, I discovered that a low-down thief had pried the locker open and had stolen all my worldly possessions."

Worked into tears over the loss of the fancy clothes that Nathan Lee had bought her and the hundreds of dollars she'd scuffled and killed for, she covered her face with her hands and cried bitter tears.

"It's going to be all right, Silk. We'll look out for you. Unfortunately, there's not a lot of room at Buddy's house, but we'll manage to squeeze you in. What do you plan to do about your teaching position?"

"I don't know. I can't take the exam without showing proof that I have a teaching certificate."

"Can't you send for another one?"

"I suppose, but that'll take some time."

"I'm going back to Biloxi after the funeral is over, and I think you should travel with me. Maybe teaching so far away from home isn't a good idea. There're lots of kids that need teaching in the South."

"I suppose," Silk said glumly.

"Don't worry about bus fare. I'm sure the Christian folks of Chester will be willing to pitch in with donations to buy you a bus ticket back home."

The small, two-story, wood-frame home on Flower Street with a stone path leading to the front door was a delight to the eyes, but the funeral wreath of dark-colored flowers and a black bow that hung on the front door was a reminder that the household was in mourning. The well-cared-for home was surrounded by numerous tall trees, high shrubs, and rosebushes, isolating it from the cluster of cookie-cutter, white brick, government houses that were on the opposite side of the street, and down-a-ways a bit.

Looking over her shoulder, she could see the shadowy figures of some of the residents of the barracks-type houses. She could hear their distant voices, and the faint sound of music. She sensed a liveliness and vitality in that area that pulled on her like a magnet.

"Come on, let's go inside, Silk," Clara prodded.

Distraught over losing her money and clothing, Silk didn't have to fake a solemn expression when she entered the house. The teardrops that trickled from her eyes were heartfelt.

Inside the house, grown-ups were drinking liquor and their plates were piled with all kinds of soul food from pig's feet and collard greens to pineapple upside-down cake and monkey bread. While the adults were drinking and filling their faces, the children were underfoot, squealing as they ripped and ran without supervision. Being stuck in a house filled with a bunch of snotty-nosed kids was not the way she envisioned her new life in the North. The thought of her predicament caused Silk to bury her face in her hands and cry.

Clara patted her on the back comfortingly. "Shh. Shh. It's okay. I know you have a sensitive heart, and seeing these little, motherless children is awfully hard to bear, but we're all trying to hold ourselves together for their sake. We told them their mother is resting with the angels, surrounded in God's glory. The fact that they'll never see her alive again hasn't hit them yet." Clara choked up briefly and then pulled herself together. "Why don't you come on upstairs with me and change out of that wrinkled dress? You're a little smaller than me, but I think you can fit my clothes. I'll introduce you to everyone after you freshen up."

Mourners who gathered in the small dining area stealthily cut their eyes at Silk as Clara escorted her up the stairs. No doubt they'd already been told of the stolen suitcase disaster and were being considerate enough not to openly stare.

Clara ran bathwater for Silk and poured in a generous amount of Jean Naté bath oil that had belonged to her dead sister-in-law. She laid clean clothes and underwear across the bed that had been shared by the deceased and her husband.

After the relaxing bath, which was a great luxury compared to the quick wash-ups she was accustomed to at home where there was no electricity or running water, Silk felt refreshed and in high spirits. Her mood quickly shifted when she noticed the drab gray dress Clara had loaned her. One glance at the brassiere and panties and she knew they were much too large for her.

Bra and panty-less, she put on the ugly dress that was several sizes too big. She tightened the belt that was attached to the garment in an attempt to make it fit better. Glancing around the bedroom, she was struck by the modern furnishings in the tidy room. She snooped in the closet and inside the drawers and couldn't help admiring the stylish clothes and colorful array of nylon panties. She quickly came to the conclusion that Ernestine had a great sense of style and flair.

Buddy was obviously a good provider, and that insurance money he had coming was an extra bonus. *I better hurry up and get myself downstairs and make his acquaintance before some other woman tries to take advantage of the fact that he's grieving and vulnerable.* The pack of brats Buddy was saddled with wasn't an ideal situation, but Silk decided to do her best to get along with her future step-children.

She smiled, imagining herself settling down with Buddy and being treated like a queen. Buddy couldn't offer her the kind of luxury that Nathan Lee had promised, but he could provide a comfortable lifestyle. With that insurance money he was entitled to, there might be enough for Silk to get herself a shiny, new car. She wondered what Buddy looked like. Was he red as clay and handsome as Duke Durnell or flabby and unattractive like Pudgy Hales? *It don't matter. I'm gonna make that hard-working widower my husband even if he's sporting a peg leg and a glass eye.*

With marriage on her mind, Silk sat down at the dead woman's vanity table and picked up her hairbrush and ran it through her hair. Instead of letting her locks hang loose, which always garnered compliments, she pulled in into a plain bun that downplayed her attractiveness. In the looks department, the average woman couldn't hold a candle next to Silk, and she didn't want to intimidate any of the plain-Jane mourners into putting up their guard around her. Nor did she want to provoke them into putting a protective circle around the grieving husband, and making Silk's goal of seducing Buddy and roping him in, much more difficult than it needed to be.

It was laughable that Clara thought Silk would get back on a bus and return to the South when everything she needed, minus the kids, was right here in this house. For starters, there was a closet filled with clothes as well as bureau drawers stuffed with undergarments and other womanly paraphernalia that wasn't currently being used. She gazed at the vanity table top and selected from an ample collection of Avon perfume, a scent called Unforgettable. Smiling, at her reflection, she spritzed herself with the fragrant mist.

Clara tapped on the door. "Are you decent?" she asked.

"Come on in," Silk replied, as if she were already the woman of the house.

"That dress is a little loose on you, but you still look like a million bucks," Clara complimented.

"Thanks, I feel much better. But I feel so silly not being able to hold on to my belongings, I dread facing your family and friends—especially your brother. I feel awful intruding on him during his time of sorrow."

"Buddy's having a rough time, but he has good manners and a charitable heart, and he told me that it was okay for you to stay here. He's at the hospital right now, visiting the twins." Clara shook her head. "Those babies are barely clinging to life, but Buddy goes to visit them for a few hours every day. Handling the funeral arrangements, going through all the red tape with that insurance business, and seeing about those twins is keeping him so busy, he'll hardly notice you at all."

That's what you think! Buddy's gonna be doing a lot more than merely noticing me.

CHAPTER 10

"Is there anything I can do to help out around here and earn my keep?" Silk asked.

"Nothing I can think of off the bat. There's lots of food on hand and the ladies from Ernestine and Buddy's church are keeping the house nice and tidy." Clara gazed upward in thought. "With you being a teacher and all, you're probably good with kids. Maybe you can keep an eye on the children and keep them in line. With their mother gone on home to glory, and their daddy distracted with funeral business and the baby twins, the boys are running around like wild heathens. My niece has always been the quiet type, but she seems to be withdrawing even more. That child is going to need a mother even more so than her brothers. And those sickly, newborn twins…" Clara's expression turned grim. "I don't know what Buddy is going to do about them."

Taking care of snot-nose kids was the last thing Silk wanted to be in charge of, but she smiled demurely and said, "I'll make sure the children spend their time constructively." "Spending time constructively" was a phrase she'd borrowed from one of her former teachers.

Though her beauty couldn't be denied, she'd made herself look as nonthreatening and innocent as possible by scrubbing her face clean of rouge, powder, and lipstick and by styling her hair in a plain bun. When Clara introduced her to small group of church ladies, Silk presented a bashful smile.

"You poor dear, we heard about your misfortune," said Sister Beverly, who was holding Clara's baby. Beverly had on a beige hat with a cluster of white flowers in the front. She appeared to be in her forties and was obviously the spokesperson for the group of church women.

"Philadelphia is full of con artists; it's not a safe place for a righteous woman to be wandering around alone," said Sister Beverly.

Silk nodded. "I found out the hard way."

"So, you're a teacher, are you? I heard you're going to be teaching at a private school."

"Yes ma'am. I am. This will be my first year teaching school."

"Where's the school located? It must be well hidden because I've never heard of any Christian School for colored children in Chester," Sister Beverly continued. The other women who were gathered around the dining room table murmured in agreement.

Silk's eyes darted back and forth as she thought up a lie. "It hasn't opened yet. The trustees are still looking for a building."

Sister Beverly raised a brow. "Who are the trustees? I know all the Christian folks in this area."

"Well, they're actually white missionaries who were traveling through Louisiana, recruiting teachers for Christian schools they're opening in different parts of the country. I already had a teaching position lined up in Louisiana, but I loved the idea of doing the Lord's work, and so I took a chance and traveled all the way here. Unfortunately, I don't know how to get in touch with those missionaries because all the information was in my suitcase." Silk shook her head pitifully. "I'll be heading south with Clara when she leaves after the funeral." Silk wiped away imaginary tears.

Clara put a comforting arm around Silk's shoulder. "Silk's beau is training to become a doctor, and I'm sure he'll be pleased to have her back in Louisiana. They're fixing to get married around Christmastime."

"Oh, you're going to be a doctor's wife?" Sister Beverly smiled in approval.

"Yes, ma'am. It's not official, but I'm guessing he's going to pop the question and give me a ring by Christmas."

"Tell the ladies about your hope chest," Clara said excitedly.

"Oh, it's nothing." Silk lowered her eyes, pretending to be modest.

"Don't be shy; tell them about all those fancy items you got stored in the chest for when you set up housekeeping," Clara prompted.

"Well, I have a set of silverware, silver candlesticks, bone china, lots of crystal, including a crystal butter dish, a ceramic serving bowl, several sets of beautiful bed linen, embroidered hand towels… oh, and I have all sorts of knickknacks and many other household items. My hope chest is filled to the brim."

"When is that boyfriend of yours going to officially become a doctor?" Sister Beverly inquired.

"He's in his last year of medical school, and after that, he has to complete a year of being an intern," Silk said, repeating what she'd overheard one of Big Mama's white clients say while speaking about her son, the future doctor.

"Hmm. Seems like colored doctors always end up marrying high-yella girls," Sister Beverly commented. Clara shot Sister Beverly a disapproving look.

Sensing hostility in Sister Beverly's voice, Silk said in a timid voice, "I'm gonna go check on the children."

"That wasn't very nice of you to say," Clara chastised Sister Beverly as Silk left the dining room. "She can't help her color no more than you or I can help ours."

"I stated a fact," Sister Beverly said, holding her ground. "Do any of you know of any colored doctors married to a brown-skinned gal? Those light-bright women tend to snatch up all the prominent colored men—doctors and preachers and such."

The flock of women muttered in agreement.

Clara joined Silk in the living room. "Don't pay Sister Beverly any mind. She can be rude at times, but that's just her way; you'll get used to her."

"It's okay; I know she didn't mean any harm."

"You're so forgiving; you're practically a saint, Silk. I'm mighty pleased to have a friend like you."

"The feeling is mutual; now introduce me to your niece and nephews."

"The boys seem to be doing fine, jumping around and rough-housing all over the place. But my niece, Dallas, she's been keeping to herself and not talking much. It's hard to know what's going on inside her head."

Silk glanced at the well-groomed little girl who was sitting on the shiny tile floor, playing jacks by herself. Gathered around the TV set, two scrawny boys with bright eyes were wiggling around, emitting squeals of excitement as they watched *The Lone Ranger*.

Getting an opportunity to watch a TV program was a rarity for Silk and she wanted to join the boys on the sofa and watch the action-packed show.

"Dallas, Myron, and Bruce," Clara said, calling the children to attention. "I want you to meet a good friend of mine from down South. Her name is Miss Silk and your daddy said it's all right if she stays here at the house with us for a while."

The boys, Bruce and Myron, gazed at Silk briefly, and then returned their attention to the TV. Accustomed to being admired by the male species in general—coloreds, whites, and even scrawny little boys—Silk didn't appreciate the quick and dismissive manner in which the boys had evaluated her. She took an immediate disliking toward them, but didn't let it show.

Reflected in the girl's eyes, Silk saw the admiration that the boys hadn't shown. In a soft voice, Dallas said, "Hi," and then returned to her solo game of jacks.

The little girl was obviously grieving for her dead mother; Silk could see the sorrow in the child's eyes. She joined Dallas on the floor. "You're pretty good at jacks."

"I'm in my foursies," Dallas said in a somber tone as she shook the metal objects in her hand and then tossed them onto the floor.

"Can I play with you?"

"Ladies don't play jacks," Dallas said, gazing at Silk quizzically.

"I do. It's always been one of my favorite games. But down South we don't get to play with shiny jacks like these."

"What do you play with?" Dallas inquired.

"Bottle caps, pebbles, and stones," Silk admitted, accidentally letting it slip out that she was from humble beginnings. She caught herself and said, "I mean, the poor little kids I taught when I was a student teacher had to play with stones. They'd love to have a store-bought set like you have."

"They play jacks with stones?" Dallas wrinkled her nose.

"Some children aren't as privileged as you are," Clara piped in.

"If you let me play, you won't have to start over. You can stay in your foursies, and I'll try to catch up with you."

"Okay," Dallas said, returning her attention to the game. She threw the ball up and scooped four jacks into her palm, and then caught the ball in the same hand. When she tried to scoop up the next set of four jacks that weren't spaced close together, she dropped the ball.

"It's my turn," Silk said gleefully. She picked up all ten jacks, rattling them around in her hand. Giving the jacks a wide toss, she began tossing the ball upward and picking up the jacks one at a time. She quickly caught up to Dallas, but instead of surpassing her, Silk deliberately dropped the ball, giving Dallas another chance.

"You're down; it's my turn again," Dallas said, excitement shining on her face as she scooped the jacks off the floor.

Seeing that Silk was coaxing Dallas out of her shell, Clara gave Silk a wink and made her way back to the dining room, rejoining the church folks.

Silk clapped her hands gleefully as Dallas progressed in the game. "You're a lot better than I thought you'd be. I'm going to have to get some practice in if I expect to beat you."

Silk's complimentary words brought a bright smile to the little girl's face.

The sound of tires crunching over gravel was heard. "Daddy's home," the boys exclaimed. "Let's ask him to help us put together our new model airplanes." Bruce and Myron raced across the room and pushed open the screen door, welcoming their father home.

The church women as well as Clara began moving from the dining room to the living room, their faces etched with sympathy. A few of them, Silk noticed, were primping their hair and smoothing out the wrinkles in their clothes. Apparently, some of the women had a little more on their minds than to simply console the grieving widower.

Showing respect, Silk rose from the floor, telling Dallas, "We'll finish the game later." Dallas stood next to Silk and Silk put an arm around the child's shoulder. Dallas rested her head against

Silk's side, a sign that she was warming up to the newcomer.

A man who was the color of blackstrap molasses walked through the door. He was medium height and weight, wearing a short-sleeved shirt that exposed muscular arms. He had a quiet dignity about him—a manly man who possessed full sensual lips and a thick head of kinky hair. His grim expression didn't disguise his good looks. In fact, the scowl that came from grieving the sudden loss of his wife made him even more attractive to Silk. He reminded her of the photographs she'd seen in movie magazines of actor Sidney Poitier.

Silk hadn't expected to be instantly attracted to Richard Dixon, but she was. And that attraction was accompanied by a flash of jealousy. If she were in Louisiana, she would have pulled out her knife and warned those church bitches to take their asses back into the dining room if they knew what was good for them. But here up North, she had to let go of her old ways and behave like a prim and proper schoolteacher.

"Daddy! Deacon Whiteside gave us new model airplanes, but we need you to help us put them together," Myron said in a rush of excitement.

"Boys! This is not the time to bombard your daddy with foolishness. He's under a lot of pressure," Sister Beverly said, shooing the boys away.

Buddy muttered that he'd take a look at the planes later, and rustled the boys' hair before they returned to their perch in front of the TV.

"Come on in the dining room and rest yourself, Buddy," Sister Beverly said. "The ladies will fix you a plate of fried chicken and a nice glass of lemonade to cool you off," she said, steering Buddy out of the living room.

Buddy stopped walking as his eyes landed on his daughter. "How's my little bunny rabbit?" he said to Dallas. Silk could tell he had a soft spot for his little girl, and she was glad that she was winning the child over.

"I'm fine, Daddy," Dallas responded. "How come you didn't bring the twin babies home?"

"They're too small right now. They have a lot of growing to do before they can come home." His gaze shifted to Silk. "You must be Clara's friend."

"Yes, my name's Silk Moreaux."

"I'm Richard Dixon but everyone calls me Buddy. I heard about your mishap in Philly, and I want you to know you're welcome to stay here."

"She's catching a bus back down South when Clara leaves," Sister Beverly interjected.

"We don't have a lot of room, but we'll make do," Buddy said. His voice was deep and rich. The sound of it made Silk feel tingly all over.

"Thank you for your hospitality, and I'm terribly sorry about your loss," Silk said.

"Miss Silk talks country like Aunt Clara," Bruce blurted. He and his brother broke into titters of laughter and Silk wanted to slap them. But instead she smiled at the boys.

"Clara and I are country girls. What you hear is called a Southern accent," Silk explained.

"Your daddy used to have a Southern accent, too," Clara reminded her nephew.

"Uh-uh, our daddy never talked country, did you, Daddy?" Myron asked.

"I was a country bumpkin when I arrived here in Chester, but I lost my accent after a while," Buddy explained to his son.

"That's enough about country-talking," Sister Beverly said. "Come on, Buddy; let's get you something to eat. You've been gone for hours, and you must be starving." She motioned for Buddy to follow her to the dining room.

More than anything, Silk wanted to kick Clara, her baby, and all the church folk out of the house so that she could have some privacy with Buddy. Before he was whisked away by Sister Beverly, she could have sworn that he'd given her a special look. A look that told her he'd rather spend time with her than be stuck in the dining room with a bunch of ol' biddies.

CHAPTER 11

The boys shared the bedroom with their father, Clara and her baby stayed in the boys' room, while Silk bunked with Dallas. Silk wondered if she'd get a wink of sleep tonight while sharing a tiny little twin bed with the youngster.

Dallas' bedroom reminded Silk of a child's room in a magazine. The wallpaper was decorated with little ballerinas. Frilly gingham curtains with sashes hung at the windows and the dust ruffles around the bed matched the curtains. On the floor beside the bed was a multicolored oval rug that was bordered with peach rosettes. Beneath the windowsill was a large, wooden toy box that was painted white and had Dallas' name engraved on the front.

There were dolls and stuffed animals everywhere: perched on shelves, clustered on top of the chest of drawers, lying in toy cradles, and life-size dolls stood like sentries in different areas of the bedroom. Silk had never possessed any shiny, new toys as a child. She'd had a crude rag doll that Big Mama had made for her out of old scraps of fabric. But Silk's most prized possession had been a Tiny Tears doll passed on to her by one of Big Mama's customers, discarded by her daughter after she'd dropped the doll and cracked its hard plastic skull. Silk had cherished that doll, feeding her lots of water and then squeezing her rubber tummy to make the tears trickle from her eyes.

Silk was fascinated by Dallas' toy collection and the little girl was fascinated with Silk's long hair. While Dallas brushed and combed Silk's hair, styling it a half-dozen different ways as if she were a real-life Barbie doll, Silk took an interest in the child's Betsy McCall paper doll set. Wearing a smile, Silk cut out the fancy paper clothes, carefully working the scissors around the tabs that would secure the clothing to the cardboard doll.

When Silk noticed Dallas yawning, she reluctantly put away the paper doll and told Dallas it was time for both of them to call it a night.

"Do you want to play with my Patti Playpal tomorrow?" Dallas pointed to the dark-haired, life-size doll that was dressed in a summer short set. "She's wearing my old clothes," Dallas said with pride.

Silk pulled back the covers. "I love toys, and we can play some more first thing in the morning. Now, get in bed, and I'll curl up at the bottom."

"I have to say my prayers first."

"Well, go ahead and say 'em."

Dallas got down on her knees beside the bed and placed her hands together prayerfully. At the conclusion of the prayer, the list of people she asked God to bless went on endlessly.

"Okay, that's enough blessings," Silk said with a patient smile. Unlike her rowdy, smart-aleck brothers, Dallas was a sweet and likable child.

"And may God bless Miss Silk." Dallas stood halfway and then returned to her knees. "And dear God, please let Miss Silk stay here with us until our mommy comes back home with the twins."

"Honey, your mama ain't coming back. Didn't your daddy explain what happened to her?"

Dallas nodded. "He said she's resting with the angels."

"That's right, and she'll be resting for a very long time."

"How long?"

"Your mama won't be coming back, ever. But don't worry; she's safe up in heaven with God and his angels."

"I don't want her to be with God; I want her to come back home," Dallas said with her bottom lip quivering, and tears spilling from her eyes. The child began to tremble, making a low, screechy sound that reminded Silk of a wounded animal.

"Shh. Don't cry, honey," Silk said comfortingly as she wiped the tears from the little girl's face. "Everything is gonna work out." She put her arms around Dallas. "Hush, now. You still got your daddy, and from what I can tell, he's a kindhearted man. He's not gonna let anything happen to you."

"But I want Mommy, too," Dallas cried. Gasping, her little chest heaving up and down, Dallas was finally releasing the grief that had been bottled up inside, but it was bad timing for her to choose the dead of night to finally let go of her sorrow. Only a wall separated Dallas' room from the room where Clara and her baby were sleeping, and the last thing Silk wanted was to hear that loudmouth baby yelping and crying.

"You gotta hush up before you wake up your baby cousin and everyone else in the house."

There was a tap on the bedroom door, and Silk wasn't surprised. "See, you done woke up your auntie," Silk said in exasperation. "Come in," she said, expecting Clara to walk through the door clutching her fussy baby. But it was Buddy who entered the bedroom, and he looked boyishly handsome in a pair of striped pajamas.

He crossed the room and sat on the small bed next to Silk and Dallas. "What's wrong, bunny rabbit?"

"I want Mommy. I want Moooommy!" Close to hysteria, Dallas' voice escalated.

Silk gazed at Buddy helplessly. "I was trying to calm her down. I told her that her mama was with the angels, but she doesn't seem to understand."

Buddy scooped Dallas into his arms. "I know you miss your mother. I miss her, too, and if I could bring her back, I would, but the good Lord called her home."

"Why?" Dallas inquired in a tearful voice.

"He needed another angel," Buddy said softly. "We're all going to have to learn how to live without her. It's not going to be easy, but we'll get through it, I promise." Buddy's voice cracked with emotion and Silk took that opportunity to comfortingly pat him on the back.

The pats turned into a circular rub along his shoulder blade and then the center of his back. She didn't look at his face, but could tell by the way his shoulders relaxed, that he was responding favorably to her touch. She cut an eye at Dallas and was relieved to see that although the child was sniffling a little, sleep was over-powering her and closing her eyes for the night.

While Dallas drifted off to sleep in her father's arms, Silk's hands were busy. "Let me get the kinks out your neck," she whispered. She scooted behind him. On her knees, she administered to his taut muscles. She squeezed and kneaded the muscles in her neck in the precise manner that Big Mama had taught her to work on her stiffened muscles after she'd put in a long day of hunting, fishing, or digging in the ground.

"That feels nice," Buddy murmured.

Silk's hands traveled to his shoulders and began to squeeze hard. "Your shoulders are so tense, seems like they've been carrying the weight of the world."

"Yeah, I got the weight of the world on me. That's exactly how it feels."

"Well, it's a good thing I'm here to lighten your burden, somewhat." She made chopping motions on his shoulder blade and across his back, working her way to his other shoulder blade.

"Mmm. Feels nice. How'd you learn how to do this?"

"My mama was a nurse. She took care of the ailments of all the folks in our community, and she taught me a few of her nursing specialties." Silk reached upward and began massaging Buddy's temples. She smiled with satisfaction when he let out a soft moan. Cutting an eye downward at Dallas, Silk was glad that the mournful child had finally cried herself to sleep.

"Dallas is out like a light. You wanna lay her down so I can finish taking care of you?" Silk used the sweetest and most innocent voice that she could manufacture.

"Uh, okay." Buddy placed Dallas at the top of the bed, gently resting her head on the pillow and then covering her with the top sheet. He resumed his sitting position at the foot of the bed and Silk continued to work on him from behind.

"Why don't you take off that pajama top so I can rub your back real good?"

"No, that wouldn't be proper. I think I better keep my top on."

"I didn't mean any harm, Buddy. You been so kindhearted toward me; I only wanted to pay you back by using my nursing skills on you." Her breasts were pressed into his back as she began to massage his scalp. Her fingers meandered to his forehead, which she lightly stroked.

"Close your eyes," Silk whispered, and then gently caressed his eyelids. She ran her fingertip along the bridge of his nose and down to his lips, outlining them, and then brushing her finger against his full lips.

When Buddy let out a groan, Silk interpreted that utterance as permission to take things a little further. She inserted the tip of her finger between his lips. Feeling the cool moisture of his tongue, she drew in a sharp breath.

"My whole body is tingling," she said, keeping her voice low and glancing over her shoulder, making sure Dallas was sound asleep.

Buddy grasped her wrist and removed her finger from his mouth. "This is wrong. My wife's not even in the ground yet." Anguished, he buried his face in his hands.

She eased off the bed and stood in front of him. "It can be our secret. No one has to know," Silk said, caressing the hands that covered his face. "You've been staying strong for your family, but everybody has a breaking point. You need to let your guard down every once in a while, and you can do that when you're with me."

She crouched in front of him and buried her face in his pajama crotch. "I know you're grieving for your poor, dead wife, and all I want to do is take some of the strain off you," she said with her lips pressed against the bulge that began to form beneath the cotton fabric. "What goes on behind closed doors, ain't nobody's business." She kissed the phallic imprint that lengthened and twitched with yearning.

"Quit it! This ain't right." Buddy patted her head briskly, urging her to stop. But instead of heeding his wishes, Silk looked up at him and smiled as she defiantly wound her hand inside his pajama fly and worked it inside his boxers.

Clutching his pulsing manhood inside her palm, she said, "Close your eyes and relax while I give you some special treatment."

Buddy leaned back a little, but remained upright with his palms pressed against the bed, his weight supported by his extended arms. Silk stroked his rigid flesh, drawing from Buddy more agonized objections, but she silenced his protests when she fitted her lips around the head of his throbbing appendage and sucked it in slowly, and then suddenly allowed it to slip from her mouth.

"What's wrong?" Buddy inquired in a desperate voice.

"I don't want to force you into anything you don't want to do. I wanna suck this big ol' thing of yours, but I won't do it if you think it's wrong."

"It's not wrong," Buddy said in an urgent, hoarse voice. Panting, he gripped Silk by her shoulders and pulled her closer. Shuddering, he groaned and clutched the bedspread as he slid in and out of her moist mouth.

After a few moments, Silk pulled away.

"Please," he uttered, jutting forward and attempting to refill her mouth with his hardness.

"You don't want Dallas to catch us, do you?"

"No."

"Then, let's get down on the floor, so she won't see us."

Lying atop the soft, oval rug on the floor, Silk lifted her nightgown and spread her legs invitingly. "Come on and get some of this poontang. It'll help with your grief."

Buddy straddled her, pushing inside her with urgency. As he humped and thrust, Silk's eyes wandered around the lovely bedroom that was overflowing with toys and dolls. She wondered how Buddy would respond if she asked him to buy her a brand-new doll. Grown women had doll collections, she reasoned. One of Big Mama's best customers had a doll collection that included a beautiful bridal doll and a Victorian doll with an elaborate hat and an umbrella. *Shoot, I want me a bunch of pretty dolls of my own. With the thrills I'm giving Buddy, he should be more than willing to spoil me the same way he spoiled his dead wife and his kids.*

CHAPTER 12

The spur-of-the-moment rendezvous with Buddy had been Silk's way of making a down payment on the comfortable lifestyle she longed for. After Buddy slipped out of Dallas' bedroom, Silk got under the covers and slept like a baby. She was in the midst of a dream where she was well-dressed and classy-looking, wearing a sleek shift dress and a pillbox hat with a veil that was similar to a Jacqueline Kennedy ensemble.

A knock on the bedroom door pulled her out of the dream. She sat up and looked around. Dallas wasn't anywhere to be found. The door opened and Clara entered, cradling her brat. She was dressed in a flared skirt, a white blouse, and clutching a pocket-book, all dolled up like she was on her way to a special outing.

"Where's Dallas?" Silk asked.

"She's downstairs eating breakfast with her brothers."

"Oh, I guess I must have overslept."

"That's okay. After all you went through in Philadelphia, I'm sure you needed the rest."

Silk nodded.

"I'm fixing to go to the hospital to check on the twins with Buddy. They don't allow children or babies to visit patients, and I was wondering if you'd be kind enough to look after Vernon, Jr. and Buddy's kids while we're out? After we leave the hospital, we have to stop by the insurance company for Buddy to sign some papers."

"Okie dokie," Silk said reluctantly. She didn't know the first thing about taking care of a baby. Had never changed a diaper or bottle-fed a baby in her life, and she wasn't in the mood to start now. But needing Clara's continued support and friendship until she secured her position as Buddy's wife, Silk thought it best to tough it out and try to care for the cranky baby.

"I saved you a plate of pancakes, sausage, and eggs. It's covered with wax paper on the kitchen counter."

"Thanks, Clara."

Clara kissed the baby goodbye, which prompted him to try and launch himself out of Silk's arms in an attempt to get to his mother.

"His bottles of milk are in the ice box. You can feed him the jar of baby food I left on the counter around noon. In a few minutes, he'll be ready to be put down for a nap."

The baby let out a sharp cry and Clara eased backward toward the open door. "I best-better sneak on out of here before my son starts a big ol' ruckus."

After Clara fled down the stairs, Silk alternated between shaking and rocking the baby, attempting to get him to take a nap. She didn't appreciate being saddled down with a baby and a pack of kids. After the good loving she'd laid on Buddy last night, she should have been relaxing—watching TV and eating from a gift box of chocolate bonbons.

All in due time, she told herself.

Vernon, Jr. finally dozed off and Silk decided to lie him down on Buddy's bed, since it was too wide for the baby to accidentally roll off. While in Buddy's bedroom, Silk did some more snooping, looking through his wife's bureau drawers and examining her clothes that were hung in the closet she shared with Buddy. Silk had to hand it Mrs. Ernestine Dixon. The deceased had been a snazzy dresser with oodles of regular clothes and maternity wear. The top shelf inside the closet was stacked with hat boxes. Silk took the boxes down and peeked inside each one. The hats were glorious, a variety of shapes and colors that were decorated with feathers, flowers, and veils.

Silk had never worn a fancy hat in her life, and she couldn't resist trying on some of the hats. She was having a good time until Bruce walked into the bedroom.

He gazed at Silk with a scowl. "Why're you messing with my mother's hats?"

"I don't think your mama would mind if I admire her hats. I'll tell you one thing, your mama sho' nuff had good taste."

Bruce grimaced. "I hate that country way you talk."

He was an insolent child, and Silk was so infuriated by the insult, she was of a mind to turn him over her knee and whip him so hard, he wouldn't be able to sit on his backside for a week. But common sense told her she needed Buddy's boys to like her as much as Dallas did. Forcing herself to grin and bear it, she smiled at Bruce and said, "I hope I can get rid of my accent while I'm up here visiting with y'all."

Taken off-guard by Silk's good-natured reply, Bruce simply shrugged. And without further comment, he turned around and exited his father's bedroom.

It was time to get dressed and start her babysitting duties, but she had nothing to wear except Clara's dowdy, old dress. She longed to select something from Buddy's wife's wardrobe but decided against it. *All in due time.*

Bruce and Myron were playing in the neatly mowed backyard that was filled with well-kept shrubs, bushes, and flowers and in the center of it all was a swing set and a sliding board. Like their dead mother, the Dixon children were spoiled rotten. Silk watched the boys with a frown for a few moments, and then joined Dallas in the living room to watch television.

Silk was in seventh heaven as she watched cartoons with Dallas. She wasn't sure what she enjoyed more, the entertaining commercials or the actual televised programs. Turning the dial and clicking from one channel to the next was a wonderful new experience. At home, she and Big Mama didn't even have a battery-operated radio. Big Mama didn't have any interest in entertainment or current events. Her own small world was all that mattered to her.

The cartoon went off and the opening music began to play, announcing a game show called *Queen for a Day.* Silk settled into a comfortable position on the sofa. At the same time that the host asked the audience and television viewers, "Would YOU like to be queen for a day?" there were three sharp knocks on the front door.

"Aw, shoot. Somebody picked a heck of a time to drop by for a visit," Silk complained as she rose from the sofa, aggravation creasing her brow. When she opened the front door and found Sister Beverly and a moose-faced, younger woman standing on the welcome mat holding large Tupperware containers, Silk was tempted to slam the door in their faces and return to the TV program.

"Hello, Satin," Sister Beverly said. She wore a large hat with lots of netting and flowery ornaments dangling around the brim. "I don't see Buddy's car in the driveway, so I suppose he's out handling funeral business."

"My name is Silk, not Satin."

Sister Beverly placed her hand to her mouth as she chuckled in mock embarrassment. "Excuse me, dear. I was close, though. I knew your name had something to do with a soft fabric."

Silk wasn't amused. "Buddy and Clara are at the hospital, visiting the twins," she said sullenly.

"Those poor little babies," Sister Beverly said, shaking her head and clucking her tongue. "Hopefully, Buddy won't stay single too long. When the appropriate amount of time has passed, he's going to need a good woman by his side." She nodded toward the unattractive woman standing next to her. "This is my niece, Henrietta. After she graduated high school, she started working as a clerk typist at the Bell Telephone Company. This girl is smart as a whip and she can cook up a storm." Sister Beverly pushed her way into the living room. "Henrietta made Buddy's favorite: neck bones and beans. I made chicken and dumplings for the children. That was one of their mother's specialties and I thought it might put a smile on their faces. Where're the boys and how're they holding up?" Sister Beverly asked.

"They're playing in the backyard, and they're doing as well as can be expected," Silk replied.

"What about Dallas?" Sister Beverly nudged her head in Dallas' direction and beckoned Henrietta and Silk to follow her into the kitchen. "It's a good thing you're looking after Dallas for now, but after you go back down South that child is going to need the company of a woman. Being the only girl in the family, she's going to need a mother much more so than the boys do."

"I thought her mama gave birth to twin girls," the moose-faced niece chimed in.

"Nobody expects those babies to make it, God bless their little souls. They only weigh a couple pounds each." Sister Beverly shook her head and then motioned for Henrietta. "Get moving, Henrietta.

Put the neck bones in the Frigidaire. Grab an apron and start heating up the chicken and dumplings for the children's lunch." Sister Beverly pointed to a row of hooks on the wall, one of which held a red-and-white apron.

Silk had hoped the women would drop the food off and skedaddle, and she was none too pleased with them sticking around.

Glimpsing Silk's resentful expression, Henrietta began to awkwardly fuss with the lid of the plastic container. "Sorry to barge in on you like this, and I hope you don't mind us poking around in the kitchen," she said apologetically.

"Why would she mind?" Sister Beverly butted in. "These kids will starve if we Christian folk don't pitch in and help keep food on the table. I want you to start getting comfortable in this kitchen because after Buddy's sister and Silk leave town, he's going to need all the help he can get with feeding those poor, motherless children of his. Buddy's a widower now, and he'll fall out of the Lord's favor if he stays single too long."

Both Henrietta and Silk shot Sister Beverly puzzled glances.

"It's in the Bible. Proverbs 18:22 says, *He who finds a wife finds a good thing and obtains favor from the Lord. It's* my Christian duty to help Buddy find a suitable wife, and my niece, Henrietta has all the qualifications."

Silk could feel her anger rising. She'd staked her claim on Buddy and had already put down a deposit last night. Sister Beverly, with her big-hat-wearing, sanctimonious self was intruding on Silk's territory, and Silk was too high-spirited to simply stand back and take it.

Choosing her words carefully, Silk spoke in a calm tone. "Buddy's worried sick about those little babies, and he's grieving something terrible over the sudden loss of his wife. Finding a new wife is the last thing on his mind right now. I'm sure your niece understands," Silk said, glancing from Sister Beverly to Henrietta.

"Yes, indeed. I understand," Henrietta readily agreed. "I heard a man should mourn his wife for a full year before he takes a new bride."

"That's ridiculous. Where the devil did you hear that crap, Henrietta?" Perturbed, Sister Beverly set the chicken and dumplings on the countertop with a bang.

Silk eased the Tupperware from Henrietta's hands. "On Buddy's behalf, thank you for your kindness, but I think it's best if you two run along. His wife isn't even in the ground yet; it's much too soon for him to even think about getting hitched."

Sister Beverly snorted. "Young lady, you're overstepping your boundaries. What gives you the right to tell us what to do when you're nothing more than a charity case. You're staying here because you don't have a pot to piss in nor a window to throw it out."

Hearing Sister Beverly's voice rise, Dallas meandered into the kitchen and leaned against Silk. Silk put a comforting arm around the child as she addressed Sister Beverly. "It's true, I suffered a terrible misfortune, and I intend to repay Buddy for his wonderful hospitality. After I return to Louisiana, my life will return to normal when my beau and I announce our engagement. He's training to be a doctor," Silk said to impress Henrietta.

"A doctor!" Henrietta's voice was filled with awe.

"Yes, and I have a teaching degree. Since things didn't work out here, I've decided to accept the position I was offered back home. Buddy understands that my current financial straits are only temporary. My future doctor husband and I will pay him back for his generosity." It was difficult for Silk to use good grammar when she was on the verge of cursing Sister Beverly out.

"Oh, you're going to pay Buddy back, huh. I'll believe it when I see it," Sister Beverly said with her lips screwed to one side. "Come on, Henrietta; let's go. We don't stick around ill-mannered folks." She glanced down at Dallas. "Honey, make sure you let your daddy know that Sister Beverly and her niece, Henrietta, stopped by with lunch and dinner for the family."

"Okay," Dallas said meekly.

With her niece in tow, Sister Beverly left in a huff.

Peeking through the curtains, Silk could hear Sister Beverly grumbling as she stood on the front porch adjusting her hat and straightening her clothes. "I feel like I've been battling with the daughter of Satan," Sister Beverly said to Henrietta.

"She seemed nice," Henrietta replied. "She's real pretty, too."

"Don't be fooled by her pretty face. That girl is sneaky and up to no good. I can feel it in my bones."

"You shouldn't say things like that, Auntie. She was as sweet as pie, and she did have a point about giving Buddy time to grieve."

"Don't be so naïve, Henrietta. Buddy earns good money. He's the only colored supervisor at the shipbuilding plant. I plan to make it my business to see to it that you get your hooks into him before other folks start parading their sisters, cousins, and daughters in front of him."

Buddy's already taken; I beat everybody to the punch, Silk thought as she discreetly closed the curtains. Smiling in satisfaction, she patted Dallas on the shoulder. "I heard you like chicken and dumplings, is that right?"

"Uh-huh."

"Well, I got some for you. Have a seat at the table while I heat up some lunch for us. I'll call your devilish brothers in after we finish eating." Silk smiled at Dallas and whispered conspiratorially,

"This is our special time. We don't like spending it with noisy, bad boys, do we?"

Crinkling her nose as she smiled, Dallas shook her head in agreement.

Silk took the red-and-white apron off the hook and tied it around her waist. The kitchen appliances sparkled like new, and the linoleum floor held a high-shine. Like the other rooms in the house, the kitchen was modern and decorated tastefully, reminding Silk of the white folks' kitchens she'd stood in while delivering Big Mama's potions.

Humming, Silk transferred the chicken and dumplings into a pot, and turned the burner on the stove. "Hot dog!" Silk exclaimed when the flame popped up. The indoor plumbing and electricity she was enjoying at Buddy's house was a dream come true, and the gas stove she was cooking on was a luxury she hadn't even considered back when she was making plans to run off to a better life with Nathan Lee.

Happily, she rummaged around in the refrigerator, looking for a vegetable to go with the main dish. She selected a sealed bowl that some church member had thoughtfully labeled with a strip of masking tape that read: "mustard greens." *This is my kitchen now, and I suppose it wouldn't hurt if I learned a thing or two about cooking, but in the meantime, I'm content to stir the pots filled with other folks' cooking.*

CHAPTER 13

On the back porch, Clara and Silk sat on the metal glider drinking lemonade while the children ran around the yard, trying to catch lightning bugs. For the kind of person who enjoyed a peaceful lifestyle, tonight would be considered a lovely evening. But Silk was bored. She'd never been too fond of tranquility; she'd always gotten a kick out of stirring up trouble and shaking things up.

Inside the house, Buddy and three men from his job were gathered in the dining room. The guys had come over to help Buddy forget his troubles, and they were all laughing and talking as they drank hard liquor. The low rumble sound of their deep voices seemed to beckon Silk.

She'd much rather be inside with the menfolk, flirting, throwing down drinks, and causing a ruckus. It wasn't uncommon for men to come to blows when they were vying for her affection. She wondered how Buddy would react if one of his friends tried to make time with her. He was such an even-tempered man, it was hard to imagine him puffed up and enraged. The idea of it tickled her.

"The mortician promised to do a good job on Ernestine," Clara said, breaking into Silk's thoughts. "Buddy wanted a closed casket because Ernestine's face was cut up so bad when she went through the windshield of the taxi cab. But the mortician assured him that he could make her look true to herself when she's laid to rest in the white, satin-lined coffin that Buddy picked out."

"Hmm." Silk figured if she uttered only a grunt, Clara would take a hint and stop jabbering long enough for Silk to get her thoughts together and figure out a plan to ditch Clara on the porch and join the menfolk who were having a good time inside the house. Each of Buddy's friends had brought along a bottle of whiskey, and the scent drifted outside, tantalizing Silk.

"My brother was very particular about the quality of Ernestine's casket. He always gave her the best of everything while she was living and I suppose he didn't want to shortchange her in death."

A hot streak of jealousy shot through Silk. She didn't like hearing that her husband-to-be was still doting on his dead wife. "Buddy was a good husband," Silk murmured. Unable to think of anything else to contribute to the unpleasant conversation, she gulped down the lemonade and rose to her feet. "That lemonade was delicious and refreshing, Clara. Would you mind if I got myself another glass?"

"Of course. You're practically family; you don't need permission to help yourself to anything you'd like."

"Thanks. That's really kind of you, Clara." Silk had one foot inside the house when the children began bickering over something. She quickly closed the screen door behind her, relieved she'd vacated the porch in the nick of time. She'd had enough of tending to children for one day. It was Clara's turn to deal with the squabbles of the little buggers.

In the dining room, the conversation stopped and four sets of eyes ogled her. Silk had washed and ironed her polka dot dress, which was much more attractive than that drab, shapeless dress that Clara had loaned her. With a subtle wiggle in her walk, she proceeded toward the sink and rinsed her glass, dried it, and put it away.

Realizing she was being admired, she gracefully opened the freezer door and took out an ice tray. She emptied the ice cubes into a bowl, and then sauntered in the direction of the dining room.

"I thought you gentlemen might need your drinks freshened. Anybody want some ice?"

Buddy's three friends held out their glasses at the same time. They'd all been drinking their whiskey straight, but were willing to switch to having it on the rocks merely to enjoy Silk's company.

Daintily, Silk picked up ice cubes and dropped them in their glasses. When each man thanked her, she exaggerated her Southern drawl when she responded, "It's truly my pleasure." Talking extra-country made her seem sweet and naïve, as if she could be easily taken advantage of. Those two con artist sailors in Philadelphia had made out like bandits with all her worldly possessions, only because she'd been as drunk as a skunk. When sober and working with her full capacities, there wasn't a man alive who could outfox Silk Moreaux.

"My name is Leon, and I don't believe I've made your acquaintance," said a squat, box-shaped man.

"I'm Silk."

"Yes, you are," said a short fellow with conk in his hair. He was the youngest in the bunch and wore a high pompadour that gave him the appearance of a rock-and-roll singer. He glanced at Buddy and said, "Richard Buddy Dixon, you sly ol' fox, you. You didn't mention that Miss Lena Horne was visiting you. If I knew a movie star was among us, I would have changed out of my grungy work uniform."

Silk blushed and giggled as all the men broke out in laughter.

She liked the playful, teasing manner of the guy with the pompadour. Although he was short in stature, his big personality made up for his lack of height. Out of the three male visitors, he was the most attractive and also seemed to be the most fun.

"My name is Cephus, and by the way, I'm the only bachelor in the crowd," he said with a charming smile. Then, he cut his eye at Buddy, dropping his smile when he remembered that tragedy had changed Buddy's status from married to single.

"Hi, Cephus. It's nice to meet you," Silk said. "In fact, it's nice to meet all of you, gentlemen. I hope to see you again before I make the trip back home to Louisiana." Silk positioned the bowl of ice on the table and waved at everyone as she exited the dining room.

Cephus followed her to the kitchen. "Uh, when are you splitting?" he inquired in a low voice.

"In a week or so. After, Buddy's sister, Clara, helps him find a full-time babysitter."

"Maybe we can catch a movie before you leave Chester."

"That sounds good. I've been cooped up in the house, and haven't had a chance to see much of this town."

"I'll make it my business to do something about that. Give you a tour of Chester after the movie. By the way, do you like monster flicks?"

Silk nodded enthusiastically. "I like all kinds of picture shows."

"*King Kong vs. Godzilla* is playing at the State Theater, over town. Or we could catch a John Wayne western. *The Man Who Shot Liberty Valance* is playing at the Apollo Theater. Oh, and the Strand Theater is showing an old flick, *Psycho*. The Strand and the Apollo are both located on Third Street, and that's where all the colored folks go. Those theaters aren't as nice as The State, but the popcorn is tasty," Cephus said with laughter.

Silk waved a hand. "Oh, I'm not particular. Wherever you want to go is fine by me." She leaned to the side so she could glance into the dining room and catch Buddy's reaction. Buddy was squirming in his seat. He didn't appear too comfortable with her being alone in the kitchen with Cephus. His uneasiness served him right. He'd been avoiding Silk like the plague after getting his thrills off of her last night.

Cephus gently grasped Silk's hand and caressed her fingers. "I'll give you a call tomorrow."

"I'll be waiting." Giving Cephus an alluring smile, she withdrew her hand. Feeling a sense of accomplishment, Silk sashayed out of the kitchen and rejoined Clara on the back porch.

"Who were you talking to?" Clara asked.

"One of Buddy's friends—a guy named Cephus. Says he wants to take me to the picture show."

"They don't call it a 'picture show' here in Chester. They say they're going to the movies," Clara informed.

"I don't think I'll ever catch on to this city-slick way of talking. It's a good thing I'm going back to Louisiana."

"How do you think that doctor of yours will feel about you courting and sparking behind his back?"

"As long as I'm faithful, he doesn't mind if I go out and have a nice time."

"My husband would never be that open-minded. He doesn't want me out of his sight. If a long-distance telephone call from Biloxi, Mississippi to Chester wasn't so expensive, he'd be calling and checking on me every day."

"My boyfriend trusts me and I trust him." Silk stared off dreamily, imagining the good time she was going to have with Cephus. She gazed at Clara. "I hate to ask, but do you think I could borrow another dress from you? Something nice that I could wear to the picture show." Silk covered her mouth and giggled. "Excuse me, I meant to say, the movies."

"I didn't pack much. The only thing I have left in my suitcase is a few house dresses and the black dress I plan to wear to Ernestine's funeral."

"Oh," Silk murmured in disappointment. Struck with a bright idea, she regarded Clara. "Do you think Buddy would mind if I borrowed one of Ernestine's dresses? I couldn't help but notice that her closet is crammed with beautiful clothes."

"I don't know, Silk. Buddy might not like that idea."

"Well, what's he planning to do with all her nice things?"

"With so much on his mind, I doubt if he's crossed that bridge, yet."

Silk and Clara sat in uncomfortable silence for a while, and then Clara called the children, informing them it was bedtime.

The boys and Dallas complained about having to go to bed. Clara had to threaten to take a strap to their behinds to get them moving. The children galloped across the yard and up the three wooden steps that led to the porch. Instead of trailing behind Clara and her brothers, Dallas stopped and clasped Silk's hand, expecting her new roommate to accompany her to bed.

"You run along with Aunt Clara. I'll be upstairs a little later."

"Are you going to come up and say prayers with me?"

"I'm going back home next week, and so it's about time you got in the habit of saying your prayers without me," Silk said, stroking the child's face

Dallas' eyes became watery. "I don't want you to go away and leave me."

"Well, you be sure to let your daddy know how you feel. Don't say anything right now. Wait until you have some alone time with him and then you tell him how much you love Miss Silk."

"Okay."

"You do love me, don't you Dallas?"

"Uh-huh. You're nice. And you're pretty like the princess in my storybook."

"Thank you. You're pretty, too."

"I want to look like you when I grow up," Dallas admitted, blushing.

Silk was tickled that Dallas admired her so openly. Having Buddy's favorite child as an ally would eventually come in handy, Silk surmised.

"Go on upstairs and get ready for bed. When you get up in the morning, I'll let you brush and comb my hair. When I was a little girl, my school friends always wanted to braid my hair, but I couldn't let them because my mama didn't allow it. You're the only little girl who's ever played in my hair. You wanna know why?"

"Why?"

"Because you're my special friend."

"I am?" Dallas beamed with pride.

Silk nodded. "Now, don't forget to tell your daddy how much you love me."

"I won't forget," Dallas said with a bright smile.

CHAPTER 14

Sitting alone on the glider, Silk heard the front door opening and closing as Buddy's friends left one by one. Cephus came outside to bid her goodnight.

"Goodnight, Cephus."

Instead of going back inside, Cephus took a seat next to her on the glider. "It's a nice night," he remarked, draping an arm around her as if they were sweethearts.

Frowning, Silk leaned to the side. "Hey, what do you think you're doing?"

"Sorry. I jumped the gun. I didn't mean any harm. I'll keep my hands to myself," Cephus said, chuckling as he folded his hands and placed them in his lap.

The screen door cracked open and Buddy stood in the doorway watching Silk and Cephus, the muscles in his face were taut with hostility. "Say, man, you promised to give Leon a ride home. He's sitting in your Rambler, waiting."

"My mistake. I was blinded by all this beauty and forgot about Leon."

"I'll walk you to the front door." Buddy opened the door wider, waiting as Cephus bade Silk a final goodnight.

When Buddy returned outside, he held a glass of whiskey. He sat next to Silk, took a swig and grimaced as he swallowed the bitter libation. The two sat in silence as Buddy clenched the whiskey glass while looking up at the starlit sky.

"Let me have a little taste," Silk said, removing the glass from Buddy's hand.

"This stuff is pretty strong," Buddy warned.

"That's exactly the way I like it." She took two sips without batting an eye.

"I didn't expect a woman as pretty and dainty as you to be able to handle hard liquor, straight out of the bottle."

Silk nudged her head toward the glass in Buddy's hand. "Store-bought liquor ain't nothing compared to the homemade moonshine I was raised on."

Buddy looked up at the sky again, and then with a grim smile, he gazed at Silk. "Can I be straight with you?"

Silk nodded somberly.

"What we did last night wasn't right. I don't know how we allowed things to get out of hand like that, but it can't happen again."

"I hope you don't think I'm a loose woman. I was only trying to ease your pain, that's all."

"I don't know what to think. After laying up with me, do you think it's okay to turn right around and allow Cephus to get fresh with you?"

"He didn't get fresh. All he did was invite me to the picture show. I never been before, and wanted to try something new before I return to the sticks."

"You've never been to the movies?"

Silk shook her head.

"But my sister told me you're in high society down South—a schoolteacher from a good family, and that you're planning to marry a doctor."

Silk covered her face and made sniffling sounds. "I lied to Clara.

When I met her on the bus, I didn't think we'd become close friends the way we have. I never thought I'd see her again, and so I made up a story about a grand lifestyle. In all actuality, where I live probably isn't even on the map. I live in a shack in the woods, so far from civilization, we don't have running water or electricity. I came up North to find myself a better life, but I ain't found nothing but adversity. Those city-slick crooks stole my worldly goods and took all my money. Since I have to return home with my tail between my legs, I at least want to be able to say that I accomplished something. Telling folks that I've been to a picture show up North is the only thing I'll be able to brag about."

Silk pretended to cry, and Buddy rubbed her back.

"Don't cry," Buddy murmured. "I'll take you to the movies."

"You will?"

Buddy nodded and Silk wiped nonexistent tears from her eyes and threw her arms around his neck with such exuberance, whiskey splattered from the glass he held in his hand. He set the glass down on the porch. Seeking out Silk's lips with his, he drew her into a tight embrace.

It was a lingering, sweet kiss, and when they finally broke apart, Silk said, "Buddy, I have a confession. I'm falling for you, and I know I shouldn't."

He took her hands in his and stared in her eyes. "I feel the same way. But I'm so confused. Although I realize I have to face the fact that Ernestine is gone, it still feels like I'm cheating on her with you."

"You're such a good man, Buddy. It would be so easy for me to love you and treat you right, and I can help you take care of those sweet little children of yours. By the way, how are the twins holding up?"

Buddy shook his head. "The doctors call them miracle babies, and I pray their luck holds out. But things aren't looking too good right now. Pamela has breathing problems and she's losing more weight. Paulette picked up some weight, but she has some kind of heart condition."

"It's a shame that those poor little babies never got a chance to meet their mother. I'd like to go with you the next time you visit them at the hospital."

"Clara usually goes with me to see the twins. I don't think it would be proper for you and me to carry on in public…at least not right now. Let's give it some time. After the funeral Saturday…" Buddy's voice trailed off. "It's hard to get used to the fact that I have to bury Ernestine. But as I was saying, after her funeral, we'll let my sister know that you're not going back to Louisiana. We'll make up a story about you waiting on your teaching papers, and tell her that you're gonna help me look after the kids until I find permanent help. Nobody needs to know about our personal business. We'll keep that to ourselves."

Silk gave Buddy a pat on the arm. "You don't have to worry about me saying a word. People wouldn't understand how we fell head over heels so fast. Tongues would be wagging, and those church folks would be spreading rumors if we broadcasted our love affair." Silk paused and scrutinized Buddy's face. "You do love me, don't you, Buddy?"

"I have strong emotions for you, but it's too soon to call it love."

Silk didn't like his answer, but she nodded as if in agreement. "Since we're keeping things under wraps, I think we should hold off from going to that picture show until it's nice and proper."

"Thanks for being understanding," Buddy muttered and then shot Silk a suspicious look. "You don't plan to go traipsing off to the movies with Cephus, do you?"

"Why shouldn't I? There's nothing between me and Cephus. I consider him a friend."

Buddy gave a wry laugh. "You don't know Cephus. That joker is always up to no good. He can sweet-talk the drawers off a woman in a matter of minutes."

"He won't get inside these drawers. This here juicy poontang is exclusively for you."

Aroused by her lewd declaration, Buddy made a groaning sound as he tugged Silk's arm, guiding her onto his lap. "You drive me crazy, Silk. I've never met a woman like you before. Since last night, I can't keep you off my mind." He groped beneath her dress and pulled her panties to the side. "Mmm. It's soaking wet between your legs," he whispered. Lifting up a little, he unzipped his pants and withdrew his hardening manhood. "God forgive me for being weak in the flesh, but I need some of your juiciness right now."

"Don't you worry, Buddy Dixon. I'm going to take good care of you and give you all the poontang your heart desires." Silk pressed down, taking in his full length. Sitting on his lap, she rode him, clenching her inner muscles as she whispered dirty words in his ear.

Buddy kissed Silk twice before he finally pulled himself away from her and crept upstairs to slip into bed with his sleeping sons. Silk lingered downstairs, emptying ashtrays and straightening up the mess Buddy and his friends had left in the living room. Her living room! The furnishings looked spanking, brand-new, but they wouldn't stay that way if she allowed the boys to continue to climb on the furniture and to roughhouse all over the place. In due time, she'd train Bruce and Myron to sit still when watching TV and to confine their rowdy behavior to the backyard. Dallas was a sweetheart who didn't require reprimanding. Silk and Dallas would get along fine as long as Dallas accepted that Silk was the new queen of the castle.

CHAPTER 15

Clara was outside hanging up sheets and towels on the clothesline while Dallas played on the swing set and the boys chased each other around the yard. Trying to get on Clara's good side, Silk kept big-headed Vernon, Jr. inside the house with her, rocking him as she watched an episode of the soap opera, *As The World Turns*.

The members of the Dixon household were in an odd state of mourning. One moment the kids would be crying for their mama, and the next moment they were racing around, playing tag. And Buddy and his moody self was as bad as the children, walking around with a long, sad face during the day, but slipping in the bedroom after Dallas went to sleep, hounding Silk for some poontang at night.

Saturday couldn't come soon enough. Silk wanted the funeral to be done and over with so she could get the household in order. It seemed to Silk that the bratty kids were running the show, but all that was going to change after she became the lady of the house.

The telephone rang and Silk hurriedly picked it up. Having a phone on the premises was another perk in her new lifestyle. "Dixon residence," she said with a smile in her voice.

"Hey, Silk. This is Cephus."

"Hi, Cephus," she said unenthusiastically. When he'd called yesterday, she'd made it clear that she wouldn't be accompanying him to the picture show. He sure was persistent.

"You bailed out of our movie date, but I have another proposition."

"Oh, yeah?"

"Every Thursday night there's a beef and beer at the Melody Lounge bar over on Third and Edgmont, and I was wondering if you'd like to go. The place is always packed with folks from Chester and other towns like Twin Oaks, Linwood, Trainer, and Marcus Hook."

The towns he named didn't mean a thing to Silk, but the idea of letting her hair down and having the opportunity to have some fun was very appealing. "Sure, I'd like to go. What time do you wanna pick me up?"

"How does eight o'clock sound?"

"Sounds good. See you later."

Silk forgot all about the soap opera she'd been riveted to. She raced up the stairs to raid Ernestine's closet. She no longer felt the need to ask for Buddy's permission—not with all the poontang she was providing him. Besides, everything that Ernestine had owned would officially belong to Silk immediately after the funeral. And that included her husband, her kids, and the insurance money that Buddy was expecting to receive very soon.

She held Vernon, Jr. in one arm and used the other to push hangers around until she found the perfect dress, a tight-fitting burgundy number that would knock Cephus dead when she stepped out of the house. Most of Ernestine's shoes were stored inside boxes, and it took Silk a while to find a color that coordinated with the dress. Next, she rummaged through the dead woman's bureau drawers, selecting underwear and jewelry. On her way out of Buddy's bedroom, her arms filled with the pilfered goodies,

Silk snatched a bottle of Avon perfume from atop Ernestine's vanity table.

Silk had persuaded Buddy into going along with her plan to start dating Cephus. No one would suspect that she and Buddy had a secret affair if she used Cephus as a front, she had explained, and then assured Buddy that he didn't have to worry about any hanky-panky between Cephus and her.

When Cephus pulled up in front of the house and honked his horn, Silk raced down the stairs. She was relieved that Buddy had two unexpected guests. Two white men—one from the insurance company and the other was some kind of politician—were sitting in the dining room with papers spread out, having a serious conversation with Buddy about the insurance money.

Silk intended to find out what they were talking about later. She was also very interested in when Buddy was going to receive the check. As she strode to the front door, Clara and the children gawked at her.

"That's my mother's dress," Myron said sullenly.

"It sure is," Bruce said with anger settling over his face like a dark cloud.

"Did you ask Buddy?" Clara inquired worriedly.

"No, I didn't want to bother him while he's busy talking with his visitors. But I'm sure it's all right with him," Silk said gaily. She could feel Buddy's eyes on her, and without seeing the expression on his face, she sensed that he wasn't happy with the way she'd helped herself to his dead wife's fashionable wardrobe. Oh, well, he'd have to get over it.

Cephus was standing outside his car. When he set eyes on Silk, he looked her up and down and let out a whistle. "I don't know how you got into that dress…looks like you were poured into it. You sure look good, baby. I should have remembered to bring along a baseball bat."

"For what?" Silk asked, playing dumb.

"To fight off the cock-hounds that are gonna be sniffing around you tonight." Grinning, Cephus eagerly opened the car door for Silk.

After he climbed into the driver's seat, he gave her another lingering look. "I wish you could slide over, so I could put my arm around you. But these bucket seats…" He trailed off and shook his head. "I knew I shouldn't have bought a car with bucket seats."

Cephus and Silk stepped inside The Melody Lounge, and male patrons murmured, "Who's that fox?" as they gazed at Silk with longing. One look at Silk, and the women inside the joint seemed to arch their backs like cats, whispering behind their hands as they glared at her.

"What are you drinking, baby?" Cephus asked after he and Silk took seats at the bar.

"Gin and tonic," Silk replied as she scanned the barroom, sending flirtatious smiles to her many male admirers.

The drinks arrived and Silk chugged hers down quickly and requested another. "Let me have some change for the jukebox," she said to Cephus with her hand stuck out. Happy to oblige, Cephus dug inside his pockets. But when he came up with only nickels and dimes, the men who were sitting nearby, quickly provided Silk with a handful of quarters.

Strutting toward the jukebox with a drink in one hand, quarters in the other, and her purse tucked under her arm, Silk was delighted by the attention she attracted. As she studied the record selections,

Cephus joined her, pretending to make small talk while he stood next to her like a bodyguard.

Out for a good time and not caring what Cephus or anyone thought of her, Silk continued to peruse the selections while leaning over the jukebox and shaking her behind to the beat of "Something's Got a Hold on Me" by Etta James.

One of the fellows who'd provided her with change, danced over to her, holding out his hand. "Come on, let's bop, girl."

Silk handed Cephus her drink, her purse, and the extra quarters in her hand and began dancing. Wiggling her ass excessively, Silk heated up the place with so much sexual energy, men abandoned their girlfriends and lined up to get the next dance with her. In between songs, Silk made pit stops to the jukebox, taking long swigs of her drink. After draining her second glass of gin and tonic, various male patrons tripped over each other, getting to the bar to refresh her drink.

Several up-tempo records played, and then "Baby It's You," a slow song by The Shirelles poured from the jukebox.

Refusing to be ignored any longer, Cephus handed Silk her purse, and said, "It's my turn," as he swept her into his arms. "I let you have your fun. I stood back and watched you while you were freshing around with every man in this bar, but I hope you didn't think I was going to let you slow drag with any of these jokers."

"Simmer down, Cephus. Don't be jealous; I'm only having fun. You're acting ornery, and there's no cause for that."

"I can't help it. I brought you out so we could have a good time together, not to stand back and watch you play around and make a fool out of me."

She whispered in his ear, "Be a good sport and I'll reward you later."

"Reward me? How?"

"I can show you better than I can tell you." She gave him a slick smile. "You'll see what I mean when we leave here and go to your place," she said seductively.

Cephus released a long sigh and pulled Silk closer. "You have no idea what you do to me. You got me steaming hot, girl."

"I plan on cooling you off as long as you step aside and let me have a little fun tonight." Silk stroked Cephus on the cheek.

"I'll step aside," Cephus reluctantly conceded.

The record ended and was followed by another slow song, James Brown's "Lost Someone," a passionate love ballad in which Brown's pleading wail coaxed dance partners into rubbing their bodies together in shameless passion.

After Cephus retreated to the background, someone caught hold of Silk's arm. The tall, well-dressed, pretty boy didn't bother to ask if she wanted to dance, and Silk didn't protest when he drew her into his arms and began dancing, slow and sensually. They seemed to stand in one place with their bodies writhing while their feet hardly moved at all.

"Hey, beautiful. You must be new here because I'd remember a fine fox like you," he said as he held her tight with his groin pressed against hers.

"Yeah, I'm new in town."

"Where you from?"

"Louisiana."

He let out a short whistle. "You're a long way from home. Say, are you one of those Geechie girls?"

Silk wrinkled her nose. "Geechies are from South Carolina and Georgia. I'm a Louisiana Creole."

"Ain't Creoles and Geechies the same?"

"Uh-uh." She shook her head.

"Geechies and Creoles know how to work roots on people, and from the looks of Cephus, over there, I'd bet you got him under some kind of voodoo spell."

"What makes you say that?"

"Look at him, sitting at the bar, twiddling his thumbs while I got you wrapped up in my arms. He must be under a spell to let you out of his sight."

Silk laughed again. She looked up and studied her dance partner's face. He was even better-looking than she'd thought. Handsome didn't begin to describe him. He was fine as hell, and almost as pretty as a girl. But the hardness in his eyes warned that only a sucker would mistake his good looks for being a pushover. His light-brown eyes, fringed by long, dark lashes, were mesmerizing.

"My name's Tate Simmons. What's yours?" he asked.

"Silk Moreaux."

"Silk, huh? That's an unusual name, but I like it." Caught up in the music, Tate closed his eyes and concentrated on their slow grind on the dance floor. His hands roamed freely over her back, waist, and hips.

Had any other man acted so familiar with her in a public place, Silk would have slapped his face or stuck him with her knife, depending on her mood. But she made no attempt to bat Tate's hand away when he stroked her hair and pushed it to the side. She involuntarily shivered when he pressed his soft lips against her neck and murmured, "You smell almost as good as you look. You got me strung out and I don't even know you. Do you feel what I'm feeling?"

She did. In fact, she was overwhelmed with the urge to devour his lips. But she refused to admit it. "I have no idea what you're feeling."

Tate pulled her even closer. "You feel that?" he crudely asked, referring to the hard-on that felt like there was a piece of steel lodged inside his pants. "Don't tease me, baby. We both want the same thing," he said knowingly.

Tate was right. She was drawn to him like a magnet, and wanted him in the worst way and her sudden, strong emotions bothered her tremendously. Silk had always used her looks and sexuality to exploit men, but the only thing she wanted from Tate was to stare into his piercing, light-brown eyes, kiss him until her lips hurt, and to surrender herself to that bolt of steel that was tucked inside his pants.

In Tate, she sensed a kindred spirit—someone she could confide all her deadly secrets and who wouldn't blink an eye. She had a feeling he'd be impressed about all the blood she'd shed.

And that's what scared her. Intuitively, she realized they were too much alike, and too much of the same thing couldn't be good. A voice in her head told her to break loose from him and join Cephus at the bar. Cephus could be wrapped around her little finger, but a man like Tate couldn't be manipulated or outsmarted. Fooling around with the likes of Tate was worse than playing with fire. As tempted as she was to lie down in the backseat of a car, a field, or an alley somewhere and spread her legs for him, her survival instincts kicked in, warning her that Tate was nothing but trouble and she should beware!

When the record stopped playing, Silk disentangled herself from his arms and left Tate standing alone as she fled in the direction of the bar. In addition to being spooked by the realization that she and Tate were both cut from the same cloth, she'd experienced an eerie feeling when he'd spoken about Creoles and Geechies working roots. Now, an image of Big Mama was swirling around in her head. In her mind, she could hear Big Mama warning her that she wouldn't find any easy living up North if she didn't settle down and stick with one man. So far, Buddy was her best bet for easy living, and she'd be a fool to mess up the good thing she had.

"Hey, Silk. Where're you going?" Tate asked, sauntering toward her with a swagger she'd never seen on any Southern boys. Involuntary, Silk licked her lips. Tate sure was a tall glass of water, but her strong attraction to him was overpowered by the memory of Big Mama making strange motions with her hands as she put a hex on Silk. There wasn't anything more potent than a dying hex, and whatever Big Mama had put on her wasn't going to come off easily. She wondered if there were any conjure women in Chester or anywhere nearby. Someway, somehow, she had to get rid of Big Mama's spell.

"Thanks for the dance, but I'm in the doghouse with Cephus, and I gotta spend some time with my date. I'll catch you later."

"When am I gonna see you again?" Tate asked.

"That's for me to know and you to find out," she said sassily, and then walked away.

"Buy me another drink and then let's cut out of here," she said to Cephus when she rejoined him at the bar.

Cephus beckoned the bartender. "Another drink for the lady." He gazed at Silk. "For a minute, I thought Tate was gonna steal you away from me."

She took a long swig from the drink the bartender placed in front of her. "Can't nobody steal something that doesn't belong to you," Silk said with an edge in her voice

"I didn't mean to tick you off, Silk. But I can't help being jealous with all these hounds trying to get next to you."

"Let me worry about the hounds. You worry about getting me back to Buddy's house, safe and sound."

"I thought you were gonna swing by my place for a nightcap."

"Some other time, Cephus. I've got a splitting headache, and I need to lie down." Silk chugged down her drink and slid off the barstool. Cephus followed suit and escorted her out of the bar.

Once Silk was situated in the car, and Cephus was behind the wheel, he made one last attempt to win her over. "I noticed you like music, and if you're feeling better tomorrow night, I'd like to take you to a live show at the Uptown Theater in Philly. Jackie Wilson, The Contours, Ike and Tina Turner, and a lot of other good acts are on the bill. You'll love it."

"I'd like to, but I can't."

"Why not?" Sounding desperate, Cephus' voice went up a pitch.

"It wouldn't be right for me to be out traipsing around town on the night before Buddy's wife's funeral. Tomorrow night, Clara and Buddy are gonna need my help more than ever with the children."

"You're right. You look so damn good, you got my head spinning, and I forgot about the funeral on Saturday. Maybe we can catch the next rock-and-roll show at the Uptown. They change the line-up every couple of weeks."

She didn't commit to going to the show with Cephus. With all the sexual tension built up by her encounter with Tate, going on another date with Cephus was the last thing on her mind. She was feeling mighty frisky, and was anxious to get back to the house so she could jump on Buddy and ride him like a stallion, while pretending he was Tate.

CHAPTER 16

The lights were out and the Dixon home was pitch-black when Cephus pulled up to the curb. To Silk's and Cephus' amazement, Buddy was sitting on the front porch with a bottle of liquor turned up to his mouth. They couldn't see his expression, but Silk sensed that Buddy was glaring at the two of them.

"Losing Ernestine is tearing Buddy's heart out. I think I should sit with my man for a spell, and have a drink with him," Cephus volunteered.

"No, you go on home. Buddy doesn't need another drink. He needs to sober up for the children's sake. They need their father more than ever. I'm gonna coax that bottle out of his hand, make him some coffee, and encourage him to call it a night."

"That's thoughtful and kind of you, Silk. You're a good woman."

"I try," Silk said, smiling as she imagined the good loving she was going to put on Buddy after she got rid of Cephus.

"Well, goodnight, Silk. I wish I could get a little kiss, but with Buddy sitting outside mourning the loss of his wife, I suppose it wouldn't be polite."

"No, it wouldn't. Goodnight, Cephus." Silk grabbed the door handle.

"You don't open doors when you're in the company of a gentleman. Hold on while I get out and open the door for you."

"Don't bother," she said, opening the passenger's door and quickly hopping out of the car. Cephus was doing everything in his power to prolong their time together, and Silk refused to go along with his silliness. She waved at him and briskly paced up the walkway toward Buddy.

Instead of driving off, Cephus sat in his Rambler with the motor idling. Silk looked over her shoulder and motioned for him to get going.

"I'll wait until you're inside the house, safe and sound," he stubbornly replied.

Now, she was outraged, but managing to keep the fury out of her voice, she said sweetly, "Go on, now. I need to sit out here and talk with Buddy for a while."

Reluctantly, Cephus drove off into the night. Silk sat next to Buddy. "How you doing, Buddy?"

"What do you care? You backstabbed me with someone I consider a friend, and had the nerve to do your dirt while dressed up in my wife's clothes. Now, that's a lot of gall." Shaking his head, he took a swig of whiskey, and wiped his mouth with the back of his hand. "One of the church ladies volunteered to look after the children, and so Clara's leaving on Monday. I think it's best if you join her; I'll pay for your bus ticket," Buddy said sullenly.

"Buddy," Silk said, touching his hand gently. "There's no reason to be upset with me. I told you that I only went out with Cephus as a front—to keep folks from getting suspicious about you and me. But I'm so crazy about you, Buddy, I made Cephus bring me home earlier than he intended. The whole time I was out with him, I couldn't keep my mind off you. Did you know that whenever I drink ice water, it's because I'm trying to cool myself off when my mind gets to wandering and thinking about you. I imagine your hands running all over my body. I imagine you sticking that big ol' thing of yours inside my mouth and between my legs. You're the best lover I ever had, and I want to lie up under your strong body morning, noon, and night."

Buddy put the bottle down, turned toward Silk and kissed her passionately. "I don't want you going out with Cephus ever again, do you understand me?" Anger flared in his dark eyes.

"I won't go out with him anymore."

"It's hard having you under the same roof. Every time I look you, I want to strip your clothes off, and take you." Buddy shook his head grimly, as if horrified by his carnal desire.

"Is that what you wanna do, right now?" Silk said in a sultry voice.

"You know I do."

"Then, take me. I don't care who sees." Silk began squeezing her breasts and licking her lips in a frenzy of sexual desire. "You make me so hot, Buddy. I need you to ram that big ol' thing inside me before I lose my mind."

Buddy groaned her name as he held her tighter, kissing the side of her face and her neck with desperate kisses.

Speeding things along, Silk hitched up her dress. "I need you, Buddy."

"Not out here. We can't risk getting caught," he whispered huskily. He took Silk by the hand. "Let's get in the car." He led her to his Oldsmobile that was parked in the driveway.

Moments later, the car rocked back and forth, and the windows steamed up quickly. For the first time, Silk and Buddy had privacy, and didn't have to be concerned about getting caught by Dallas. Secluded inside the confines of the car, she could be as loud, wild, and unruly as she wanted to be. Taking full advantage of their privacy, Silk cursed and used lewd words to express herself during the heat of the moment.

"I ain't never been with a wildcat like you before, and I can't get enough of you," Buddy admitted, reaching to pull his pants up after they'd finished.

"You can have me anytime you want if you make me your wife."

"I thought we agreed to keep our affair a secret for at least a year."

"No, I can't wait that long for you. I want to get married right away." She reached downward, caressing his privates and lightly scratching his balls.

Buddy shuddered as he became aroused once again. "That feels good. Don't stop."

Silk removed her hand. "My tongue down there will feel even better."

"You'll lick my balls?" Buddy asked disbelievingly.

"I'll do whatever it takes to make you feel good and forget your troubles. Didn't your wife lick your balls, Buddy?"

"Heavens, no!"

"Did she take it in the ass?"

"Of course not." He sounded appalled.

"Well, I do. You wanna try it?"

"Uh, I don't know."

"Come on, baby, try something new," she urged as she positioned herself on her hands and knees. "Let me take you on a little trip to paradise."

CHAPTER 17

The day before the funeral, Buddy received the insurance money for his wife's taxicab accident. Silk convinced him to take her to look at engagement rings. In a small town like Chester, their visit to Morris Jewelers didn't go unnoticed, and the gossip spread like wildfire. They were also spotted shopping in Rodger's Department Store and Kay's Women's Dress Shop.

When they returned home, the house was filled with food-bearing mourners, who had whipped up meals in a hurry in order to get a bird's-eye view of the diamond ring that Silk was allegedly sporting on her left hand.

Clara didn't believe one word of the gossip and as soon as Silk waltzed through the door, toting an armful of fancy shopping bags, Clara escorted her up the stairs

"Folks are gossiping about you and Buddy. They say you two have been carrying on right under my nose, and that you're planning to get married. Is this true?"

Silk took a deep breath and nodded.

"When did you and Buddy..." Clara shook her head without finishing the question.

Silk placed her bags on Dallas' bed. She clasped Clara's hands. "I should have told you, but it all happened quite suddenly. Buddy and I are deeply in love, Clara. We're getting married next week."

Clara gasped.

"Don't fret. I love your little niece and nephews, and I'm gonna be a good mama to those children."

"But when…how did this happen?"

"I think it was love at first sight. I tried to fight it. I even went out on a date with Buddy's friend, Cephus, hoping to get Buddy out of my mind. But being with another man made me want Buddy even more. He didn't want this to happen any more than I did, but when Cupid shoots an arrow at two hearts, there ain't much that can be done about it."

"What about the doctor who's waiting for you back home?"

"I sent him a telegram today and broke it off with him. And I sent my mama a telegram, telling her to ship my bridal chest to Chester."

"Are you and Buddy planning a big wedding?"

"No. We'll have a small affair at the justice of the peace."

"What about teaching? Are you gonna give it up?"

Silk nodded. "I love Buddy so much, I'm gonna devote myself to being a good wife and good mama to his kids."

Surprisingly, Clara threw her arms around Silk's neck. "Welcome to the family. This is wonderful news. I'm gonna miss your company on the long bus ride home, but I'll have peace of mind knowing that my brother and his children are being loved and cared for."

Silk hugged Clara back. "Fate brought us together on the bus, and we're sisters, now."

"Those church folks are gossiping about you and Buddy something terrible, they said he bought you a diamond ring, today. Can I see it?"

"The one we picked out is too large, and the jeweler is fixing it to fit my skinny, little finger. It won't be ready until Wednesday, and unfortunately, you'll already be gone."

"Well, make sure you send me a picture of you and Buddy's wedding day."

"I will." Silk opened one of her bags. "Your sweet brother is so kindhearted. He felt bad that I had to borrow clothes from you and from his deceased wife's closet, and so he bought me some fancy, new getups." Silk began pulling one item after another out of the bags, and Clara seemed genuinely delighted that Buddy had splurged on his bride-to-be.

When Clara and Silk returned downstairs, Silk had changed into one of her new outfits, a pair of Bermuda shorts and a shell top with fancy beading around the neckline. Silk was a knockout whether she was dressed casually or decked out in heels and a tight-fitting dress. It was a known fact that Silk had arrived at Buddy's house with only the clothes on her back, and after taking note of her new clothes, curious eyes drifted to her left hand.

Sister Beverly, who was fussing over Buddy and the children, preparing their plates with generous portions of barbeque spare-ribs, fried cabbage, and biscuits, looked visibly relieved that Silk's ring finger was bare.

"I want you to meet my niece, but she couldn't make it today because she had to work. She's a fine, upstanding young woman, and she's willing to help you out with the children. I'll be sure to introduce you two after the burial tomorrow," Sister Beverly said to Buddy.

"I won't be needing a sitter, after all," Buddy said as he chowed down on the ribs.

"Who's going to help you to tend to the children? They're too young to look after themselves." Sister Beverly gazed around the dining room at her fellow church members for support.

"They sure can't," Sister Yvonne agreed, cutting a disapproving eye at Buddy for even suggesting such a thing.

"I didn't want to share my good news until after the funeral, but I'm bursting with happiness. The Lord blessed me with Ernestine's love and now he has blessed me with the love of another good woman." He beckoned Silk. She crossed the room and stood next to Buddy's chair.

"What are you saying, Buddy? Don't tell me that terrible rumor is true?" Sister Beverly said, looking aghast.

"It's not a rumor. I asked Silk to marry me, and she said, yes." He gazed at Silk and smiled.

Stunned silent, Sister Beverly went limp and eased into an empty chair. It took a few moments for her to find her voice. "But…she's not a suitable wife," Sister Beverly blurted. "I heard she was in the Melody Lounge bar the other night, shaking her rear-end and drinking liquor."

"That was a one-time thing. Silk plans to join the church, get saved, and put any type of fast-living behind her. She's gonna make a good mother for my children."

Displeased with his father's announcement, Myron mumbled under his breath, "She's not my mother."

Bruce blinked rapidly as he took in the shocking news. "I don't like her. I want my real mother to come back."

"Watch your mouth, boy," Buddy chastised his son. "You're getting too big for your britches anytime you think you can sit at my table and complain about grown folk decisions. We're going to miss your mother terribly; she'll always be in our hearts. But we have to move forward as a strong Christian family, and now that Miss Silk will be helping me raise you children, I expect all of you to give her respect. Do you hear me, Bruce?"

"Yes," the boy said grudgingly.

"What about you, Myron?"

Myron poked out his lips resentfully. "Yes, Daddy," he mumbled. "Dallas?"

"I love Miss Silk, Daddy."

Dallas' brothers grumbled and rolled their eyes at their sister. Silk smiled at Dallas and the shy little girl lowered her eyes and blushed.

"Well, I suppose I should be getting over to the church to make sure everything is in order for the funeral tomorrow," Sister Beverly announced, gazing around the dining room and giving the other church members significant looks. Taking a cue from Sister Beverly, Deacon Whiteside cleared his throat and muttered that he needed to head on over to the church, also.

One by one, the church members filed out of Buddy's home to meet up at the church where they could openly discuss the scandalous upcoming wedding of Buddy and the woman he barely knew.

CHAPTER 18

lara escorted the children up to the casket where their mother lay, dressed in blue and appeared to be merely sleeping. She lifted Dallas in her arms and held the child hovering in the air above her mother's body.

"Wake up, Mommy. Please wake up," Dallas pleaded.

"She's gone, Dallas. Kiss your mother goodbye," Clara said.

"No!" Dallas screamed. "She needs a doctor to make her better."

Clutching each other, the boys crept up to the casket and both said, "Bye, Mommy," and then collapsed into tears. There wasn't a dry eye in the church after Dallas' sorrowful outburst and the boys' woeful farewell.

Quietly weeping, Buddy was being comforted by Silk. After the children were back in their seats, Buddy and Silk approached the coffin together. A hush came over the room. Spectators sat on the edges of their seats, capturing every detail of the scandalous couple's behavior.

One look at his wife and Buddy had an unexpected outburst. "Not my wife! Not my wife! Ernestine, you were too young to die!" His knees buckled and a horde of pallbearers and deaconesses rushed to his aid, holding him up and fanning his face. Escorted back to his seat, Buddy was comforted by a host of attendants.

Silk remained standing at the coffin, whispering something inaudible as she stood over the body of her predecessor.

Gossipers would put their own imaginative spin on Silk's final words to the woman she had replaced, but what Silk actually said was:

I always wanted to live up North in a home of my own, and although the one you left me is rather nice, it's kind of small and not exactly what I had in mind. Maybe we'll add some more rooms with that insurance check we collected from your accident. Don't worry about your kids; I'm gonna try to do right by them. Dallas is sweet, but those boys of yours pluck my nerves. If they can abide by my rules, we'll get along fine and dandy. As you can see, Buddy is feeling a little emotional, but don't worry about him. He'll be all right after we get hitched. Once I officially move into your former bedroom, Buddy's gonna keep a smile on his face. Well, that's about all I have to say. Sleep tight, chickadee. Silk concluded by patting Ernestine's folded hands.

When Buddy pulled up in front of the Greyhound Station at five-thirty in the morning, Clara hugged Silk tight, promising to stay in touch.

Clara offered Silk some last-minute advice in a whispered voice. "I know you're the curious type, but promise me you won't venture down Twelfth Street to those project houses. I heard some of the church folks say that those Fairground Project people aren't up to any good. They sit out in their yards cussing and drinking while they play Pinochle until the wee hours of the morning. I'm only warning you because you tend to be such an innocent little lamb, and I don't want you mixing in with a bad crowd. If you stay on Flower Street, you'll be fine. For your own safety, please don't travel to Twelfth Street unless Buddy is with you."

Silk nodded. She let out a sigh of relief when Clara and her baby finally boarded a bus that was Mississippi-bound.

"Bye, Buddy and Silk. Bye, kids," Clara said, sticking an arm out the open window and waving. "Tell Aunt Silk, Uncle Buddy, and your cousins bye-bye," she said to Vernon, Jr., holding his wrist and waving for him.

Aunt Silk, my ass. I ain't no kin to that little rugrat. Silk smiled sweetly and waved vigorously.

On the way back home, Silk scooted close to Buddy, and they drove back to Chester snuggled up together like teenage lovebirds. Buddy ran his fingers through Silk's hair and she caressed his hand as he shifted the gears. The three children sat in the backseat, quiet and forlorn. They appeared lost and bewildered, but Silk and Buddy were so wrapped up in each other, neither seemed to notice.

Buddy had to return to his job after being off for over a week on bereavement leave. Before dropping Silk and the kids off at home, Buddy reached in his pocket. "Here's your household money for the week," he said, slipping Silk twenty-five dollars. It was a generous amount, and Buddy smiled proudly.

Silk was disappointed, but didn't show it. She'd seen Buddy's checkbook that had both his and Ernestine's name engraved on every check. She wanted Ernestine's name replaced with her own, but would wait until after they were married before she brought up the subject.

"Don't forget to call the hospital to check on Pamela and Paulette," Buddy reminded. "Let the head nurse know that I'll stop by as soon as I get off work today."

Standing on the front porch with an arm wrapped around Dallas and with the two boys standing uncomfortably at her side, Silk waved to Buddy. "Have a good day at work, darling," she said, mimicking the behavior of a loving mate.

"Bye, Daddy," Dallas said, but the sullen boys didn't open their mouths.

"Tell your father, goodbye," Silk prompted Bruce and Myron through gritted teeth.

Solemn-faced, the boys held up their hands limply. When Buddy's car roared away, Silk glared at his sons. "I can see that I'm gonna have to teach you two boys a lesson about plucking my nerves. Get in the house...both of you," she said, giving Myron a shove and smacking the back of Bruce's head.

"Ow!" Bruce hollered and flinched as if he'd been bopped upside the head with a brick. His overreaction aggravated Silk.

"Hush up before I give you something to holler about," Silk threatened.

"You're not my mother, and you're not allowed to hit me." Bruce scrunched up his lips and stared daggers at Silk.

His insolence infuriated her, and she was of a mind to gather switches from the backyard and whip his behind. But she had second thoughts about that. Buddy might not take too kindly to her beating the living daylights out of his kids before they were married, and so she decided to punish Bruce in a different way.

Silk and the three kids filed into the house, and the children went straight to the living room and turned on the TV set and changed the channel to cartoons.

"No television for you, Bruce. You're punished for sassing me, so march your butt upstairs and sit in your room."

"Sit in my room and do what?" Bruce demanded.

"I don't care what you do, but you'd better get out of my face. Now, get up those stairs!"

The loud volume of Silk's voice caused Dallas to jump in fear. Myron stared at Silk, wearing a shocked expression while Bruce dragged himself up the stairs with his head hung low.

"Don't look at me like that, Myron."

"Like what?"

"Don't play dumb. Keep on sassing me with your eyes and you gonna find yourself on punishment right along with your brother."

Silk exited the living room and ventured into the kitchen to figure out what to fix for breakfast. Countless Tupperware containers and foil-covered plates were stacked in the refrigerator. There was enough ready-made food to feed the family lunch and dinner for weeks. But there wasn't anything suitable for breakfast. Nor were there any snacks that would satisfy Silk's sweet tooth.

With the spending money Buddy had given her, she supposed she could spare a few dollars for milk and cereal for the kids and a few dollars more for her personal stash of treats.

"Where's the closest store?" Silk asked Myron.

"Max's store is right over there on Twelfth Street." Myron pointed toward the window, while his eyes were glued to the TV screen.

"Glass's store is a little further down Twelfth Street," Dallas added. "Mommy likes to buy from Mr. Glass because he's colored."

Since *Mommy* preferred the colored store, Silk decided to patronize Max's. "You kids stay in the house and don't budge until I get back," Silk instructed.

Silk was excited about exploring Twelfth Street, the raunchy part of the neighborhood that Clara had warned her about. Besides the people she'd met in The Melody Lounge the other night, Silk had only become acquainted with stuffy, church folks in Chester, and she was itching to meet some folks who knew how to kick up their heels and have a good time.

She peered out the front door, trying to get a look at Max's store, but the elementary school that sat on the corner blocked her view. "I don't see any store, Myron; all I see is a school and those government homes," Silk said irritably.

"The store is on the other side of the school. Do you want me to show you where it is?"

"No, I'll find it. Keep an eye on your sister until I get back." Clutching her purse, Silk left the house, eager for an adventure.

CHAPTER 19

Max's grocery store was located on a property lot that included Freddie's Barbershop, the Flower Hill bar, six apartments, and the Office of the Magistrate was situated on the far-right corner of the lot.

The patrons of the barbershop craned their necks to get a look at Silk as she promenaded past the plate-glass window of the shop, swaying her hips and tossing the men a confident smile.

The grocery store was small, dimly lit, and junky. Max, a Jewish man who looked to be in his mid to late thirties, was behind counter. A woman with pink sponge rollers in her hair stood at the counter waiting for Max to tally up her purchases. Instead of giving him money, she handed him a miniature, black-and-white composition book in which Max jotted down some numbers and returned the book with a smile.

"Hello, there. You must be new around here. I'd remember a pretty face like yours," Max, the store owner, greeted. From the shabby appearance of the store, Max wasn't worth getting to know better, and Silk refrained from conversing with him or even bestowing him with a smile.

Browsing, she moseyed to the back of the store where a colored boy in his late teens or maybe early twenties was stocking shelves with canned good. Silk found it odd that the stock boy wore sunglasses inside the dimly lit store. The right side of his head was scarred and dented, and when he held up his hand and said, "Hi," in a childlike voice, she realized he was slow or possibly brain damaged.

"My name is Sonny Boy. I work here," he said sluggishly.

"Good for you," Silk replied with a sneer. She had no patience for mentally retarded people.

"Can I help you with anything?" Max asked, coming from behind the counter.

"Where's your milk and cereal?"

"Cereal's over there." He pointed to the far wall. "I'll get the milk for you. Do you want a quart or half-gallon?" Max inquired as he went behind the meat counter to get to the refrigerated products.

"Make it a half-gallon." Silk picked up a box of Cheerios, a five-pound bag of sugar, and a box of Oreo cookies, and a package of Fig Newtons. "I'd like a Coke while you're back there…no, make it two Coca-Colas, and a quart of orange juice," she called to Max.

"Two Coca-Colas and a quart of orange juice," Sonny Boy repeated, irking Silk with the sound of his thick voice.

Max brought the milk, sodas, and orange juice to the counter and Silk added an assortment of candy bars, a pack of Tastykake Krimpets, a box of Cracker Jacks, and a family-size bag of barbecue potato chips to her order.

"You've got a large order here. If you need help with your bags, Sonny Boy won't mind carrying them for you," Max offered.

"I don't mind carrying them for you," Sonny Boy parroted.

Silk surveyed Sonny Boy. The way he talked was pissing her off, and his dented-in head was hard on the eyes. "What's wrong with him?" she asked Max with a scowl.

"Something happened to him down South when he was only a boy. He's not right in the here." Max tapped on his temple. "But he's harmless," he quickly added. "Sonny Boy's as innocent as a child."

"Why's he wearing them sunglasses? Is something wrong with his eyes, too?"

Max nodded. "He's blind in one eye, and uh, partially blind in the other. But he gets around just fine."

"Was he born like that?"

"No," Max said grimly. "His eye sight was damaged also during that very unfortunate incident that happened while Sonny Boy was living in the South. I'd rather not discuss it. It's a good thing for Sonny Boy that his parents sent him to live with his aunt here in Chester. At least in the North he won't have to suffer any more racial injustice."

Silk shrugged indifferently. She didn't give a damn about Sonny Boy's problems. "Okay, well, sure he can carry my bags. So, what's the damage?" Silk asked lightheartedly, nodding toward her groceries.

Max rang up her items. "Your total is three dollars and eighty-nine cents. The orange juice is on the house. You're a first-time customer and I hope you'll return. I can extend credit if you need it."

"No, thanks, I don't need credit." She extracted a five from her purse.

After Max gave Silk her change, he called out to Sonny Boy. "Stop what you're doing, Sonny Boy. I want you to carry the lady's bags home." Max turned to Silk. "Where'd you say you live?"

"Oh, I'm only a hop, skip, and a jump away. The white house on the corner of Twelfth and Flower," she said.

"Oh, that's where the Dixons live. Shame about Ernestine; she was a nice lady. Are you a family member?"

"I guess you could say that. In a few days, I'll be Buddy's new wife."

Max looked surprised. "I thought Buddy would be in mourning for a while. I can't believe he's getting married, so soon. Well, congratulations, uh, I didn't catch your name."

"It's Silk."

"Sonny Boy, this is Silk. She lives in the white house across the street from the school. I want you to carry her bags home and then come straight back, you hear?"

"Yes, sir, Mr. Max," Sonny Boy replied.

With Sonny Boy toting two large shopping bags, Silk led the way home, and then she suddenly stopped walking. "Take those sunglasses off and let me see your eyes, Sonny Boy."

He shook his head. "My Aunt Verline told me to always keep these glasses on when I'm out in public."

"What your Aunt Verline doesn't know won't hurt her. I bet you have nice eyes, Sonny Boy. Come on, let me see 'em," Silk cajoled. She was morbidly curious about the damage that the violent crackers down South had done to Sonny Boy.

"One eye can't see nothing, and the other one sees things fuzzy."

"Stop blabbing about it and let me see for myself what kind of shape your eyes are in. If you wanna carry my bags home, you gotta let me see what's underneath them glasses. Now, take 'em off and show me."

Sonny Boy carefully placed the bags on the ground. Slowly and hesitantly, he removed his sunglasses. Silk inhaled sharply. She hadn't expected his eyes to be as damaged as they were. The right eye was a hazel-colored, stray eye that didn't appear to be able to focus on anything for very long. The left eye was gone, and Sonny Boy was left with an empty eye socket.

Silk was reminded of how she'd gouged out the eyes of Mr.

Perry with a pair of ice tongs. During her fit of rage, the gory result of her actions hadn't turned her stomach at all, but looking into an empty eye socket, unexpectedly, had her on the verge of vomiting. Averting her gaze, she asked, "What happened?"

"They pulled it out." The memory caused Sonny Boy to tremble.

"Who pulled it out?"

"Mean white men yanked my eye out. They said they'd fix it so I couldn't look at any more white women."

"What else did they do to you?"

"They beat me and kicked me. Hit me over the head with a baseball bat. And they broke both my legs." The horrifying recollection caused Sonny Boy to throw a fit. He began whining unpleasantly, turning in fast circles, and smacking the dented side of his head. "I ain't looked at no white woman. I kept my eyes down. I ain't looked at no white woman. I kept my eyes down," he continuously repeated.

"Simmer down and stop acting the fool, Sonny Boy! Put your sunglasses back on, pick them bags up, and let's go," Silk said sternly.

Responding to Silk's sharp tone, Sonny Boy pulled himself together. "Are you gonna tell my Aunt Verline that I showed you my eyes?" he asked meekly.

"No, that's gonna stay between you and me. It'll be our little secret." She gave Sonny Boy a sneaky smile. "You wanna keep secrets with me?"

He nodded briskly. "Okay."

She leaned in and planted a kiss on Sonny Boy's lips. "Now, our little secret is sealed with a kiss."

Sonny Boy grinned and seemed to be hyperventilating. "Are... are...are you my girlfriend, Silk?"

"Uh-huh. But that's a secret. You gotta keep our romance between you and me," she said teasingly. "I'm gonna be getting married soon, and we don't want my new husband to find out, do we?"

"No." Sonny Boy shook his head.

When they reached her house, Silk gave Sonny a dollar tip for carrying her bags.

Sonny Boy looked at the dollar and frowned. "This is too much. I only charge a quarter to carry bags. Mr. Max is gonna get mad if he thinks I stole your money."

Silk dug around in her purse and retrieved a quarter. "Here you go. Show this to Max and hide that dollar in your other pocket. That's another secret between us."

Sonny Boy stuffed the dollar bill in his pocket and lingered on the stone walkway. "You're real pretty, Silk, and I love you."

"Yeah, all right, but don't go around blabbing about how much you love me. Keep that information to yourself, you hear me? Nobody is supposed to know our secret."

"I won't tell anyone," he said earnestly, and then whispered, "I love you."

Silk cracked up laughing. Poking fun and playing mind games with the town idiot was somewhat pleasurable. "Go on, now, Sonny Boy. Get back to the store before Max comes looking for you."

CHAPTER 20

S ilk filled two bowls with cereal and called Dallas and Myron
into the kitchen. One look at the box of Cheerios and Myron
wrinkled his nose. "Mommy buys us Frosted Flakes."

Without a word, Silk picked up Myron's bowl and dumped the
cereal back into the box. "You done earned yourself a punishment,
so get on upstairs with your brother."

"But…"

"Don't backtalk me, boy. Get upstairs before I grab some switches
and go to town on your bare legs and backside."

Myron skulked off toward the stairs. He looked over his shoulder
and forlornly watched Silk pouring milk into Dallas' bowl.

"You want some sugar on your cereal, Dallas?" Silk asked in a
sweet tone.

"Yes, ma'am," Dallas responded, quickly learning that agreeing
with Silk was the best way to get along with her.

"I don't like it when you say, *Yes, ma'am,* it makes me seem old.
Being that I'm your new stepmother, you need to give me a proper
title." Silk stared up at the ceiling thoughtfully. "Do you wanna
call me, Mommy?"

"Um…" Dallas fidgeted with her spoon, not wanting to say
anything that would cause her to be banished to her bedroom.

"I realize I'm not your real mother, so you don't have to call me,

Mommy." Silk squinted as she contemplated a suitable name for the children to call her. "How about Mama?"

Risking punishment, Dallas hesitantly shook her head no.

"You're trying my patience, Dallas. You gotta call me something, so what's it gonna be?" Silk's voice took on a hard quality, and Dallas' winced in fear.

Silk smiled suddenly. "I got it! I know exactly what I want you and your brothers to call me. Y'all can call me, M'dear. That's the shortcut way of saying, my dear. It's nice and classy, don't you think?"

"Yes."

Silk arched a brow. "Yes, what?"

"Yes, M'dear."

"Good girl. Now, eat your breakfast." While Dallas ate cereal, Silk put away most of her goodies, storing them in a hiding space behind the canned goods. With a Hershey's chocolate bar and a Coca-Cola in hand, she sat across the table from Dallas. She removed the wrapper from the chocolate bar and popped the cap off the bottle of soda pop.

Silk was delighted to have a cabinet full of goodies all to herself. Back home, Big Mama hardly ever allowed her to have sweets. Whenever the white folks stopped by for their remedies and brought along treats for Silk, Big Mama would keep the goodies for herself, telling Silk she didn't want her getting cavities because she was trained to nurse folks, not to pull out teeth.

It was rare, but every now and then, after giving Big Mama her thrills, Silk would earn a piece of candy or a slice of cake. When Silk grew older and had money in her pocket, she used to buy all sorts of goodies. She tried to stash them in secret places in the shack, but Big Mama, having a nose like a bloodhound, could always sniff out Silk's treats. She'd take a strap or a couple of switches to

Silk's behind to break her out of the habit of hiding goodies from her.

Silk's mind began to wander back in time.

"Ain't nothing worse than living under the same roof as a liar and a cheat," Big Mama complained after whipping the daylights out of Silk.

"I won't hide goodies, anymore, Big Mama."

"Shut yo' lying mouth! Now, go lay your yella tail on that bed and gap your legs open for me. You done worked my nerves something terrible, and I gotta get me some thrills in order to calm myself down."

"You want me to give you the special treatment before I lay down on the bed and gap open my legs?"

"Yeah, I guess so. Get on over here and sit on this chair," Big Mama said, kicking off her boots. Next, she took off her skirt and let it float down to the floor.

Silk sat on the chair and Big Mama pulled it close.

"Don't I teach you right from wrong, Silk?"

"Yes, Big Mama."

"Then, why you so bad and ornery?"

"Because I was borned bad," Silk said, repeating what Big Mama had always told her.

"Is you ready to be good?"

"Yes, Big Mama."

Following the steps of a ritual she'd been participating in for as long as she could remember, Silk tugged down the woman's big bloomers and when they pooled around her ankles, Big Mama stepped out of her underwear and kicked them out of the way. She propped a big, meaty foot on the seat of the chair that Silk sat upon.

"Welp, get to it, girl."

Eager to get Big Mama out of her foul mood, Silk palmed the wom-

an's enormous buttocks as she used her tongue to provide pleasure.

Big Mama shuddered and widened her fleshy thighs. "You getting better and better at giving me the special treatment."

Encouraged by the compliment, Silk worked harder, sucking with her lips and penetrating deeply with her tongue.

Suddenly angry, Big Mama yanked Silk's hair. "Slow down, you lil' yella heifer. You think you slick, trying to take me over the edge before I'm ready. I don't know where you learning this stuff, but you getting mighty tricky with them nasty lips and that wicked tongue of yours. That's enough special treatment. Go lay your fresh-butt on the bed, so I can get me some poontang.

Back in the moment, Silk gazed at Dallas curiously. "Hey, Dallas, did you give your mama thrills at night?"

Dallas looked at Silk, puzzled. "Did I give her what?"

"Thrills. You know, in the bed?"

"We said our prayers kneeling by the bed, and she taught me how to make up my bed. Sometimes she put my stuffed toys on the bed—"

"That's not what I'm talking about. You ain't never lay underneath your mama in the bed…you know, so she could get thrills?"

Completely perplexed, Dallas shrugged. "I don't think so."

"Y'all Northerners sho' is strange. Kids talk back to their elders and complain about what they don't want to eat for breakfast." Silk shook her head. "I had a strong Southern mama. She didn't take any mess off of me. She taught me right from wrong, and most importantly, she taught me how to keep her nerves calmed down by giving her thrills and special treatment. She told me it's a secret that's kept between little girls and their mamas." Silk pondered briefly. "Maybe it's a Louisiana tradition."

Having no idea what Silk was referring to, Dallas asked, "Does giving thrills mean you made your mother laugh?"

"I suppose you could say that. Actually, what I gave my mama was way better than laughter." Silk looked at Dallas. "Can you keep secrets, Dallas?"

The innocent little child gazed into Silk's eyes and nodded her head.

CHAPTER 21

Wearing Ernestine's blue apron with white ruffles around the edges, Silk greeted Buddy at the door with a kiss and a glass of Jack Daniel's. She noticed that on many of the TV programs she enjoyed watching, the wife greeted the husband with a drink and made sure the children were quiet and orderly.

"It sure is quiet. Where are the kids?"

"They already ate dinner and they're upstairs in their rooms. The boys are building something with their Erector Set and you know, Dallas, she's fooling around with her dolls."

"We always ate together as a family when Ernestine..."

Silk winced, and Buddy's voice trailed off as he noticed the hurt look on Silk's face.

"Forgive me, sweetheart. I didn't mean to compare you to my ex-wife."

"It's okay. We can all eat together tomorrow, if you'd like," Silk said quietly. "I figured it would be nice to have a romantic dinner with just the two of us on the first night that your sister isn't here. It's nice to have some privacy from all those church folks that were hanging around the house."

"You're right. This is our first night having our home to ourselves. You know, I'm really looking forward to making you Mrs.

Richard Dixon. Out of tragedy came an unexpected blessing, and having you makes me feel like the luckiest man in the world."

"Tell me more," Silk said, grinning.

"You're beautiful on the inside and out, and I already know you're the best mother I could have found for my children."

"Thank you, Buddy. I'm so glad you appreciate the effort I'm putting into helping you rear your children. I know I can't take the place of their natural mother, but I plan to always do the best I can. The children were calling me Miss Silk, but that sounds like I'm no more than a neighbor lady, so we decided together that they would call me, M'dear. What do you think about that?"

"I like it. It sounds loving and respectful." Buddy sniffed the air. "Whatever's on the stove cooking, sure smells good."

"I wanted to whip up some Creole cooking for you. You know, some good ol' gumbo or jambalaya, but we have so many leftovers that the church folks gave us, I simply heated up something that was already in the ice box."

In actuality, Silk didn't know how to fry an egg. Big Mama had prepared all the meals at home, cooking up her remedies and supper out of the same black kettle.

"I've never tasted Creole food. I've heard a lot about gumbo and I can't wait to taste it. So, what's for supper? All this talk of food has my stomach growling."

"Chili con carne, rice, and corn bread. Peach cobbler for dessert. I froze a lot of the leftovers that the church folks brought, but there's too much to fit in the freezer. Do you want me to throw it all out or keep heating up leftovers for supper until it runs out?"

"Those good people toiled over those meals, and it would be a sin to throw away good food." Buddy peeked inside the refrigerator and whistled in surprise when he saw the stacks of plastic containers.

"You won't have to worry about cooking a meal for quite a while, Silk."

"I'm looking forward to cooking for you, Buddy," she said, lying through her teeth.

"Make sure you put gumbo at the top of the list after we get through the leftovers."

Silk set a steaming plate of chili in front of Buddy and prepared another plate for herself. She sat across from him, eating daintily. Stuffed from cookies and candy, she stirred the chili mixture around with her fork.

"You eat like a bird, Silk."

"Never had much of an appetite."

Buddy ate heartily, and then pushed his plate away. His jovial expression turned sad. "I have some bad news I was saving until after supper."

"What is it?" Silk feared Buddy was going to tell her that they had to postpone their wedding plans.

"The twins aren't doing well at all," he said solemnly.

She let out a sigh of relief, and then quickly painted on a concerned expression. "Are they gonna make it?"

"They're fighting hard and holding on. But they're gravely ill with heart and respiratory problems. The doctors don't think they got enough oxygen when they were born, and there's probably something wrong with their brains." Choked up, Buddy dropped his head. "My little babies aren't going to be normal. They're never coming home because they'll need medical care for the rest of their lives." Buddy looked distraught.

Silk had to contain herself from clapping her hands with glee. It was a stroke of luck that life-threatening ailments had worked their way into the twins' bodies, preventing them from ever entering the Dixon household. Adding two sick babies to Buddy's brood of kids was more than Silk could handle.

"Would you like me to call the children downstairs so you can tell them the sorrowful news?"

"Yes, it's gonna break their little hearts, but I have to tell them."

While Buddy sat in the living room, sipping Jack Daniel's, Silk went upstairs and escorted the children down. Myron, Bruce, and Dallas stood with their hands folded in front of them. "Hi, Daddy," they said quietly in unison.

Buddy was too broken up over the twins to notice that his sons weren't behaving like their normal rambunctious selves, and Dallas wore a straight face instead of greeting him with a smile.

After he gave them the sad news, Dallas started to cry, but when Silk gave her an evil look, she quickly wiped away her tears. The boys shifted from one foot to another, but didn't say a word.

"Well, it's time for bed, kiddies. Go on upstairs, put on your pajamas, and hit the sack," Silk said with a sweet smile and a sugary tone of voice. "We'll all say a prayer for your baby sisters."

"Mommy makes us take a bath before we go to bed," Myron interjected.

"Oh, all right. I'll run the bathwater." Silk smiled at the three children adoringly.

When Silk got Myron and Bruce alone in the bathroom, she pinched Myron's arm. He opened his mouth to yell, and Silk whispered, "Hush up or I'll make it hurt worse. Did *Mommy* pinch you every night before your bath?" Silk asked in a spiteful tone.

"No, Miss Silk," Myron said, looking contrite.

Silk gawked at the child. "What did you say?"

"I mean, no, M'dear."

"That's better. Now, get in that bathtub. Both of you. Before I spank your little, black asses."

She walked toward the bathroom door, and then turned around and glared at them. "How's it feel going to bed on an empty stomach?"

"It feels bad." Myron's lips trembled.

Silk chuckled. "I bet you two hard-heads won't sass me tomorrow, will you?"

"No, M'dear," they both said at the same time.

Satisfied that the boys were sufficiently chastised, Silk closed the bathroom door.

While the boys were in the tub washing up, Silk went to Dallas' room. "You're the only good one in the bunch; that's why I love you."

"I love you, too, M'dear. Are you going to say prayers with me tonight and stay in my room with me?"

"No, not anymore. I have to sleep with Daddy from now on. I have to treat him good and give him lots of thrills."

"Are you gonna make Daddy laugh?"

Silk snorted. "Yeah, something like that."

CHAPTER 22

After their early morning wedding ceremony at the justice of the peace in Upper Darby, Pennsylvania, Buddy and Silk drove to Atlantic City, New Jersey for an overnight honeymoon. After checking into a hotel, they walked the boardwalk hand-in-hand. The boardwalk with all its shops and neon lights was fascinating to Silk. They bought saltwater taffy and fudge, and so many souvenirs, they had to make several trips back to the hotel to drop off the heavy bags.

At the Steel Pier, they rode the Ferris wheel and other rides, played carnival games, and took in a rock-and-roll show.

Silk had never had so much fun in her life. Back in the hotel room, Silk gave Buddy the special treatment to try and convince him to stay over one more night.

"We can't stay, Silk. We have to leave at checkout time tomorrow morning. Our neighbor, Mrs. Sudler, was kind enough to watch the kids overnight, but she has her own household to tend to. Besides, I have to be on the job first thing Monday morning. I missed so much time after everything with Ernestine, I can't miss another day this year. Not if I want to keep my job."

"But you got all that insurance money, now. With that kind of money, you can afford to miss a day's work here and there, can't you?"

Buddy's face clouded. "About the insurance money…" Buddy looked down guiltily. "I struck up a deal where I'd accept a smaller settlement instead of fighting in court. When my lawyer stopped by last week, he told me that a court fight with the cab company could last for years."

"I've been meaning to ask you how much you got out of that accident."

"Eleven thousand dollars."

"That's a lot of dough." With eleven thousand dollars, Silk could get a new car, build on extra rooms, get herself an electric clothes dryer, go on endless shopping sprees, and get the basement remodeled to look like a honky-tonk with a full bar and a Magnavox stereo console. She'd throw parties in the basement every Saturday night. There were unlimited ways to spend eleven thousand dollars once she weaseled the money away from Buddy.

"No amount of money could make up for the loss of Ernestine," Buddy said gravely. "But it doesn't matter. I had to sign most of it over for the twins' medical bills. My health insurance doesn't cover all the care they need."

"What are you saying? We lost all of the insurance money?" Silk's mouth went dry and her heart plummeted to her stomach. That sneaky-looking lawyer had come by the house while Buddy was in deep mourning. The crooked lawyer and that politician had probably gypped Buddy out of most of the dough he was entitled to. Silk was pretty certain that the lawyer and the politician had pocketed most of the insurance money for themselves and Buddy was too grief-stricken and gullible to realize it. Had she been married to Buddy at the time, those two crooks would have had to get past her before they could get their grubby fingers on one thin dime of that insurance money.

"The money's not lost," Buddy said. "It's keeping the twins alive and I used some of the money to pay off the mortgage on the house. I also signed up for new policies for me and the children. I'll have to add you on now that we're man and wife," he said as an afterthought.

Silk was raging mad over Buddy wasting good money on brain-dead babies. She'd had her heart set on getting a shiny new car ever since Nathan Lee had promised to buy her one. But she didn't say anything. Instead of complaining like she wanted to, she patted Buddy's hand comfortingly. "You're a good man, Buddy. The way you look after me and the kids makes me proud to be your wife."

"I truly love you, Silk. I don't want you worrying about money because I earn a decent living. With the house paid off, that's one less bill. You'll never have to worry about being provided for. You're the queen of my house and I'm going to do my best to always treat you like royalty."

"You're making me blush, talking all sweet and tender."

"You'll see, Mrs. Dixon. I plan to pull as much overtime as possible to make sure you have the finest things in life."

"Thank you, Buddy. But I don't want you breaking your back over me."

"Shoot, you're well worth breaking out a little extra sweat over. Didn't you notice how every man on the Boardwalk, both white and colored, couldn't keep their eyes off you? I felt like poking my chest out with pride. I could hardly keep myself from shouting out loud, 'This beautiful woman is my new bride.'"

"Aw, Buddy, you say the sweetest things."

"I only speak the truth. Now, get back under these covers, woman, so I can show you how much I love you."

Silk wondered if Buddy was finally going to give her the special treatment to demonstrate his love. Back home, white men loved pleasuring her with their lips and tongues, but colored boys always acted real funny-time about it. Most flat-out refused, and others hesitated and required a lot of persuading.

"In my time of need, you were good to me, Silk. And I want to return the favor. I always thought oral sex was something only white fellas with little peckers did. You've opened up my eyes and shown me sexual pleasures I'd only heard about. I love you so much, I'm willing to try most anything to keep you satisfied."

"I'm already satisfied."

"I want you to be even more satisfied," Buddy said softly, moistening his lips in preparation for the task ahead.

"Okay, Buddy," Silk said, leaning back and widening her legs. "The main thing you need to know about oral sex is that it feels better to the woman when you don't rush through it. It's much, much better when you take your time."

"I'll take my time," Buddy agreed as he lowered his head between Silk's smooth thighs.

Monday morning before leaving for work, Buddy gave Silk her weekly house money. She had yet to spend all of last week's money, and since the money wasn't doing any good sitting in her purse, she decided to go over town and browse around, and maybe buy herself some more new clothes, some shoes, and personal items.

"Boys!" Silk called. Myron and Bruce rushed to her bedroom.

"Yes, M'dear?" they both said.

"You're both old enough to look after yourselves. I'm going over town, and I'm taking Dallas with me. You two can eat peanut butter and jelly sandwiches after you finish your chores. I better not see a speck of dust on anything when I get back, or I'ma take switches to y'all little narrow behinds. Do you hear me?"

"Yes, M'dear," the boys chorused.

Holding Dallas by the hand, Silk walked along Flower Street until she reached the bus stop on Ninth Street. When the bus arrived, she and Dallas boarded, and Silk gave the bus driver a quarter. From a metal case that was strapped to his waist, he gave her five cents change. Silk and Dallas took seats in the front of the bus, and Silk felt like a grand lady.

The last stop was Seventh and Sproul Streets. Silk and Dallas walked along the street and gazed through the window of the YWCA, where little white girls were dressed in tights and leotards, taking ballet lessons. With money to burn, Silk was ready to start spending.

"Do you want to be a ballerina, Dallas?"

"I don't know how to dance like that."

"The ballet teacher will show you how. I think you'd make a pretty ballerina, so let's go in and see about getting you signed up for some lessons."

Inside the building, there was an older woman at the desk. She gazed at Silk and Dallas as if they were intruders.

"I want to sign my little girl up for ballet lessons," Silk said.

"Uh, you're at the wrong branch. The West branch Y at Seventh and Yarnall Streets is where the Negroes go," the woman said.

"Do they give ballet classes at the colored Y?"

"No, but there are tap dance classes as well as interpretive dance."

"My little girl wants to be a ballerina," Silk said stubbornly. "Is there a law that says she can't dance with those little white girls?" Silk pointed to the girls standing at the ballet bar.

Flustered by Silk's bluntness, the receptionist turned a pinkish color. "There's no law. But historically, here in Chester, the coloreds tend to congregate among their own kind."

"I didn't come in here for a history lesson. How much is the ballet class, and how soon can my daughter start?"

Red-faced, the woman shuffled through some papers, and then handed Silk a card. "Your child will have to become a member of the Y in order to take dances classes or use any of the facilities, such as the pool. Fill out the information and bring the card back on Saturday, along with the five-dollar registration fee. The summer session begins Saturday at two."

"Okie-dokie," Silk said, with smug satisfaction.

"She's going to need dance attire. Soft ballet slippers, black tights, and a black leotard."

"Why do they have to wear all that black? I thought ballerinas wore pink leotards with pink crinoline skirts."

"They wear tutus when they perform at their dance recital, but the girls rehearse in standard tights and leotards. Black only," the woman said pointedly, clearly annoyed by Silk's lack of knowledge.

"So, what store carries ballet getup?"

The receptionist sighed. "Weinberg's carries the tights, leotards, and slippers. But if she makes the cut for the recital, you'll have to get her costume from Baum's Dancewear in Philadelphia."

"I suppose we'll be traveling to Philly to pick up a tutu because my little girl is a natural born dancer. She's gonna make the cut and put all those other children to shame. Isn't that right, Dallas?"

"Yes, M'dear."

Giving the receptionist a look of triumph, Silk tucked the registration card in her purse and escorted Dallas out of the building.

"I didn't expect to encounter a bunch of prejudiced people up North, but I suppose they're everywhere," Silk said.

"What do prejudiced people look like?" Dallas inquired in a wary tone.

"They look like crackers."

Dallas scowled. "Like Saltine crackers?"

Silk sighed. "Never mind. You don't need to concern yourself about prejudiced people because I'm gonna protect you from them."

Silk and Dallas approached the State Theater and gazed at the advertisements for the coming attractions. An animated movie, *101 Dalmatians*, was scheduled to show the upcoming Saturday.

"You want to see that picture about those spotted dogs?" Silk asked Dallas.

"Uh-huh."

"I'll tell you what. If you're a good girl, and if you give me lots of thrills, we'll go to the picture show after your ballet class next Saturday."

"Okay," Dallas said with a giggle, thinking that all she had to do was tickle Silk or tell her jokes.

They entered Weinberg's Department Store, which Silk noticed had a hoity-toity air. "I need ballet slippers and a dance getup for my daughter's ballet class. Oh, and I want a slew of satin ribbons for her hair," Silk added, giving Dallas' hair a critical look. The babysitter, Mrs. Sudler, had fixed her hair in two thick braids with a part down the middle. Silk didn't like that style—it looked too country. She wanted Dallas to wear her hair in ponytails and pig-tails, tied up with bright ribbons.

They left Weinberg's with Silk proudly carrying the bag with its prestigious logo by the handles. She spotted Woolworth five-and-dime on the other side of the street. "I'm ready for lunch, how about you?" she asked Dallas.

"I love Woolworth. Mommy always let me pick a balloon—"

Dallas caught herself, and her eyes widened in fear. "I didn't mean to talk about Mommy. I'm sorry, M'dear," she said in a scared voice.

"It was an honest mistake, but don't let it happen again."

"I won't."

"Good. Now, let's go get us some food, sweetiekins. I could go for a cheeseburger or maybe a double-decker, ham and Swiss cheese sandwich. You can get a hot dog, French fries, and a root beer float, if you'd like."

"Ooo. Yummy!" Dallas responded, looking relieved that Silk wasn't upset with her.

Sitting at the lunch counter amongst white folks was another new experience for Silk. The North was strange in many ways, but it had its good points. Above the counter was a bouquet of colorful balloons, and despite Dallas' *Mommy* slip-up, Silk was as gleeful as a child about the prospect of picking out a balloon that the waitress would pop with a pin. Inside the balloon was the surprise cost of lunch—for kids only. The cost could be as low as a penny or as high as a dollar, depending on the customer's luck.

"Do you feel lucky, Dallas?"

"Yes, M'dear."

"Which balloon do you want to pick?"

"The red one, over there," Dallas said, smiling and pointing.

The waitress popped the balloon and announced, "The grand total for the little lady's lunch is five cents."

Sitting on the swivel stool, Silk and Dallas clapped their hands happily.

Silk had to admit, she had a good life, and even without the insurance policy money, she couldn't complain. Buddy worshipped the ground she walked on, and now that she had those bratty sons of his straightened out, she didn't have to worry about them acting up or giving her any lip. Timid, little Dallas was so well-behaved, she was the apple of Silk's eye. And the child adored Silk almost as much as her daddy did. If Silk told Dallas to jump off a cliff, she was pretty certain, Dallas would do so with a smile.

The waitress placed their food in front of them, and Silk and Dallas dug in. After they finished eating, Silk paid the tab and reached down to pick up her Weinberg's bag, when a familiar voice said, "I'll get that for you."

Butterflies fluttered around in her stomach, and she drew in a sharp breath. It took a few moments for her to get the nerve to look up, and when she did, she found herself staring into the gorgeous, light-brown eyes of Tate Simmons.

CHAPTER 23

"Well, well. If it isn't the New Orleans Geechie girl," Tate said with a smirk.

Even though Tate was dressed as sharp as a tack in a crisp, short-sleeved shirt, a white cap, and white pants, Silk scowled at him like he was trash. "I'm not from New Orleans, I'm from another part of Louisiana. And I done told you that I'm not a Geechie, I'm a Creole."

"And I told you that you voodoo ladies are all the same to me," Tate said with teasing laughter.

Silk slid off the stool, and helped Dallas off hers. "I don't know anything about voodoo."

"That's a relief because you already got my nose open, and I would hate to think what would happen if you put some roots on me. Would be a shame if I started barking like a dog every time I saw you or smelled your perfume." Laughing, Tate lowered his head to Silk's neckline and took a whiff. "Man, oh, man. That perfume you wear drives me wild."

"There ain't no reason for you to go wild over me. I'm already spoken for." Silk held up her left hand that sparkled with her new diamond ring and gold wedding band.

Visibly disappointed, Tate said, "I thought what I heard about you and Buddy Dixon was only a rumor. His wife's body is barely cold, but he didn't waste any time. Oh, well, I guess he beat me to the punch."

"He sure did," Silk said snidely. "Nice talking to you, Tate. I'll catch you later." She took Dallas by the hand and walked away.

Unwilling to give up easily, Tate followed Silk and Dallas out of the store. "Say, it's pretty hot out today, and I'd hate for you to burn up while you're standing around, waiting around for the bus. I can give you a lift home."

"That's okay. I have plenty more shopping to do."

"I bet that insurance money Buddy collected is burning a hole in your pocketbook," Tate said scornfully.

"You need to mind your business. I don't want a ride from you. In fact, I don't want anything to do with you, so leave me alone and stop talking to me." As Silk's voice escalated, Dallas nervously squeezed her hand tight.

"Calm down. I was only kidding around. Where's your sense of humor? Can't you take a joke?" He eyed Silk up and down. "Look, I know all the fellas got you thinking you're hot stuff, and maybe you are. But all I did was offer you a ride home, and that's no reason for you to bite my head off."

"You're right. I'm s…"

"Save it," Tate interjected before Silk could apologize. "If there's one thing I can't stand, it's a stuck-up broad." With anger flashing in his eyes, Tate was more handsome than ever, and Silk had to briefly look away.

"I tried to apologize, but if you don't wanna accept it, then don't. It's no skin off my back," Silk spat, her own temper beginning to flare.

"I'll catch you later." Tate wheeled around and walked away.

"Tate, wait a minute," Silk called out. But he kept on moving, with a dip in his walk that was so smooth, Silk could feel her heart beginning to flutter. "Ugh. I hate that cocky bastard," she muttered under her breath.

Dallas squeezed Silk's hand again. "Are your nerves bad, M'dear?"

"A little bit, sweetiekins." Silk stroked Dallas on the cheek. "But I'll be much better after you give me some thrills."

Dirty laundry was piling up, and Buddy had started complaining that his work uniforms needed washing. Bruce had run out of clean clothes, underwear, and pajamas. And for some unknown reason, bed linen from the boys' room was being stuffed inside the clothes hamper on a daily basis. The laundry situation had Silk stumped. There was a shiny washer in the small room off from the kitchen, but Silk didn't have the first idea of how to operate it. Big Mama had done their washing in a metal tub with a washboard, and at times, she lugged dirty laundry down to the lake.

Wanting to keep her ignorance a secret, Silk considered hand washing Buddy's uniforms, but she doubted if she'd be able to get the grease and grime out of his coveralls. Her delicate hands had no experience with toiling. Back home, Silk wasn't required to labor. Her only job was to deliver Big Mama's remedies to the white folks.

Big Mama came home looking particularly tired after a long day of hunting. "Dragging that hog through the wood done sapped me of all my strength."

"I can help you hunt hogs, Big Mama."

"No, I want you sitting right here in this house looking pretty when I come home. I don't ever want you getting your pretty, little hands dirty." Big Mama held up her hard, roughened hands. "Do you see my hands?"

"Yes, Big Mama, I see your hands."

"This tough ol' leathery skin was made for hard work and healing. Your soft, gentle hands was made for rubbing the kinks out of my neck and squeezing and loving up on my titties on nights like tonight, when I'm too dog tired to climb on top of you." Big Mama plopped wearily onto the wooden chair. "Go fetch a cool rag and wipe the sweat off my face."

Twelve-year-old Silk dipped a square cloth into a basin of water and wrung it out. Carefully, she dabbed the beads of perspiration from Big Mama's face and the creases in her neck. "You want me to get the kinks out your neck, Big Mama?"

Big Mama began unbuttoning her mannish shirt. "Nah, skip that and get right to squeezing on my tits." She closed her eyes in anticipation. "I'm awful tired, so use your hands real gentle, the way I taught you, and make Big Mama feel extra good tonight."

"Okie-dokie."

Untrained in domestic work of any kind, Silk abandoned the idea of trying to hand wash a week's worth of laundry. Struck with the idea of asking the neighbor lady and babysitter, Mrs. Sudler, to show her how to operate the machinery, Silk picked up the phone and called her.

"This is Silk, Mrs. Sudler. How are you doing? Listen, we have so much leftover food from the funeral, I was wondering if you'd drop by and take some of it off my hands."

"Merciful Jesus. Thank you, Silk. My husband got laid off from his job, and our food was starting to get low."

"I had no idea, but you know the Lord works in mysterious ways. I'll see you shortly."

It took a less than ten minutes for Mrs. Sudler to arrive with a large shopping bag. After Silk filled the bag to capacity, she casually said to her neighbor, "That washer that Ernestine used ain't the kind we use down South. Do you think you could show me how to run this thing, so I can wash Buddy's work uniforms?"

"Sure, I can show you. What did you use down South—those old wringer washers?"

"Yup, that's exactly what we used."

"You're gonna love the automatic washing machine. It's fast and convenient, and less dangerous. I've heard tales of quite a few women getting their hands caught up in the wringer," Mrs. Sudler said with a shudder.

Silk listened and watched closely as Mrs. Sudler walked her through the steps of washing a load of clothes. Filled with Buddy's uniforms, the washer hummed and vibrated as it went through the various cycles. After the load of clothes was washed, Silk walked Mrs. Sudler to the door.

The kids were out back, splashing around in a wading pool their father had recently purchased for them. "Myron!" Silk yelled out the back door.

The boy jumped out of the pool immediately, and came inside the house. "Yes, M'dear?"

"Dry off, and then go upstairs and bring down the hamper of dirty laundry in you boys' room."

An odd expression came over Myron's face.

"Are you deaf, boy? Don't stand there and gawk at me." Silk yanked hard on Myron's earlobe.

"Ow!" With a hand covering his ear, Myron bounded up the stairs. It took him longer than it should have to bring down the wicker clothes hamper from his room, and when he did, he tried to slip it into the wash room and then dart out the back door, unnoticed. But Silk caught him.

"Where are you running to?" She pointed to the wicker basket.

"Explain to me why there's a bunch of sheets and pajamas and things in that laundry basket?"

Myron avoided eye contact with Silk. "Bruce changes his sheets every morning as soon as he wakes up. And, um, he throws his pajamas and underwear in the hamper, too."

"Why does he do that?"

Myron shrugged.

"There's something you're not telling me. I'ma whoop Bruce's ass and I'ma whoop yours, too, if you don't spill the beans and tell me what you know."

"Bruce pees the bed," Myron blurted.

"That boy is too old to be pissing the bed." A hot rage blazed through Silk. "Go back upstairs and get me one of your daddy's leather belts. I'ma light a fire to Bruce's ass."

Myron scampered back up the stairs and came back down quickly, holding a brown leather belt.

Silk flung the back door open and shook the belt threateningly. "Get out of that pool, Bruce. Your ass is grass!"

"No, M'dear. Please. I didn't do anything," Bruce wailed with a look of terror in his eyes.

"Did you hear what I said? March your ass in this house, right now," Silk said through clenched teeth.

Bruce climbed out of the pool. Wet and shivering from fear, he slowly walked toward the back porch. When he got close to Silk, she grabbed him by the arm and yanked him inside the house. "Go outside and look after your sister, Myron."

Myron raced out of the back door, leaving Bruce alone with Silk.

"So, you done turned into a little pee-pot just to spite me, haven't you?"

"No, M'dear. I don't know why I keep having accidents."

"That's bullshit, you lying little bastard." Silk moved closer to the boy, and bent low, putting her face only an inch or so away from his. "You don't like me, and you never did. You and your brother had it in for me from the first day I set foot inside this house. Well, you don't have to like me, but you're damn sure gonna respect me. Do you hear me, you little bastard?"

As Bruce nodded briskly, Silk raised the belt and brought it down on his wet back. An angry welt appeared immediately. Bruce screamed and jumped around, exaggerating his pain.

The way he was acting the fool made Silk want to beat the skin off his back, but she didn't think Buddy would approve of her leaving his son scarred and bloody. It took a great deal of willpower for Silk to put the belt down. But she wasn't finished with Bruce. He'd never learn a lesson if she let him off the hook with only one lashing.

"Nasty, evil alley cats go around pissing on things when they're mad about something. You wanna act like an alley cat, well, I'm gonna treat you like one. Do you want me to get a litter box for you to squat down and do your business in?"

"No, M'dear." Tears rolled down Bruce's cheeks as he stood in a puddle of water that had dripped off his wet swimming trunks.

Silk looked down at the puddle of water, and then glared at Bruce.

"I didn't pee on the floor, M'dear. I swear to God."

"Hmph. Tell that to a fool that don't know any better. You about as nasty as they come, and I'm gonna break you out of your disgusting habits. Go upstairs to your room, and strip out of them wet trunks. I'll be up there to finish your punishment in a few minutes."

"What are you gonna do to me, M'dear?" Bruce asked through chattering teeth.

"That's for me to know and you to find out. Now, get up those stairs."

Silk had a brilliant idea, and all she needed was a few items that Clara had accidentally left behind when she returned to Louisiana. Silk scratched her head, wondering where Buddy had stored Clara's junk. Then, she recalled that there was a box on the top shelf of the hall closet with Clara's name written on it.

Carrying the box, she raced up the stairs. When she burst into the boys' room, Bruce was dried off and sitting on the edge of his bed, wearing a white undershirt and white briefs.

"Take them drawers off," Silk said, motioning impatiently.

"Why?"

"Because you ain't nothing but an overgrown pee-pot, and I figured out a way to break you out of that bad habit. Now, get out them drawers like I said."

Bruce removed his briefs and self-consciously covered his private parts with both his hands.

Silk shot Bruce a cold stare. "Your little ding-a-ling don't faze me none. I ought to cut that lil' weenie off and throw it in the frying pan. I bet that would put an end to all that bed wetting."

"Please, M'dear. Don't cut my wee-wee off." More tears spilled from Bruce's eyes and rolled down his cheeks. With his knees locked together, he protectively shielded his private parts.

"Move your hands!" Silk shouted.

"What's in the box? What are you gonna do to me, M'dear?"

"Stop asking so many questions." She opened the box and retrieved a cloth diaper, a pair of jumbo-sized safety pins, and a pair of yellow rubber pants. "Since you wanna pee all over the place like a big ol' baby, you better start getting used to wearing your little cousin's diapers. No more drawers for you until you start pissing in the toilet like a normal seven-year-old boy."

"I don't wanna wear Vernon, Jr.'s diapers. Please don't make me. I won't pee the bed anymore. I swear to God."

"Hush up. You should be ashamed using the Lord's name in vain. Now, lift up your behind, so I can get this diaper on you." Silk had watched Clara change Vernon, Jr. more times than she'd cared to, but now the unwelcome tutorials had come in handy. She shook baby powder on Bruce's genitals before pinning up each side of the diaper. "Here, put these rubber pants on yourself."

"They're too little," Bruce protested.

"Squeeze into them. If you're uncomfortable enough, maybe you'll stop being such a nasty pee-pot."

Crying his heart out, Bruce did as he was told.

"Now, put some clothes on before your brother and sister discover you have to wear baby diapers."

Bruce quickly put on a pair of pants and a shirt.

"When you have to go to the bathroom, open up one side of the diaper, and then pin it back up after you finish. There'll be hell to pay if I find out you took that diaper off and put your drawers back on."

Sniffling and wiping tears, Bruce nodded. "How long do I have to wear this thing?"

"Until you stop pissing the bed."

CHAPTER 24

Whenever there was a household dilemma that she couldn't handle, Silk always called on Mrs. Sudler. This time, Dallas was the source of her grief. The child was crying and shrieking in pain, and Silk didn't know what to do.

"How are you, Mrs. Sudler? I hate to bother you, again, but I need some help with Dallas' hair."

"What's the problem?" Mrs. Sudler asked.

"Well, her hair was smelly from being under that bathing cap in the pool every day. So, I shampooed her hair twice. I dried it with a towel, and then I let her play in the backyard, to let it air-dry the rest of the way. Now, her hair is standing all over her head, and it looks and feels like steel wool. It's so tangled up and knotty, I can't even get a comb through it. She's bawling her eyes out while I'm trying my best to tackle her wild head of hair."

Mrs. Sudler chuckled over the phone. "Dallas' hair doesn't take water. Ernestine always gave her a hard press, and while Buddy's sister was visiting, she ran the hot comb through the child's hair several times. You should have combed through it and braided it up while it was still damp…then it would have been easier to handle when you pressed it out."

"Should I wash it again?"

"Do you know how to use a hot comb, Silk?"

"No," Silk admitted.

Mrs. Sudler chuckled again. "You don't know the first thing about taking care of kinky hair, so it would be best if you take Dallas to see Carmalee."

"Who's that?"

"She's a beautician. She lives over in the projects on Ruby Street. Her salon is set up in her kitchen. Carmalee charges three dollars for a press and curl, and two-fifty to only press hair."

"I'm taking Dallas to her right away. Where's Ruby Street?"

"You can't drop in on Carmalee. She's always booked up, so you're gonna have to make an appointment."

"Do you have her phone number?" Silk asked desperately.

"No, I don't, but why don't you walk on over there and introduce yourself. Maybe she'll squeeze Dallas in tomorrow."

"Tomorrow! I need Dallas' hair straightened out today. Buddy will think I'm a bad mother if he comes home and sees his daughter looking like Buckwheat."

"Yeah, I know what you mean. One thing about Ernestine, she kept herself and those children well-groomed at all times. I never saw Dallas with a hair out of place."

Silk was ready to fly off the handle and curse Mrs. Sudler out for bringing up Ernestine's name, and for singing her praises, but she held her temper. Through gritted teeth, she asked, "Can you give me directions to Ruby Street?"

"Sure, honey. Walk down Twelfth Street, and on the other side of Max's store is Nooker Street. Next to Nooker is Morris Street. Keep walking, and you'll bump smack into Ruby Street. If you pass by a kiddy playground, you'll know you walked too far. Turn onto Ruby and walk almost to the end of the block. Carmalee lives on the left-hand side. Folks will be sitting out on their stoops and kids will be outside playing. Ask anybody to point out Carmalee's house for you."

"Okie-dokie." Silk had heard there was never a dull moment in the projects, and she'd been itching to be right in the midst of all the excitement, and it looked like her wish was about to come true.

Avoiding Sonny Boy, who always got overly excited and stopped whatever he was doing and tried to follow her around if she came into Max's store or even if she merely walked past, Silk traveled on the opposite side of Twelfth Street. Following Mrs. Sudler's directions, she reached Ruby Street in a matter of minutes. As predicted, people were out in droves. Little girls jumped rope in the middle of the narrow street while adults sat on stoops and lawn chairs, smoking cigarettes and chatting.

All conversations ceased when Silk made her way down the street.

"Hellooo! Are you lost, miss? Are you looking for somebody?" asked a plump woman with bulging eyes, and whose hair was styled in finger-waves. Shiny metal clamps decorated her head, holding the waves in place. Grinning broadly, she fluttered her fingers, greeting Silk.

Right off the bat, Silk disliked her. She could tell the woman was pretending to be friendly when she really wanted to get in her business and find out all she could about Silk.

Silk bypassed the nosey woman with the finger-waves and approached two women who were thumbing through magazines, while stealing glances at Silk. Both of the women had on duster dresses with snaps down the front and wore bedroom slippers on their feet. The one wearing the blue duster was looking through a copy of *True Confessions* and the one wearing an orange duster with flowers and birds embroidered around the neckline, was glancing at a copy of *True Romance*.

As Silk grew closer to the two women, she heard one of them

say, "That must be that high-yella gal from New Orleans that everybody's talking about."

"She don't look like a voodoo lady to me," the other woman said.

"No, she don't. But you can tell by the way she walks that she thinks she's high and mighty."

"Mm-hmm."

"Excuse me, can you tell me where I can find Carmalee?" Silk asked in a kindly tone that she hoped would distract them from envying her looks.

The two greeted her with hard expressions while their gazes traveled from Silk's recently purchased, two-tone, stack-heeled pumps and all the way up to the stylish chignon bun on the top of her head.

While the women checked Silk out with their faces twisted in scowls, the nosey neighbor got up from her stoop and ambled over. "You looking for Carmalee? I'll show you where she lives. Come on with me, I'll walk you over there." Guiding Silk by the arm, she steered her away from the unfriendly duo.

"My name is Franny. You must be the New Orleans gal who married Buddy Dixon," the plump woman said.

"I'm not from New Orleans. I'm from another part of Louisiana."

"Oh, yeah? Whereabouts?"

"I lived near the swamps in a part of Louisiana you ain't never heard of." Silk didn't mind giving out vague information about herself. She was no longer concerned about Sherriff Thompson. He would search high and low in all the surrounding towns and boroughs near Devil's Swamp, but it would never enter his mind to look for her up North in Chester, Pennsylvania.

"You're the talk of the town. Folks say you put some roots on Buddy, and that's how you got him to marry you before Ernestine was even in the ground."

"That's a lie. We didn't get married until after the funeral. And for your information, I don't know the first thing about working roots, so tell all the gossipers that they can kiss my high-yella ass," Silk said in a tone loud enough for the two women on the stoop to hear.

Taken aback by Silk's spunk, Franny said, "I didn't expect you to be such a firecracker."

"I speak my mind, and I don't take shit off anybody." Under normal circumstances, Silk would have at least made an attempt to present herself as innocent and harmless, but she was ticked off by the way those two biddies wearing house dresses and slippers had called her names under their breath and then snubbed her.

"That's just how I am, honey chile. I don't talk behind nobody's back, either. Anything I have to say, I'll say it to your face."

"Yeah, well, you better watch what you say to me because I'll cut your ass if I don't like the shit you're talking."

Franny laughed nervously. "I was speaking in general. I don't know you well enough to talk trash about you."

"Mm-hmm," Silk murmured doubtfully.

"Here we are. This is Carmalee's house." She pointed to a house with pretty flowers in the yard. "What do you want to see Carmalee about? I know you're not thinking about letting her put a straightening comb in all that bone-straight, pretty hair of yours."

"No, I need to make an appointment for my daughter."

"You got kids?"

"I consider Buddy's three children as my own flesh and blood."

"Oh."

"Thanks for walking with me. I'll catch you later." Silk left Franny behind and walked up the steps, and knocked on Carmalee's door. She put on her most endearing smile and thickened her Southern accent when Carmalee opened the door.

"Hi, there, Carmalee. My name is Silk Dixon and I'm new around here. I'm in a heck of a pickle and would appreciate it so much if you could squeeze my little girl in for a hair appointment."

Taken in by Silk's beauty and Southern charm, Carmalee smiled and welcomed her inside. Sitting in a kitchen chair was an older woman with half a head of nappy hair and the other half was straight. On top of the kitchen table was an assortment of hair pomade, hair pins, and silver clips.

"I had a cancellation. You can bring your daughter over at one o'clock if you'd like. You have to wash her hair first, though."

"Thank you. We'll be here at one o'clock sharp," Silk said with an appreciative smile.

Outside, Silk was surprised to see Franny still hanging around.

"Did she give you an appointment?" Franny asked.

"Yep, she's gonna fit my daughter in at one this afternoon."

"Shoot, it's only a little after ten. You got almost three hours to kill." Franny fanned her face with her hand. "It sure is hot today. I could go for a cold beer; what about you?"

Although Silk didn't care too much for Franny, she didn't mind relaxing over a beer and picking the woman's brain to find out where the excitement was on this side of town. "You got some beer in your ice box?"

"No, but I saw Sweet Daddy pull up to the Flower Hill bar in his Thunderbird. He's the numbers runner, and the pockets of his sharkskin suits are always full of cash. He'd buy plenty of drinks for a pretty girl like you. You wanna stop by the bar for a little while?"

"Sure, why not?" Silk could drink like a fish when she wanted to. Being a good wife to Buddy, she'd been trying to lay off the hard stuff, but after battling Dallas' kinky hair, she felt she deserved a drink or two. She checked her wristwatch, one of the many trinkets she had inherited from Buddy's dead wife. "I can't stay long, though. I have children to attend to, you know."

"One beer," Franny assured her, guiding her along Ruby Street. When they approached the woman who had snubbed Silk, Franny flashed a smile and clutched Silk's arm as if she'd won a prize. The women buried their heads in their magazines, pretending not to notice Franny and Silk.

"Those two biddies don't like me and I don't care," Silk said bitterly.

"Don't pay them any mind. They're jealous because you're as pretty as Dorothy Dandridge and you're dressed to kill. Plus, they both had their eye on Buddy. He's a decent man and would have made good husband material for the women in the community who ain't got one. Folks are upset about you swooping in and stealing him before anyone got a chance to try to win him over."

"It was love at first sight between Buddy and me. That's the only way I can explain it."

"That's nice," Franny said dismissively. "Now, listen, Silk, I wouldn't expect you to play around behind your husband's back, but it wouldn't hurt if you were nice to Sweet Daddy. Smile at him and act sociable after he buys us a beer."

Silk didn't need any lessons from Franny on how to get what she wanted out of a man, but she nodded, pretending to go along with Franny's instructions.

Franny pointed to a flashy, yellow Thunderbird parked in front of the bar with its top down. "That's Sweet Daddy's car. It's something else, isn't it?"

"It's all right," Silk said, sounding unimpressed, but in actuality, her heart skipped a beat when she got a close look at the flashy vehicle. The glimmering yellow convertible was the kind of car she'd been dreaming of. The kind of car Nathan Lee had promised to buy her when they were planning to run away together. Well, she was up North now, and the car was staring her in the face, which she took as a sign that by hook or by crook, she would soon get a pretty car of her own.

Buddy owed her a wedding present, and she decided in that moment to start working on her husband, and to figure out a way to entice him into taking out a loan to buy her something that outshined the yellow Thunderbird.

CHAPTER 25

Sandwiched between the bar and the barbershop was an area with a set of rusted metal stairs that led to six apartments that were up high, above the bar.

"A colored man, Mr. Bob Lewis, owns the bar and those apartments," Franny pointed out. "His wife, Arvetta—she's a former beauty queen. She won the Miss Sepia beauty pageant back in the day. Anyway, she runs a speakeasy up there in one of the apartments after the bar closes," she said in a lowered voice. "All kinds of illegal carryings-on take place in those apartments. So, honey chile, make sure you keep your distance," Franny cautioned.

"What kind of illegal carryings-on?"

"You didn't hear it from me, now…" Franny paused.

"I won't say anything."

"Well, aside from allowing his wife to sell booze after-hours, Mr. Bob lets her use those apartments for illegal gambling like crap shooting and poker. And I hear there's prostitution going on up there," Franny added in a whisper. "Every weekend there's some kind of trouble that requires a visit from the police. But Mr. Bob has political connections. He's in real good with the white politicians, and no matter how much trouble happens at the Flower Hill, the place never gets shut down."

Franny sidled up close to Silk and spoke conspiratorially. "Sweet Daddy works for Mr. Bob and his wife, Miss Arvetta. Rumor has it that Sweet Daddy and Miss Arvetta have a thing going on. I don't know if it's true, but that's what people say."

Silk didn't give a damn about Sweet Daddy or Miss Arvetta. She wanted to roll her eyes at Franny for wasting her time with idle gossip, but instead she merely gave a little shrug.

With her metal hair wave clips gleaming in the sun, Franny gripped the door handle of the Flower Hill. "Time to get us some free drinks," Franny said with a broad smile.

Back home, the honky-tonk didn't open until the sun went down, and Silk was excited to enter a bar during morning hours. There wasn't much of a crowd inside the Flower Hill, but the distinct smell of alcohol, music from the jukebox, and the sound of billiard balls smacking into each other livened up the place enough to suit Silk just fine.

The bartender's eyes lit up when Silk sat down at the bar. "How you doing, Franny? What can I get you and your friend?" he asked, unable to tear his gaze away from Silk's face.

"Hey, Wally. This is my new friend, Silk. We'll have two cans of Schlitz beer."

"How you doing, Silk. You look like a ray of sunshine, and you done brightened up my entire day," Wally said, grinning.

Silk barely cracked a smile at the bartender. Wally was too portly and unattractive to warrant her exerting any energy.

"Where's Sweet Daddy?" Franny asked, stretching her neck, looking in the back area where the pool table was located.

"I believe he's upstairs in the apartments, making his rounds. You can leave the number you want to play with me, and I'll make sure he gets it," Wally offered.

"Nah, I don't play the numbers 'cause I never hit. I wanted to talk to him about something else," Franny said, giving Silk a knowing smile.

The bartender placed the cans of beer and glasses in front of

Silk and Franny. "These are on the house, Sunshine," he said, pointedly to Silk. "My way of showing appreciation for you coming in here and brightening up the place."

"Hey, Wally, can I bum a cigarette off you?" Franny asked, taking advantage of the bartender's good mood and unexpected generosity. Any other time, Wally would have pointed to the cigarette machine if Franny had asked him for a smoke, but wanting to make a good impression on Silk, he shook a Marlboro out of his pack and not only handed it to Franny, he lit it for her, also.

Franny sat back and sipped her beer and took a deep and satisfying puff on the cigarette. Blowing out a stream of smoke, she wondered what else she could get out of Wally. It seemed that being friends with Silk came with lots of perks and she didn't want to miss any opportunities.

"Say, Wally. Isn't Carrie Pettiford selling dinners out of her house today?" Franny inquired.

"I don't think so. She usually sells dinners on Saturday."

"And the first Wednesday of the month, which would be today," Franny replied. "You should treat me and my good friend to a dinner." Franny looked at Silk. "You want fried fish or chicken?"

"Uh, it's pretty early for one of Carrie's dinners," Wally said, looking a bit angry and somewhat flustered, realizing that Franny was trying to spend his money and play him for a sucker.

Silk laughed to herself. She could tell that the bartender didn't want to give Franny anything, but he also didn't want to make a bad impression by appearing stingy in front of Silk.

"I could go for some fried fish," Silk said, enjoying putting Wally on the spot.

"In that case, I'll give Carrie a call and tell her to drop off a couple of fish platters." Wally came from behind the bar and reluctantly meandered toward the pay phone in the corner.

Franny elbowed Silk. "Wally's sweet on you. Maybe you can get him to buy us tickets for the rock-and-roll show tonight."

"What rock-and-roll show?" Silk's ears were perked. She loved listening to live music. The rare occasions when musicians came from out of town to play at the Low Moon, Silk would dance up a storm and drink more liquor than usual. Not to mention, getting cozy with one or more of the band members when they finished playing for the night. Being married to Buddy was cramping her style. Silk was ready to let loose and have a good time.

"There's a bus excursion going to the Uptown show in Philly. Don't you listen to the radio? It's been announced on WDAS all week long. They got Patti LaBelle and the Bluebelles on the show, Barbara Mason, The Marvelettes, The Vibrations, and Little Stevie Wonder." She gazed at Silk curiously. "You know who he is, right?"

Silk shook her head.

"Little Stevie Wonder is that little blind boy who has that new hit song called 'Fingertips.'"

"I never heard of that song."

Franny poked out her lips as if insulted. "Where you been? 'Fingertips' is number one on all the stations. But anyways, the headliners of the show are the Miracles. And honey chile, I loves me some Smokey Robinson. Ain't no way I'm gonna miss that show."

Thinking back, Silk realized that Cephus had mentioned taking her to the Uptown Theater back when they'd gone to The Melody Lounge together. "Do you mean to tell me, all those famous people are gonna be in the same place at the same time?" Silk asked incredulously.

"Mm-hmm. The Uptown stays packed. Standing room only!"

"Do the entertainers come off the stage and mingle after the show is over?" Silk asked, delighted to have the opportunity to make time with the likes of Smokey Robinson, the lead singer of The Miracles.

"When the curtains closes, the show is over, and you get back on the bus," Franny informed, gazing at Silk curiously. "What kinds of shows have you been to where the singers hang around and mingle with the audience?"

"Back home at the honky-tonk. We dance, drink, and party with the musicians that come to town."

"Oh, we ain't going to no honky-tonk. We're going to a theater," Franny said, pronouncing the word, *thee-ater.* "No liquor unless you sneak it inside your purse. But liquor or not, you have a real good time at the rock-and-roll show."

Franny looked over her shoulder at Wally who was placing the call for their fish platters. "You need to work on Wally when he gets back behind the bar. If you make eyes at him and pretend to like him, he might drive us to Philly, and we won't have to waste money on bus tickets."

Silk was tickled that Franny thought she was stupid enough to work the bartender over on her behalf. Silk could pay for her own bus ticket to the Uptown, but if she felt the need to work somebody over, she'd do it for herself, and not for some poppy-eyed, fat heifer she barely knew. Silk was about to put Franny in her place when the door opened emitting a streak of blinding sunlight.

"That's him!" Franny said with awe in her voice. "That's Sweet Daddy."

Silk shielded her eyes and squinted in the direction of the door, curious to get a gander of the infamous Sweet Daddy. She gasped in shock and nearly choked on her beer. Strolling into the Flower Hill bar was none other than Tate Simmons. As usual, he was looking good and was as clean as the board of health.

"I know him. He told me his name was Tate," Silk whispered to Franny as Tate pompously glided toward her.

"Tate's his real name, but everyone around here calls him Sweet Daddy, and you can see why. Ain't he fine, honey chile?"

"Hmph," Silk grunted. "I don't see what's so sweet about him. He don't look like much of nothing to me." Silk may not have had Big Mama's gift of vision, but she could clearly see that Tate was nothing but bad news. Clutching her purse, Silk eased off the barstool. "I'll catch you later, Franny. I gotta go."

"Wait a minute. Wally's ordering our food."

"Fuck that food," Silk spat as she breezed past Tate.

"Where are you running off to?" Tate inquired.

"None of your damn business," Silk exploded and rushed out the door.

"Can I talk to you?" He grasped her arm.

"Hell, no." She snatched her arm away. "You might think you're God's gift to women, but you ain't nothing but a pain in the ass to me."

"Whatever you say, baby," Tate said with arrogant laughter in his voice as he kept on strolling toward the bar.

The cocky look on Tate's face had infuriated her and when Silk got home, she took her anger and frustration out on the boys. She yelled at them for having the volume of the TV up too loud. She pulled Myron over to her, put him in a headlock and then ground her knuckle into the side of his head, causing him to flail about and holler. When she finished with Myron, she grabbed Bruce and shook him until he was breathless.

"Now, take y'all ornery asses upstairs and stay out of my sight."

The boys quickly scampered upstairs.

Trying to alter Silk's bad mood, Dallas changed the channel from the cartoons she'd been watching with her brothers to *The Price Is Right*. "Do you want to watch this show, M'dear?"

"Yeah, I guess so," Silk responded, flopping down on the sofa while Dallas sat Indian-style on the floor in front of the television.

"We have some time to kill before I take you to the beautician who's gonna straighten out your knotty hair. Come over here and sit next to me, Dallas. Your bad-behind brothers done upset me and plucked my nerves." Silk patted the sofa cushion, and Dallas rose from the floor and dutifully sat next to her.

When Dallas's tiny hand and arm disappeared beneath Silk's dress, Silk closed her eyes and let out a sigh of satisfaction. "That's my good girl. You're the only one in this family who cares about my feelings."

CHAPTER 26

With Buddy putting in overtime and working the third shift as well as his regular morning shift, and with Mrs. Sudler staying overnight to babysit the kids, Silk had the entire night to kick up her heels and have a good time.

Dressed to kill, Silk turned heads as she walked along Twelfth Street, en route to the corner of Twelfth and Engle Streets where the charter bus was picking up folks who had tickets for the midnight show at the Uptown Theater.

Silk's steps faltered when she drew near the Flower Hill bar. She saw Tate's canary-colored convertible in the parking lot. She picked up speed and swept past the bar, relieved that she'd gone undetected by Tate. Tate had a way of rattling her nerves, and she didn't want him and his smart-alecky remarks interfering with the good time she planned on having at the rock-and-roll show tonight.

"Hey, honey chile," Franny greeted cheerfully when Silk reached the bus stop on Engle Street.

There was a large crowd waiting for the charter bus, and she noticed that most of them were coupled off with only a few single people among them. As was usually the case, all eyes were on Silk. Women looked her up and down with envy, and the men appraised her with lust in their eyes.

It wasn't Silk's fault that the men tended to try and undress her with their eyes, and so she shrugged off the dirty looks she received from their female counterparts and struck up a conversation with Franny.

"I can't wait to meet Smokey Robinson. That man makes me weak in the knees with his pretty, cat eyes."

"I already told you that you're not going to meet any of the singers that perform at the Uptown. After they perform their sets, they go to their dressing rooms back stage. They don't mingle with the regular folks."

"Speak for yourself, Franny. You may not get to mingle with Smokey, but I'm damn sure gonna hobnob with the stars. I'm gonna get Smokey's autograph and maybe a little extra something," Silk said with a wink.

"I don't know how y'all do things down South, but you're in for a big disappointment if you think you're gonna party with record-ing artists after the show."

"We'll see about that," Silk said with confidence.

"The only way you can even get a glimpse of the performers after the show is over is by hanging around the back-stage door. Those fast-ass, Philly girls don't mind walking down that dirty alley near Susquehanna and Dauphin Streets to get to the stage door, but Chester women have a little more self-respect."

Silk sucked her teeth. Franny, who wasn't too proud to beg for free dinners and drinks at the Flower Hill, was a fine one to talk about having self-respect.

"I'll take a walk down an alley in a heartbeat, if that alley leads to Smokey and his cat eyes," Silk said with a chortle of laughter.

The bus pulled up and everyone piled on. Franny plopped down in the seat next to the window.

Silk gave Franny a look of indignation. "Uh-uh, get your big ol' butt up. I gotta sit there so I can see the scenery, chile."

Without making a fuss, Franny slid over and allowed Silk to have the window seat. As the bus rolled along, Silk could hear low murmurings of discontent. She listened carefully and overheard several women grumbling in low tones.

"That's the woman that Buddy married while his wife's body was still cold."

"Hmph. She's pretty and everything, but she seems like a fast number, if you ask me."

"I heard she's a Geechie girl and she worked roots on poor Buddy."

Silk's ears began to burn as she listened to the jealous biddies openly gossiping about her. Temper flaring, she stood up and squeezed past Franny and stood in the aisle with a hand on her hip.

"You have to sit down, miss," the bus driver advised.

"I'll sit down in a minute, sir. But first, I have to make an announcement."

There was a hush and the chattering people on the bus went silent as they waited for Silk's announcement.

"I'm giving all of y'all who are whispering under your breath about me the opportunity to speak your mind and say whatever you have to say to my face."

The silence continued.

Silk's expression was a chilling mask of hatred. "Okay, well, since nobody has anything to say, I'm gonna sit back down. But if I hear another word of gossip about me, I'ma put my foot up somebody's ass right here on this bus. Don't let this pretty face fool you. I know talk is cheap, but you best believe, I can back up every word that comes out of my mouth. So, y'all can try me if you want to." Silk gave the onlookers a contemptuous, sweeping gaze, and then rolled her eyes at the lot of them before returning to her seat.

"Ooo, you told those bitches off, and now all of a sudden nobody has shit to say. It's so quiet on this bus, you could hear a mouse pissing on toilet paper," Franny said with a giggle.

Inside the Uptown Theater, Franny wanted to stop at the concession stand and buy snacks, but Silk grabbed her by the arm. "We don't have time for that shit. We have to get ourselves some good seats."

With Franny in tow, Silk pushed past people as she made her way to the front of the theater, close to the stage. After securing choice seats in the center of the front row, she gazed at Franny with a smug expression.

"I never sat near the stage before," Franny said in awe.

"Okay, now that we're situated, you can go back to the candy stand and get us some goodies." Silk handed Franny a five-dollar bill and recited her order. "You can get yourself whatever you want out of that money," Silk offered.

By the time Franny made her way back to her seat, loaded down with two cardboard containers filled with large cups of soda, hot-dogs, popcorn and packs of Goobers, the lights had gone down and Georgie Woods and Jimmy Bishop, two handsome local DJs, were on stage together, warming up the crowd.

Electricity seemed to crackle in the air. Silk hadn't been this excited since the night of her killing spree. Goosebumps ran up and down her arm. Franny attempted to hand Silk one of the cardboard containers, but Silk held up a hand, letting Franny know that she didn't want to be bothered. Silk's eyes were glued to the stage, and it didn't go unnoticed that both deejays' eyes were glued on her. They were both tall and good-looking with processed hair and wearing snazzy suits. She gave them an alluring smile, because it was in her nature to flirt with handsome men, but she hadn't traveled to Philly to make time with any DJs. She wanted Smokey Robinson and no one else would do.

Act after act made their appearances on stage and their performances had the house rocking. Finally, The Miracles came out on stage. The crowd roared and Silk thought she would pass out from excitement. She couldn't believe she was looking directly in her heartthrob's pretty, hazel eyes.

Smokey quickly ran through his past hit, "Shop Around," and when the band played the beginning chords of "You Really Got a Hold on Me," Silk, along with every other woman in the house, screamed at the top of her lungs. The screams drowned out Smokey's sweet, falsetto voice. Finally, the women quieted down and while Smokey sang, he gazed at Silk.

They locked eyes for the entire song. Mesmerized, Silk was trapped in Smokey's spell until Franny whispered, "That woman singing backup with the Miracles is his wife."

"How do you know?" Silk snapped.

"I read it in *Hit Parade* magazine. They been married for a long time."

"Hmph!" Silk was ready to pout, but she perked up when Smokey yelled, "All right, is everybody ready?"—the beginning words to the group's new hit, "Mickey's Monkey." When the band started playing, Silk found herself out of her chair and on her feet, doing the dance that was called the Monkey.

"Come on up here," Smokey said invitingly and Silk ran up on the stage. Smokey and Silk did the Monkey to the delight of everyone in the audience. Having her big moment, Silk wasn't letting it go easily. When Smokey stopped dancing and refocused on singing, she kept on dancing. But instead of sticking to doing the Monkey, she launched into the scandalously sexy new dance called The Philly Dog. Swerving down to the floor and humping like a dog, Silk created chaos inside the Uptown Theater. Men threw their hats toward the stage and whistled loud and vigorously.

When the song ended, Smokey asked her name and told the crowd to give Silk another round of applause. He also whispered that he wanted her phone number. "I'll send my road manager to get it when my set is over."

Next, Smokey and The Miracles sang "I've Been Good to You" and "I'll Try Something New." He sang one love song after another, and he seemed to be singing each song to Silk, personally.

He ended his set with "What's So Good About Goodbye" and then the lights came up, indicating that the show was over. Silk didn't budge. She remained in her seat, waiting for Smokey's road manager. If things went the way she intended, Smokey would ditch his wife and get together with her tonight.

"What are you waiting for? We have to be on the bus back to Chester," Franny reminded her.

"Go ahead. I'll catch up with you later." Silk didn't bother to look at Franny. Her mind was focused on having a secret rendez-vous with Smokey Robinson. Hell, if he was willing to get rid of that wife of his, she'd gladly leave Buddy and travel around the country with him. She envisioned herself taking his wife's place onstage. Sadly, Silk had to admit that she'd never be his background singer since she couldn't sing worth a damn.

After waiting for about fifteen minutes, the road manager, an older man with a big gut and a pock-marked face, approached her. On Smokey's behalf, he asked for her number.

Silk handed the road manager a piece of paper that she'd jotted her number on. "When is he gonna call?" she inquired anxiously.

He scratched his head. "Well, he sleeps pretty late. I suppose you'll hear from him around three or four in the afternoon."

"Okie-dokie," she said with disappointment. Although Silk had wanted badly to get together with Smokey tonight, she derived a modicum of pleasure from the fact that she'd be wrapped in Smokey's arms tomorrow night, feeling his luscious lips pressed against hers. And possibly, he'd sing sweet love songs directly in her ear.

Hopefully, Buddy wouldn't mess up her plans. Lord, if that man didn't work the midnight shift again tomorrow night, she'd have to slip out of a window after he went to sleep. She'd find a way to go meet up with her dreamboat. Nothing could keep her away from Smokey.

CHAPTER 27

Two days passed and Silk hadn't heard a word from Smokey. She sat around waiting for his call like a lovesick school-girl. On the third day, she took a bus over town to Lee's record shop and bought five 45 records and two LPs by The Miracles. When she returned home, she played the records back to back, all day long. She damn near wore the grooves off of "Who's Loving You," even shedding a few tears as she listened to Smokey croon.

When the phone rang, she nearly jumped out of her skin, and snatched up the receiver on the first ring. Concealing her desperation, she spoke in a sultry tone. "Hello?" she answered breathily.

But it wasn't Smokey on the line. It was Buddy.

"Silk, there's been an emergency with the twins," he said in a voice filled with dread.

"Oh, yeah? What's wrong with 'em?" She didn't bother to hide her lack of interest.

"The doctor said they both have pneumonia and real high fevers…" Buddy paused and then said, "The doctor doesn't think their little bodies can survive pneumonia. They're not going to make it this time," Buddy said in a choked voice. "I'll be home to pick you up in about twenty minutes. We have to get over to the hospital right away."

"Uh. Who's gonna watch Dallas, Bruce, and Myron?" Silk asked.

It wasn't that she cared, but feigning concern over Buddy's children could possibly spare her the burden of having to visit the dreary, pediatric ward at the hospital. She was already in a funk over Smokey Robinson, but being in such close contact with sickly children would only worsen Silk's mood.

"Myron is old enough to look after his brother and sister during an emergency," Buddy said impatiently. "I'll be home shortly. When I blow the horn, please come right out. I'm at my breaking point, Silk, and I don't want to see the kids to see me like this."

"All right, Buddy. I'll be at the front door waiting for you."

Silk hung up. *Buddy chose the worst possible time to force me to stand by his side.* Angrily, she grabbed the tea kettle from the stove and banged it so hard on the kitchen table, the record that was playing on the turntable in the living room began to skip. She whisked into the living room and placed the needle at the beginning of the record, "You Can Depend on Me."

Those damned sickly twins were causing her to miss an important phone call, and it wasn't fair. A call from Smokey Robinson could change her life. She could get out of the little hick town of Chester and lead a glamorous life traveling around the country with The Miracles. A man like Smokey would have her dripping in diamonds and wearing all kinds of full-length furs. Hell, she could be Smokey's next wife and be on the cover of *Jet* magazine, standing next to Smokey while they cut their five-tier wedding cake.

It burned her up that Buddy was inconveniencing her like this—standing in the way of her getting the kind of riches she truly deserved. Hit by a wave of fury, she kicked a leg of the coffee table, startling Dallas so badly, the child dropped the doll she was holding.

"Would you stop being so jumpy all the time? Always acting nervous and dropping shit," Silk yelled at Dallas.

"I'm sorry, M'dear."

"Yeah, yeah, yeah. Take your ass upstairs to your room and play with your stupid doll."

Dallas slinked away and Silk didn't feel a bit of remorse. Dallas was by far her favorite of Buddy's children, and she hardly ever raised her voice to the child. But in this moment of blind rage, Silk was livid and was mad at the world.

I'm not the mother of those goddamn twins, so why in the hell do I have to stop what I'm doing to go with Buddy to the hospital? I don't feel like sitting around that dreary hospital, pretending to be sad. That damn Buddy gets on my fucking nerves. He loves to pretend to be Mr. Nice Guy, but he can be a selfish bastard at times. Does he really think I don't have anything better to do with my life than to sit around in a hospital, watching a pair of sickly twins slowly die?

With great reluctance, Silk took the needle off the record she was playing and turned the hi-fi off. She went upstairs to freshen up, and when she found Bruce in the bathroom floating a toy boat in the sink, she pinched his arm, hard. He whimpered, but knew better than to cry. She twisted his skin and watched with satisfaction as he bit down on his bottom lip, trying to fight back the tears. After a few moments, she released his tortured flesh and gave him a shove.

"Get out of this bathroom, playing with a goddamn boat, you ornery, little brat!" Before Bruce was able to scurry out of the bathroom, Silk added insult to injury by kicking the boy in his buttocks. He let out a tiny yelp.

"You wanna play in water, huh? I'm gonna put you back in those diapers if I catch you messing around in this sink again."

"Please don't put me back in diapers, M'dear. I won't play in water again," Bruce wailed, sniffling and shaking.

She glared at Bruce with disgust and then rolled her eyes at him. "I should hold your head under this here water to teach you a lesson, shouldn't I?"

Not knowing how to respond, Bruce wore a puzzled look. "Uh. N-no?"

Silk sighed. "If I catch you playing with toys in the bathroom again, that's exactly what I'm gonna do to you." Silk took the toy boat out of the sink and threw it at Bruce. "Where's Myron?"

"He's in the backyard playing with his friend, Billy."

"Go outside and get your brother. Tell him I want to have a talk with him."

Bruce picked up his boat from the floor and scampered away, eager to escape any additional pinches or kicks in the behind.

A few minutes later, as Silk gazed in the mirror while brushing her teeth, Myron appeared in the doorway of the bathroom. "Yes, M'dear?"

Silk continued brushing her teeth without responding. She allowed Myron to stand in the doorway squirming while he waited for her to state the reason she'd sent for him. She leisurely brushed her teeth for approximately two minutes and after rinsing her mouth, she finally acknowledged Myron's presence.

"I have to go out and I don't have time to get a sitter for you kids. You're gonna have to look after your brother and sister. When they get hungry, fix them bologna and cheese sandwiches and a glass of milk."

"Yes, M'dear."

"And don't mess with my new records. If I find a scratch on any of them, I'm gonna tan you and your brother's hide. Do you hear me?"

"Yes, M'dear. We won't touch your records."

"You better not. Oh, by the way, I'm expecting an important phone call. If a gentleman calls and asks for me, I want you to take a message and write down his number so I can call him back. Guard that number with your life. Don't you dare let your father find out that a gentleman called the house for me."

"I won't, M'dear," Myron assured her.

"You better not or I'll skin you alive. If you think I'm lying, try me. Now get out of my face. Scram!" She made shooing motions with her hands and Myron darted away.

Twenty minutes later, Buddy was outside the house, honking his horn. Silk gave the silent telephone a lingering look before walking out the door.

Nothing was more depressing than the pediatric ward. Silk would rather stick needles in her eyeballs than sit up in that place. The twins, with all their maladies, looked like death warmed over. Silk averted her gaze as Buddy rubbed their scrawny little hands and uttered comforting words. They lay in separate cribs, hooked up to monitors by wires and cords, which excused Silk from having to hold them in her arms.

"I wonder where their doctor is. I need to speak to him," Buddy said, pacing agitatedly. "No one seems to be attending to my baby girls," Buddy said, wringing his hands.

"Why don't you go to the nurses' station and try to get some answers," Silk suggested.

"Good idea."

The moment Buddy left the room, Silk walked over to the crib where Pamela lay. She was only able to identify one twin from the other by the tiny name bracelets on their wrists. Silk bent over the crib and felt the baby's forehead. The child was as hot as an oven and her lips had a blue tint.

You're not doing yourself or anyone else any favors by clinging to life, little girl. Do you realize that every day you're alive, you and your sister are costing your daddy and me a fortune? And for what? Neither one of y'all will ever be worth a plug nickel.

Considering herself showing the child mercy, Silk covered the baby's little face with a pillow. The baby squirmed and kicked. Her little legs were much stronger than Silk had expected. She put up a valiant fight for life, but finally, Pamela's tiny body went still.

Silk peeked out the door and discovering that the coast was clear, she hurried over to Paulette's crib and began working on her next. She used the same pillow on Paulette. Being the weaker twin, Paulette didn't put up much of a struggle, making it easy for Silk to smother her, while keeping one eye on the open door.

Feeling perkier than she'd felt all day, Silk took a deep, exhilarating breath. Killing gave her a rush that was slightly better than good sex.

While waiting for Buddy to return with the doctor, she found herself humming a song. Excitement surged through her, and although Silk tried to occupy her time reading a newspaper that one of the nurses had left behind, she found that she couldn't concentrate on the newspaper print—not with the melody and the lyrics of one of Smokey Robinson's songs running through her head.

Wearing a concerned expression, Buddy walked in with an Asian doctor at his side. The name on the physician's lab coat, read: *Dr. Dongsheng.* A funny name that forced Silk to stifle a giggle as the doctor introduced himself.

Silk accompanied Buddy and the doctor as they walked over to Paulette's crib.

"Oh, my God! What's wrong with her?" Buddy asked, his voice filled with dread.

The doctor checked the baby's pulse. "I'm sorry, Mr. Dixon. Your daughter has expired."

"Oh, God, no!" Buddy wailed and then hastily made his way over to Pamela's crib. "Jesus! Why?" Buddy screamed, looking up at the heavens after surveying Pamela's unmoving body. "I didn't get a chance to say goodbye to my babies," he lamented while Silk rubbed his back and murmured soothing words.

"It's a miracle that your daughters lasted this long, Mr. Dixon," the doctor said, trying to comfort Buddy.

Nodding her head, Silk agreed with the doctor. "Let's go home, Buddy. There's nothing else we can do for these precious babies." With the twins out of the way, Silk was in a hurry to get back home and continue waiting for her phone call.

"If you need a moment for spirituality, the hospital has a chapel on the fifth floor. Some families seek comfort in the chapel," the doctor said in a gentle voice.

"That's a good idea." Buddy grasped Silk's arm. "Let's go to the chapel and pray for the twins' souls."

Silk wanted to slap the dog shit out Dr. Dongsheng for making such a time-wasting suggestion, but she had to grin and bear it. Standing by her grieving husband's side, she joined him on the elevator that would take them to the chapel on the fifth floor.

CHAPTER 28

Getting rid of those money-draining twins had a surprise benefit that Silk hadn't anticipated. Buddy had life insurance policies on the babies for twenty-five hundred dollars each. Five thousand dollars would improve Silk's life, and she'd be damned if any thieving lawyer or crooked politician was going to get one nickel of it.

But she hadn't banked on having to wage a war against the head honcho at the funeral parlor.

Speaking in gentle tones, the funeral director steered Buddy toward miniature caskets. Silk was shocked by the price tags on those itty-bitty, little caskets. They cost an arm and a leg!

The somber-faced mortician made it a point to find out from Buddy exactly how much cash he was working with. Buddy revealed that he had five thousand dollars, and the greedy mortician seemed to be trying to spend up every penny, suggesting deluxe this and top-of-the-line that. He even tried to get Buddy interested in special little kiddy flower arrangements, among other costly funeral expenses.

Silk took the liberty of asking the cost of cremating the twins. Buddy gasped and the mortician tilted his head, surveying Silk as if to determine if she had lost her mind.

"You want to break tradition and burn up those innocent little babies?" the mortician asked in a reproachful tone. Shaking his head as if distraught, he walked over to his desk and fell into his seat.

"Cremation is out of the question," Buddy interjected. "My children deserve a proper burial."

"I didn't think you'd agree to something so outlandish." The mortician cast a disapproving glance at Silk. He picked up his pen, prepared to begin tallying up the cost of a double funeral.

"I'd like to speak to my husband privately. Can you give us a moment," Silk said to the mortician. The mortician cut an eye at Buddy, as if expecting Buddy to insist that he be allowed to remain in the room.

"Can we have a moment?" Buddy asked politely, and the mortician stood. He straightened his tie and walked to the door, reluctantly leaving the couple alone in his office.

Silk clasped Buddy's hand. "Listen to me, Buddy. You've been working so hard, you haven't had time to notice that your three surviving children are suffering. I try my best to be a good mother to them, but they're still mourning the loss of their mother. They all had nightmares after seeing her lying in that coffin. Bruce was so upset, he started peeing the bed every single night, but being that you were going through so much, I kept that unpleasant information to myself. Poor Dallas...she cries herself to sleep, crying for her mama. And Myron...he's quiet and jumpy. He don't hardly open his mouth to talk anymore. Do you really want to put those poor children through another funeral when they're not finished grieving over the first one?"

Buddy rubbed his forehead. "I hadn't thought about how another funeral would affect the kids."

"The twins, precious as they were, were only a few months old, and since the children never even laid eyes on them, why would you make them suffer through looking at their dead bodies? It appears to me that the mortician is trying to spend up all your money. He's not looking out for what's best for your children. But I'm with your kids—*our kids*—night and day. I want what's best for them. And I'm pleading with you not to make them suffer through another funeral so soon after their mother's death."

"But the church members will gossip."

"Did any of those church members go to visit those sickly babies while they were in the hospital?"

Buddy hung his head. "No, they didn't."

"So, why do you care what they think? When you end up having to cart your three remaining kids away to a children's mental ward, don't say I didn't warn you."

Buddy covered his face. "Don't say that."

"It's the truth. They're not the same, Buddy, but you don't want to face it."

"I did notice they were all sort of withdrawn, but I thought time would heal them."

"Time, along with my motherly ways, will heal them one of these days, but you've got to stop springing funerals on them. Their delicate little hearts can't take any more. Now, you need to stand up to that mortician and tell him that we're not interested in any burial plots, caskets, printed funeral programs, newspaper announcements, flowers, or embalming fees. You tell him that we want those babies cremated for two hundred dollars each and that's that. Out of decency, he should give you a special, two-for-one deal."

The Uptown show came to an end after its two-week run, and all the performers moved on to their next gig. Silk never heard from her idol, Smokey Robinson, and it was heartbreaking. Thankfully, Buddy took away some of the sting of lost love when he used the twins' insurance money to open a new, joint bank account for him and Silk, telling her that she could spend the windfall of money from the twins' insurance policy any way she saw fit. Silk didn't know how to write out a check or balance a checkbook, but she sure enjoyed seeing her name printed on the new checks.

"You're a wise young woman and I want you to be able to run our household without having to ask me for money every time you need something. You're an angel in my life, Silk. I've been getting hit with one tragedy after another, and I doubt if I could have made it through if you weren't by my side."

Later on that night, when they got in bed, Silk gave Buddy the deluxe version of the special treatment, which drove him to groan loudly and to bellow with such passion, Myron and Bruce ran to the master bedroom and pounded on the door.

"Daddy! Are you all right?" the boys asked with terror in their voices.

Buddy cleared his throat in embarrassment. "Everything's fine, boys. Go back to bed."

Silk narrowed an eye at the closed door. She'd deal with those meddling boys in the morning. In the meantime, she had to finish sending Buddy on a trip to paradise that was unlike any other.

Silk pressured Buddy to teach her how to drive. Too busy putting in overtime to take her out on the road, Buddy signed her up with the Apex Driving School.

On her first day of driving lessons, Silk dressed demurely in a shirtwaist dress, but when she saw her young instructor, a young white guy with movie-star good looks, she wished she'd worn something more revealing.

"Hi, there, Mrs. Dixon," the blond-haired instructor greeted. "My name is Edward Brenner; you can call me, Ed."

"And you can call me, Silk," she said, offering a provocative smile. Ed gave her a lopsided smile that was sexy as hell. White fellas had always had the hots for Silk, and she wasn't surprised by Ed's flirtatious demeanor. Silk never discriminated when it came to her male lovers. Heck, she would have been setting up housekeeping with Nathan Lee at that very moment, if he hadn't come to the Low Moon on that fateful night, roughing her up and acting the fool.

Ed took a pack of Parliament cigarettes out of his shirt pocket. "Smoke?" he offered.

"No, thanks." She watched him out of the corner of her eye as he shook a cigarette out of the pack. The way Ed slouched in his seat with the cigarette dangling out of his mouth while he steered with one hand, gave him a *Rebel Without a Cause* persona, reminding her of James Dean.

"You look kind of young to be a driving instructor," Silk commented.

"I'm twenty-five, and I've been driving since I was thirteen. My dad made the mistake of teaching me how to drive, and I liked it so much, I used to steal his car keys every night after he went to bed." Ed looked at Silk and gave her another sexy smile. "You're in the hands of a highly skilled driver with twelve years' experience."

"I'm impressed," Silk said and then opened her purse and took out a compact and checked her reflection.

"You look pretty as a picture. Did anyone ever tell you that you favor Lena Horne? You could be her daughter."

"I've heard it every now and then. Anyone ever mention that you look a lot like James Dean?"

"Couldn't you have thought of someone who's still alive? Why'd you have to compare me to a dead movie star?"

"Sorry," Silk said with laughter. Ed's sense of humor was appealing. She'd lucked up with her driving instructor. They were going to be spending a lot of time together, and she couldn't have asked for a cuter or more personable teacher.

Ed drove out of Silk's neighborhood and took her to an area where there was less traffic. He pulled to the curb and parked. "The only way to learn how to drive is for you to get behind the wheel. So, let's switch seats."

"No! I'm not ready for that. I need you to explain a few things, first." She pointed downward to the pedals. "I don't know the brake from the gas pedal."

"I'll tell you what. You can sit on my lap and turn the steering wheel while I work the pedals. Think you can manage that?"

Silk scooted over and eased onto Ed's lap. He immediately popped a boner, and she was immensely pleased. "Are you okay?" she teased.

"Uh, I've been better." Ed wiped imaginary sweat from his brow, which drew more laughter from Silk.

Sitting on Ed's erection, Silk placed her hands on the wheel, concentrating on steering while Ed felt her up, squeezing her breasts, grinding on her ass, and kissing her neck while he worked the foot pedals.

Ed slammed on the brakes. "I'm overheating, Doll Face. If you don't do something to cool me down, my engine's gonna blow." Ed was red in the face, laughing a little as he groped Silk's body with more fervor.

"I don't want you to blow your engine," she teased, and then wrapped her arms around Ed's neck. She planted a kiss on his lips, and said, "It's been awhile since I've had any white cock, and I miss it."

Silk's brazen words caused Ed to turn beet red. "Man, oh man, you're quite a little sexpot. I've never been with a colored girl before."

"Well, we're gonna have to do something about that." She ran her fingers through his hair.

"I know a quiet spot, where we can have some privacy. A woodsy area with wild blackberry patches."

"I'm game. Let's go." Silk moved over to the passenger's side of the car. Reaching out, she caressed Ed's erection as he tore through the peaceful neighborhood, leaving a trail of exhaust fumes.

The idea of making love outside in the open air didn't bother Silk at all. In fact, she looked forward to it. Lying on the ground and spreading her legs and getting a hard fuck and expert sucking from a horny cracker would be a nostalgic reminder of home. She wondered if Ed could eat poontang as good as Nathan Lee could.

Her body yearned for good head. Buddy was so terrible at oral sex—causing her nothing but frustration and irritation—that Silk no longer allowed him to stick his tongue anywhere near her vaginal area. And Buddy didn't put up a fight. He seemed relieved not to have to take any more trips downtown.

Ed parked the car and took a tarp out of the trunk. He and Silk journeyed into the woods on foot. The scratches she received on her legs from blackberry thorns were worth the discomfort once Ed laid down the tarp and mounted her. He undid the buttons at the front of her dress and yanked the cups of her bra upward, baring her breasts. Heat raced across her skin as his lips brushed against her nipples. At his touch, her flesh burned and tingled. She inhaled sharply, and then cried out with carnal hunger.

"You're getting me all hot and bothered. Now, I need you to do something about it." Her chest heaved up and down with passion as she nudged the top of Ed's head with one hand and lifted the hem of her dress with the other.

"You want me to eat your cunt?"

"Yeah, I want that real bad."

Men like Buddy made halfhearted attempts at eating poontang, but a man like Ed put his whole heart into the act, savoring the distinctive taste of pussy like a wine connoisseur. After a while, Silk began pleading with Ed to stop.

"I can't take any more. Fuck me, Ed. Please, baby. Stuff that white cock in this here poontang and go to town on it!"

But Ed wouldn't fuck her. Ignoring her pleas, he lashed and punished her pussy with his tongue. No amount of begging or bargaining would stop him. Unable to bear another moment, Silk lifted her ass from the tarp and clutched his head tightly between her hands as she felt an orgasm building inside her. With her muscles tensed, she strained and moaned as Ed slurped out her pent-up passion.

"Are you ready for me, Doll Face?" Ed asked, licking the sheen from his lips.

Silk gave him a smug smile as she readjusted her clothes. "It's too late. I told you to get it while it was hot. It's not my fault that you couldn't pry your lips away from my sweet poontang."

Hurt and confusion clouded Ed's eyes. "Are you gonna leave me hanging like this?" He looked down at his stiff dick.

"You better handle your business before you get a case of blue balls," she said, laughing maliciously.

"You want me to whack off?"

"You can do whatever you want as long as you finish giving me my driving lesson."

Ed began to masturbate while Silk took out her compact and powdered her nose and put on a fresh coat of lipstick.

"Can't you help me out a little bit?" Ed asked in a whiny voice.

"What do you expect me to do?" Silk replied, irritated.

"It would help if I could see your cunt."

Silk sighed as she stuffed the compact inside her purse. "Okay, but you have to speed it up. I paid for a driving lesson, and I still don't know the first thing about handling an automobile."

"Don't worry," Ed said with panting breath. "I'll give you all the driving lessons you need—free of charge if you open your legs and let me see your cunt."

"You got a deal!" Silk pulled her dress up and widened her legs. She pulled her panties to the side, revealing her most intimate part.

Ed jerked on his dick hastily. "Open it up. Let me see the inside."

Silk pulled her pussy lips apart, smiling broadly as she stretched it open as wide as possible.

"Christ! Sonofabitch! Goddamn!" Ed bellowed as he ejaculated into the open air.

Silk couldn't stop giggling at Ed's outburst when he shot his load.

"You're the best, baby. When can we get together again?"

"We can do it again tomorrow—after my free driving lesson," Silk said with smug satisfaction.

CHAPTER 29

Rubbernecking motorists and pedestrians gazed at Silk with awestruck expressions when she pulled up in front of the parking meter, driving her brand-new, red, convertible Cadillac with white-wall tires.

With her hair flowing down her back and wearing a tight-fitted dress, Silk felt like the colored version of Marilyn Monroe as she swiveled her hips, walking along Sproul Street with Dallas in tow.

"You look beautiful, M'dear," Dallas said adoringly.

"And you're beautiful, too. Now pick up your step so we can make it to your ballet class on time. We don't want those crackers saying colored folks are never on time. I want you to show those little white girls that you can do those ballet moves way better than their asses can."

"Yes, M'dear."

Silk walked Dallas inside the YWCA building. "I can't stay to watch you practice today. After dance class, I want you to go straight to the locker room and change into your swimsuit and get in the pool. You better make sure every strand of your hair is tucked under your swim cap because I can't deal with any nappy-ass hair, ever again. Do you hear me?"

"Yes, M'dear."

"Okay, then. I'll be back to pick you up after your swimming

lesson is over. Now, go put those no-dancing, white girls to shame."
Silk patted Dallas on the back, urging her to get moving. With a
wave of her hand, Dallas proceeded to the room where her ballet
class was held.

Ed had yet to see Silk's new car, and over the phone, they'd made
plans for Silk to take him for a little spin, and to also get into
some hanky-panky while Dallas was taking classes at the Y. But
Silk changed her mind, realizing she wasn't in the mood for Ed to
be slobbering between her legs.

Instead of driving toward the blackberry field where she'd promised to meet up with Ed, she steered the Caddy back toward her
own neighborhood and glided into the parking area of the Flower
Hill bar.

Had Buddy been at home instead of working overtime on such
a gloriously sunny Saturday afternoon, he could have stood out
on their front porch and easily spotted Silk's car.

On Saturdays, folks started filtering into the Flower Hill as
soon as it opened in the morning. Silk sat in her car, reapplying
lipstick and brushing her hair. She felt a shiver of excitement each
time the door to the bar opened, emitting raucous laughter and
thumping music. The place was already in full swing and she was
in the mood for a good time.

A peek in her side mirror, revealed pesky Sonny Boy coming
out of Max's store, carrying a load of boxes, which he stacked next
to the trash can. Silk sank down in her seat, but she wasn't quick
enough. To be half-blind, Sonny Boy sure had good vision when
it came to spotting Silk.

Siiilk! Siiilk!" Sonny Boy waved excitedly as he yelled in his
thick, sluggish voice.

Lord knows I don't feel like being bothered with this retarded mother-
fucker today!

Limping at a fast pace, Sonny Boy rushed over to Silk's car.

Panting with excitement, he grinned at Silk. "Is this your car, Silk?"

"Yup, and it's spanking, brand-new. Do you like it?"

"It's purty. I can wash it up and shine it for you when I get off from work."

"It's already clean and shiny. It don't need any polishing," Silk said with annoyance.

"I can run a rag over it, and wipe off any smudges or dust. I'll keep it nice and spiffy for you, Silk."

"Not today, Sonny Boy. Why don't you stop by my house in a few days and I'll let you clean it off."

"Thank you, Silk. I'll be knocking on your door in two days." He held up two fingers.

A glance in the rearview mirror exposed Franny crossing the street, heading for the bar. The closer she got, the clearer her features became. And she wasn't smiling like Sonny Boy. The evil way she glared at the Cadillac made Silk wonder if Franny was contemplating putting sugar in her gas tank.

By the time Franny had approached, her hard expression had been replaced with a cheerful smile. "Did your husband buy you this car?"

"He sure did."

"It's gorgeous," Franny said, stroking the car door.

"Watch it, girl. Don't be putting smudges on my baby," Silk said irritably.

Franny snatched her hand away. "Sorry."

"Sorry don't cut it. You better be more careful." Rolling her eyes, Silk opened the door and got out of the Cadillac.

"I'll run and get a rag and wipe the smudges off the door," Sonny Boy chimed in.

Franny put a hand on her plump hip and glowered at Sonny

Boy. "Shut up and mind your business, Sonny Boy. I ain't put any smudges on that car door."

Silk patted Sonny Boy on the arm. "You better get on back to work before Max comes looking for you."

"Okay, Silk. But remember, I'm gonna shine up your car for you in two days." Again, he held up two fingers, and then limped back in the direction of Max's store.

Cozying up to Silk, Franny kept in step with her. "Honey chile, I swear you look like a film star. You remind me of that girl in the movie, *Carmen Jones*. That dress you're wearing is sharp, and it fits you like a glove. Did your husband buy that for you, too?"

"Of course he bought it. Buddy likes to see me dressed glamorously, and he loves spoiling me," Silk said, rubbing her good life in Franny's face. Franny had four crumb snatchers at home and there wasn't a man in sight to claim nary a one of her brood.

"Shame about the twins," Franny mumbled. "They didn't stand a chance what with being born so small and sickly."

"Yeah, it's heartbreaking for my family and me. During these sorrowful times, I have to stay strong and be the rock for everyone to lean on."

"Buddy's a lucky fellow." Franny jerked on the handle of the bar door.

"That's exactly what Buddy tells me every single day," Silk replied boastfully as she entered the Flower Hill. As always, eyes darted in her direction. Male eyes lit up in delight. But the women, with facial features as hard as marble, sized her up through wary, narrowed eyes.

While Franny stopped to chat and mingle with a few people she knew—no doubt trying to bum a cigarette and a free drink—Silk sauntered over to the bar and took a seat.

"How you doing, Silk? You're looking good, baby," Wally, the bartender, greeted in a welcoming tone. "What are you drinking—Schlitz beer?"

"No, I done moved up in the world. I'll have a scotch and soda on the rocks. But I don't want the cheap stuff. Pour me a double shot of Chivas Regal," Silk said, recalling what Nathan Lee used to drink.

"We don't carry Chivas Regal. How about Johnny Walker Red?"

"That'll do."

"I heard Buddy bought you a new Caddy; is that true?"

"You heard right. She's parked out in the lot. One of these days, I'll take you for a spin."

Wally set the drink in front of her. "I'm gonna hold you to that, Silk."

One sip of scotch and Silk's insides became warm. She felt amorous and there was a tingling sensation in her loins. There weren't any interesting-looking men in the place, Silk noticed as she glanced around the bar. She wondered if her cute white boy, Ed, was still hanging around their meeting spot, waiting for her. She thought about chugging down her drink and racing to the other side of town so that Ed could suck on her poontang, but she decided against it. She'd be enraged if she drove all the way to their special spot in the blackberry field only to discover that Ed had grown tired of waiting.

With a cigarette clamped between her fingers, Franny meandered over to the bar and took a seat next to Silk.

"Say, Wally, give me a Schlitz, and put it on Mr. Blackwell's tab." Franny pointed to a white-haired gentleman who walked with a cane.

Franny sipped her beer and smacked her lips in satisfaction. But Silk wasn't doing so well. She squirmed in her seat, realizing that something needed to be done about her tingling pussy. She gazed at Wally and shook her head. His big, ol' protruding belly was a sign that he probably wasn't working with very much dick.

A glimpse at Franny as she wrapped her lips around her cigarette, gave Silk the bright idea of trying to talk Franny into putting those juicy lips to good use. But before she uttered enticing words that would encourage Franny to slip inside the ladies room with her, the door opened and Tate sauntered in.

"Here comes trouble," Franny alerted Silk, recalling Silk's adverse reaction the last time Tate had entered the Flower Hill.

"I don't see any trouble. All I see is a tall drink of water." Silk fluttered her fingers at Tate and sent him a smile.

Tate's expression brightened as he glided across the barroom, heading in Silk's direction. He didn't bother to glance at Franny as he maneuvered into the space between Franny and Silk.

"I can't believe you finally decided to speak to me. You're a some-timey broad, you know that?" Tate spoke in a humorous tone.

"An experienced lady's man like yourself should understand that being moody is a woman's prerogative."

"You're something else, Silk," Tate said with a smile as he beckoned the bartender. "Give the lady whatever she's drinking." He nodded at Silk.

"There's more than one lady sitting here," Franny piped in.

"Yeah, well, I only have eyes for Silk," Tate retorted.

"But me and Silk came here together; how you gonna just ignore me?"

Tate gave Franny a menacing look. "Do I have to smack you in the mouth to get you off my back?"

Franny flinched and muttered to herself as she pulled another cigarette from the pack that old man, Mr. Blackwell, had bought her.

"Why don't you scram, Franny. Give me and Silk some privacy," Tate suggested with a sneer. The menace in Tate's voice prompted Franny to grab her beer and vacate the barstool next to Silk.

Watching Franny skulk off, mumbling and rolling her eyes, tickled Silk. "You're a real charmer, Tate," Silk said with sarcastic laughter.

"That skank tried to get new with me. She knows damn well I don't give her the time of day, so why would I buy her a drink?"

"Can't blame her for trying."

Tate waved his hand dismissively, indicating he was through with the subject. "So, what's good, Silk? Everybody's talking about your new ride. I'm parked next to you in the lot. That Caddy is sharp; makes me want to trade in my Thunderbird."

"You can't keep up with me, Tate. So don't even try."

Tate laughed. "You're probably right. You're a real humdinger, you know that? And I like your style." His expression turned serious. "I'd like to get you alone. Do you think you could slip away from Buddy one night this week?"

"What's wrong with right now?"

Wally placed Silk's drink in front of her, and gazed at Tate as if he wished he were in Tate's place.

"Right this moment?"

"Yeah, no better time than now." Silk gazed at Tate challengingly.

Tate rubbed the side of his neck. "I, uh, I have some business to attend to."

Silk laughed. "You're all talk and no action, huh?"

"I've got plenty of action. Give me a few minutes to make some phone calls. I have to rearrange my schedule." Walking toward the pay phone, Tate glanced over his shoulder and winked at Silk.

She ran her tongue over her lips.

CHAPTER 30

S ilk followed Tate to a row house on Tilghman Street. Kids were out in full force, riding bikes and scooters up and down the pavement.

"Is this where you live?" she asked after parking behind Tate's car.

"This is one of my spots."

"How many do you have?"

"You ask a lot of questions."

"I'm the curious type."

"Curiosity killed the cat," he said with a sly grin.

"Hey, Mr. Tate!" a little boy called from across the street. "Do you need anything from the store?"

"Not today, Junebug, but I have another job for you. I want you to keep an eye on both these cars—my T-bird and the red Caddy behind it. Make sure none of the kids ride their bikes too close to our cars, and don't let anyone lean up against them, either."

"Yes, sir. I'll guard the cars," Junebug replied, grinning.

"All right, little fella. I'll pay you when I come out."

"Okay!" On foot patrol, Junebug paced back and forth between the two convertibles. The little boy, who looked to be around eight or nine, wore a serious expression as he kept guard.

Inside the neat house, the tiled living room floor was polished to a high shine and there was a faint smell of floor wax, which Silk found rather pleasing. The sofa and chairs were protected with clear plastic covers, giving Silk the idea to have her living room furniture covered to prevent Buddy's children from wearing out the fabric. She looked around the environment, noticing numerous framed photographs of Tate at various ages that were displayed on the mantel, table tops, and some were hung on walls.

"Somebody sure loves you. Is this your mama's house?"

Tate nodded. "She's out of town at a social function, and she likes for me to check on the place whenever she's away from home."

Tate took Silk by the hand and led her from the living room to a hallway with shellacked, hardwood floors. As he guided her up the stairs, she admired the paintings of geese in flight that decorated the wall going up the stairs.

"I've been jonesing for you since the day I met you," he said, embracing Silk at the top of the stairs and covering her mouth with his. Kissing her passionately while reaching for the zipper at the back of her dress, he backed her into a wall in the upstairs hallway. "I have to have you," he muttered, yanking the bodice of her dress down and then groping with the hooks of her bra.

Silk helped Tate remove her bra and then she flung it on the floor. The open door of the middle bedroom revealed a well-ordered room with a large bed that beckoned them. But overcome by lust, neither Tate nor Silk could find the strength to make it to the room.

Tate's hands roamed over her bare breasts, and Silk's skin tingled at his touch. She buried her head in his chest, breathing him in as her eager body rubbed against him. He smelled deliciously manly—like soap, a hint of sweat, and aftershave. The ache between her legs demanded attention, and her restless hands whizzed downward and stroked his crotch, creating a hard lump of flesh inside his pants. She urgently struggled to unfasten his pants and take hold of his dick in her trembling hand.

Her gaze dropped to the throbbing flesh that felt hot against her palm, and a range of desires overwhelmed her. Her tense fingers yearned to fondle his erection, while at the same time, her lips puckered at the sight. It was difficult to resist the urge to draw his beautifully formed appendage inside her mouth and lather it with her tongue. The very core of her body tightened expectantly, craving the sensation of him gliding slowly into her and then upping the tempo with deep, driving strokes that were certain to send her over the edge of madness.

Not knowing what pleasure to partake in first, Silk was relieved when Tate made the choice for her. With his pants falling past his firm thighs, he eased her down to the floor and mounted her. Hot kisses on her lips persuaded her to arch her back and open her legs for him as wide as possible.

She'd had many sex partners in her young life, but the way Tate made love to her was beyond anything she'd ever experienced. Maybe the alcohol that was coursing through her system made her body extra sensitive to his touch. Maybe her body hungered for a skilled lover with finesse. Whatever the case, the sexual connection between Silk and Tate was unlike anything she'd ever known, and she wanted to feel him inside her every day and every night.

When Tate and Silk emerged from his mother's house, Silk hung on to him with both arms wrapped around his waist, and her head resting on his shoulder, making it clear that she didn't want to ever let him go.

Despite having Silk cling to him like a conjoined twin, Tate managed to dig inside his pocket and wrestle out a dollar bill. "Here you, go, Junebug."

"Oh, boy! A dollar!" Junebug broke into a toothy grin. "Thanks, Mr. Tate," he said, scampering off to the corner where the Mr. Softee truck was parked with a flock of children and a few parents standing at the serve window.

After walking Silk to her car, Tate disentangled himself from her and gave her a kiss. "I'll see you again tomorrow night, baby. Keep that thing hot for me," he said with a self-assured smile.

When Silk returned to the Y to pick up Dallas, the child was looking forlorn, sitting on the steps of the building holding her satchel filled with dance attire and swimwear.

"I'm sorry I'm late, sweetiekins. Were you scared?"

"A little bit."

"Aw." Silk caressed her hair. "I'll bet you're hungry."

Dallas nodded.

"If you want, we can stop by Woolworth and see if the lunch counter is still open. If it's closed, we can go up the street to John's Doggie Shop and get ourselves a chili dog. What do you think about that?"

"I never had a chili dog."

"They're delicious. I had one the other day when I was out joy-riding in my new car."

As they approached Silk's Cadillac, she took Dallas' satchel and put it in the trunk, and then took her by the hand and continued walking. "No point in moving the car. John's Doggie Shop is right on the corner of Seventh and Sproul." Silk pointed in the direction of the hot dog shop. "Those chili dogs are some kind of good, sweetiekins, especially when they load on the cheese and raw onions."

Dallas made a face. "I don't like onions."

"Okay, I'll tell them to hold the onions on your hot dog."

After getting served chili dogs, fries, and Coca-Colas, Silk and Dallas took seats at a round table with high stools that were located in front of a large, picture window. They peered out the window, watching the passersby as they munched on their food.

"Miss Wickers, my ballet teacher, said I caught on quick. She gave me a solo to perform at the dance recital. Do you know what a solo is, M'dear?" When Silk didn't respond and continued to stare out of the window dreamily, Dallas went on chattering. "A solo is when you dance all by yourself onstage. I hope I don't mess up. Miss Wickers said you should buy the record of the music I'm dancing to so I can practice at home. She wrote the name of the song on a piece of paper. It's in my dance bag."

"That's nice," Silk said absently. Dallas was talking a mile a minute, and although Silk had hoped that she'd eventually break out of her bashfulness, now was not a good time for the child to be striking up such a lengthy conversation. Silk's mind was much too preoccupied with thoughts of Tate to pay attention to Dallas' silly jabbering.

Reminiscing about the passionate love she and Tate had made caused butterflies to flutter around in her tummy, and a chill ran up her spine.

That doggone Tate ain't nothing but trouble, she reminded herself, again. Then she thought about his soft lips and his slow, sensual hands. *Mmm*. He was the kind of trouble a girl didn't mind getting into, Silk decided.

CHAPTER 31

The food that church members had donated when Silk first arrived was long gone, and Silk had been paying Mrs. Sudler fifteen dollars a week to cook and clean for the Dixon family. For extra money, Mrs. Sudler also kept an eye on Myron, Bruce, and Dallas whenever Silk needed her to.

Buddy still had no idea that Silk didn't know the first thing about cooking. He was oblivious to the fact that she couldn't even boil an egg. Silk led him to believe that taking care of his three children kept her hands full, and that there was no time for cooking and cleaning. Eager to lighten the load of his beautiful, new wife, Buddy didn't mind paying for a little extra help.

But Mrs. Sudler had become a problem. One look at Silk's new Cadillac and she decided that fifteen dollars a week wasn't enough.

"I've been thinking," Mrs. Sudler said, shifting her eyes downward. "For all I do around here, I deserve twenty dollars a week."

Enraged, Silk saw red. "Oh, really? Well, I don't think so. Fifteen dollars a week adds up. A lot of women in this community would love to earn the sixty bucks a month that I've been paying you. And they probably could whip up much better meals than the tasteless food you throw together," Silk said with a sneer.

Mrs. Sudler was taken aback. "You never complained about my cooking before."

"Didn't want to hurt your feelings, but it's high time that I expressed my true sentiments. And if you don't like it, you can lump it," Silk said sassily, with a hand on her hip.

Mrs. Sudler began backpedaling. "Well, I suppose I could add more flavor." She chuckled embarrassedly. "I tend to forget that you're from Louisiana and most likely prefer to eat very spicy food."

Silk's mouth curled with distaste. "The amount of spice ain't got nothing to do with it. What I prefer is that you take your ungrateful, raggedy ass out of my house and don't try to come crawling back."

Mrs. Sudler huffed up in indignation. "Now, Silk, there's no cause for name-calling. Why can't we discuss this money matter like civilized people?"

Silk reached into her bosom and pulled out her knife. She held it up to the corner of Mrs. Sudler's mouth. "You've been smiling in my face with that fake grin ever since the day we met. Don't tempt me into giving you a permanent big smile," Silk threatened, drawing a few droplets of blood with the blade of the knife.

"You're crazy!" Mrs. Sudler broke away and raced to the front door, knocking into furniture along the way.

Silk doubled over in laughter. "You better take your ass out of here!" When the door slammed, Silk cackled again, this time, slapping her hand on the kitchen counter. After her laughter subsided, she began banging on the Formica countertop in fury. *The nerve of that trifling hussy to come to my home demanding more money. If I was in Louisiana, I would have cut the bitch without hesitation. Sheriff Thompson never gave a shit about what coloreds did to each other. But here in Chester, they got constables and magistrates and all sorts of lawmakers ready to punish Negroes for harming one another.* Angry that she had to restrain herself from doing bodily harm to Mrs. Sudler, Silk kicked a kitchen chair, toppling it over.

Alerted by the commotion, the children scrambled down the stairs. Silk stalked over to the bottom of the staircase. With her arms folded, she glared at the children, stopping them in their tracks.

"What happened, M'dear?" Myron inquired. Behind him, Bruce and Dallas gawked at Silk with wide, curious eyes.

"None of your beeswax. Now, take your nosey asses back upstairs before I cut some switches and light fire to your scrawny hind parts and ashy legs."

With that threat, the children practically knocked each other over, racing up the stairs.

"Get back here, Dallas!" Silk shouted.

Dallas halted. "Yes, M'dear?" she said fearfully.

"Oooh, Dallas is gonna get it," Bruce and Myron taunted in whispery voices.

"You two knuckle-headed boys better get up those steps. Hurry up before I beat y'all asses until they're black and blue!" Softening her expression, she beckoned Dallas. "I want you to come down here with me, sweetiekins." With a gentle smile, Silk reached for Dallas' hand, and then led her to the living room.

"Do you want me to give you some thrills, M'dear?"

"Shh. The walls have ears, and you know better than to talk about our secret."

"I'm sorry. Do you want me to give you some thrills?" Dallas repeated, this time in a whisper.

"What do you think?" Silk's tone was sarcastic. Hastily, she ushered Dallas toward the sofa. She hitched up her dress, and then exhaled in exasperation. "That doggone Mrs. Sudler is a pain in the butt. She done got on my last nerve, but thank goodness I have such a sweet little girl to calm me down."

Dallas looked up at Silk, her eyes sparkling with innocence and the eager desire to calm down her edgy stepmother.

Needing help around the house, Silk put out feelers. She received word that Carrie Pettiford who sold dinners every Saturday and the first Wednesday of every month was available to cook for the Dixon family. Carrie couldn't do any housework due to her allergies and heart condition, but she assured Silk that she'd bring her teenage daughter, Sharita, along to handle the cleaning chores.

Silk was none too pleased when she was introduced to Sharita. With her knock-knees, her wide, boxy-shape, and an unsightly cleft lip, the girl wasn't easy on the eyes. Furthermore, she was somewhat simple-minded. Unable to keep up with her classmates, Sharita had repeated grades so many times, she was now sixteen years old and only in the eighth grade, which made her a target for ridicule. But despite her flaws, Sharita could scrub and clean like nobody's business. She kept the Dixon household as neat as a pin and sparkling from top to bottom.

Silk noticed that Myron and Bruce enjoyed giving Sharita orders, and they teased her mercilessly. Silk didn't bother to intervene. Figuring that Sharita needed to learn how to stick up for herself, she allowed the boys to have fun at the cleaning girl's expense.

Whenever Carrie left for the day after finishing up her cooking duties, the boys considered Sharita fair game for taunts and mockery.

Gathered around the kitchen table, Myron, Bruce, and Dallas ate dessert while Silk had her face buried in the daily newspaper, reading the comics. From the corner of her eye, Silk saw Bruce sneakily hold up his water pistol and take a shot at Sharita as she stood at the kitchen sink washing dishes. Silk couldn't help cracking a smile at the boy's devilishness.

"Cut it out," Sharita mumbled without turning around.

"Do it again," Silk whispered, encouraging Bruce with a wicked grin on her face. Bruce's eyes glinted with mischievousness. With Silk's permission, he aimed the water pistol at Sharita.

Sharita was wearing Bermuda shorts and Bruce squirted each of her thick legs, prompting her into an awkward dance that brought out titters of laughter from Silk and the boys.

Pitying Sharita, Dallas kept her eyes lowered and concentrated on eating her Jell-O pudding and fruit cocktail.

"Shoot Sharita in her big ol', wide behind," Silk suggested maliciously.

"I don't have enough water." Bruce pressed the trigger, proving to Silk that he could only generate drips and dribbles of water.

"Well, go on over to the sink and fill it up."

Bruce got up from the table. At the sink, he rudely pushed in front of Sharita.

"Ow!" Sharita exclaimed when Bruce stepped on her Keds while in the process of maneuvering the water spigot toward his toy. "Excuse you," Sharita said indignantly.

"Sharita, watch your mouth. I don't want you speaking to the children using that tone of voice. I won't stand for it," Silk admonished.

"Bruce stepped on my foot, and he's trying to get water so he can keep squirting me with his water gun, Miss Silk," Sharita complained.

"He's only having fun, Sharita. A little bit of water can't hurt you. Stop being such a big baby. And remember, no one likes a tattletale."

"Yes, ma'am," Sharita mumbled and continued scrubbing pots and pans with her lips poked out in displeasure. Every so often, she'd flinch when a shot of water hit her on the neck or the arm.

Not wanting to be left out of the fun, Myron asked, "M'dear, can I be excused from the table to go get my water pistol? I wanna shoot Sharita, too."

"Go ahead and get it, but fill it up with water from the bathroom sink. I can't allow you boys to keep getting water from the kitchen spigot and interrupting Sharita while she's trying to get through her chores."

After getting water from the upstairs bathroom, Myron returned to the kitchen with mischief gleaming in his eyes.

Silk pointed to Sharita's broad backside and whispered, "Shoot her where I told you to."

Side-by-side, the boys stood a few feet behind Sharita. They aimed and fired until their guns were empty and the back of Sharita's Bermuda shorts were drenched.

"Looks like she peed on herself," Myron remarked derisively.

"She probably needs to wear a diaper and rubber pants, doesn't she, M'dear?" Bruce exclaimed, cutting an eye at Silk.

"A normal-size diaper wouldn't fit Sharita's big ol' butt. We'd have to find her some jumbo diapers," Silk said, giving Bruce a wink as she affectionately rustled his hair. She'd stopped forcing Bruce to wear diapers a long time ago, but she could tell that he was eager to inflict upon Sharita the same embarrassing and cruel punishment that he'd endured.

"I ain't pee myself, and I don't need to wear diapers," Sharita said in protest.

"You probably pee the bed every night," Myron added spitefully.

"Now, now, boys. That's enough. Stop teasing Sharita. She can't help it if she's a big-behind oaf."

The boys broke into giggles at Silk's scornful words. Meanwhile, Dallas cast a sympathetic glance in Sharita's direction.

Realizing that she'd finally found a way to bond with her step-sons, Silk gazed at Bruce and Myron with fondness.

Her eyes cloudy with tears, Sharita approached the table and began clearing away the dessert dishes.

"Come on, kids. Let's go out on the back porch and catch a breeze while Sharita finishes cleaning the kitchen."

As they exited the kitchen, Dallas reached for Silk's hand, and her two brothers who normally tried to stay as far away from Silk as possible, were jockeying for position, each trying to grab a hold of their young and playful stepmother's free hand.

Sitting on the glider next to Silk, Dallas played paddle ball. Hitting the wooden paddle with the rubber ball that was attached by an elastic string, Dallas counted aloud each time she successfully struck the ball.

"Be quiet," Silk hissed and yanked the toy from Dallas' hand. "I can't think straight with you hitting on that thing right next to my ear. Go play with it down in the yard."

Out of pure orneriness, Silk tossed the paddle ball out into the yard.

"Are you mad at me, M'dear?" Dallas asked with her bottom lip trembling. She wasn't accustomed to being on Silk's bad side.

"Damn right, I'm mad at you. The next time I sic your brothers on Sharita, you better not act like little Goody Miss Two Shoes. I expect you to join in on the fun."

"Okay," Dallas reluctantly agreed, her face contorted by a frown.

CHAPTER 32

Buddy worked six days a week and put in long hours of overtime to keep his family comfortable, and on Saturday night and most of the day on Sunday, he expected to be rewarded for his generosity. Buddy wasn't nearly as good a lover as Tate was, but he sure had stamina. Too much stamina for Silk's taste. As he pounded into her body for the fourth time Saturday night, she squeezed her eyes shut, pretending that Tate was on top of her. But her little game of pretense wasn't working. Tate had finesse and was a gentle lover. He used the soft touch of his hands and the honeyed sweetness of his kiss to get her riled up and in the mood.

Silk supposed that putting up with Buddy's brutishness in bed was the price she had to pay for her shiny Cadillac, her fashionable wardrobe, and the comforts of her lovely home. But she wasn't sure how much longer she could suffer through Buddy's bad lovemaking when she yearned to be lying in bed next to Tate.

But Tate was a mystery. He had sets of keys to six or seven different places, yet none was his home. He claimed to have a bachelor pad in Philadelphia but hardly ever went there due to the amount of business he had to conduct in Chester. Silk suspected there was more to Tate's story, but she kept her suspicions to herself. Over time she'd come to learn that Tate had a quick temper, and common sense told her it was unwise to nag him with her doubts.

Somewhere along the line she'd slipped up and fallen in love with Tate. Unfortunately, being a married woman with responsibilities, she couldn't keep tabs on her lover man the way she wanted to.

Though her mind was a million miles away, Silk's arms were secured around Buddy's waist as he grunted and powerfully thrust into her. "Your dick is so good," she said mechanically as she wondered what Tate was up to tonight.

"You like the way I'm giving it to you?"

"You know I do. I can't get enough of you, Daddy."

Buddy groaned with pleasure. He loved it when Silk called him, Daddy.

Pleased with herself, Silk smiled and then returned to her thoughts. *Is Tate secretly married? He had better not be shacking up with some floozy.* Being a fast-living, numbers runner, Tate had plenty of women in his life, but the idea that there might be a special one—a woman who had papers on him or even a special place in his heart—caused Silk's blood to boil. Tate had her nose wide open, and she was liable to claw a bitch's eyes out and slash both sides of her face if she ever caught Tate messing around behind her back.

Remembering that Buddy was on top of her, ramming his dick in and out of her, Silk half-heartedly participated in the fuck-session by crying out, "Give it to me, Daddy!"

"Ahh! Oh, shit! Oooo." Buddy gasped, dropping yet another deposit inside her body. "Whew! You really whipped it on me!" Winded, he collapsed on his back, his chest rising and falling rapidly.

"Don't tell me you're plum-tuckered out, already?" Silk teased, while secretly hoping her words were true. She couldn't take another round of Buddy lying on top of her, sweating profusely and pumping away.

"No, I'm trying to catch my breath, and then I'm gonna put some more good loving on you."

Silk ran her hand across his damp forehead. "I want you to rest up. You've been working so hard on your job, it's not fair for you to have to come home and put in more work."

"I gotta make sure my pretty wife is happy. Besides, this ain't work; this is pleasure." Buddy smiled at Silk and ran his fingers through her hair. "Despite all the sorrow I've been through in the past few months, one look in your eyes lets me know that I should count my blessings. I love you, Mrs. Dixon, and I'm well aware that I'm the luckiest man in the world."

"Aw, I love you, too, Buddy. Now, listen," she said sternly. "I want you to lie back and relax. It's my turn to make you feel good." Silk slithered over to Buddy, licking her lips, and letting him know what she had in store for him.

Preparing for the unbearably delicious pleasure he was about to receive, Buddy grimaced and grit his teeth as Silk buried her face in his groin, peppering his flaccid flesh with soft kisses that would bring his dick back to life. She licked the head, causing Buddy to gyrate and whine, and when she pulled his dick inside her warm mouth, in a matter of seconds, it began to swell up and inflate like a balloon.

Silk detested having to suck Buddy's poontang-flavored dick, but if she expected him to sleep through the night, then she had no choice but to try her best to put him in a coma by giving him the best blowjob she'd ever given.

She whipped it on her husband. Sucked the cum out of him and had him curling his toes up and calling on the Lord. Afterward, she lay cuddled next to him, stroking the hair on his chest until he began to snore like a bear. On cue, Silk slipped out of the bedroom and hurried to the bathroom down the hall, where she took a quick whore's bath.

Back in the bedroom, she kept an eye on Buddy as she tiptoed around, getting dressed in the dark. Getting fucked badly by her husband caused her to hunger for Tate's wonderfully rhythmic dick strokes. Silk fled down the flight of stairs. Tate was no doubt having drinks and handling his business at the Flower Hill, and she had to get to her man before the place closed up for the night.

"Damn!" she spat when she realized Buddy's car was blocking her Caddy in the driveway. Oh, well, she'd have to hoof-it on down to the bar. The Flower Hill was only a hop, skip, and a jump away, but walking on a gravelly road in high-heels required her to put on a hell of a balancing act. *Love sure makes me do foolish things!*

Her eyes lit up and her heart fluttered in excitement when she spotted Tate's car. With a wobbly walk, she did her best to hurry across the parking lot that was uneven and dented with potholes.

She'd never been inside the Flower Hill on a Saturday night. With Buddy working only a single shift on Saturdays, she wasn't able to get out of the house on Saturday evenings. Silk was delightfully surprised at how crowded the place was. It was packed to the rafters. Colored folks were wall-to-wall, standing around drinking while shooting the breeze, whooping and hollering, and having a good ol' time.

She recognized some folks, but most she didn't. She anxiously scanned the crowd but didn't see Tate's handsome face anywhere.

Wally wasn't working, and she didn't recognize the guy working behind the bar. As she made her approach, she heard low whistles and a male voice murmur, "Who's that fox?"

Another man responded, "I don't know who she is, but she looks good enough to eat. Yessiree, I could sop her up with a biscuit." The remark was followed by a chorus of laughter.

Hearing men express appreciation for her good looks wasn't anything new to Silk, and their admiration had little meaning since the praise wasn't coming from Tate's mouth.

Giving her male admirers an eyeful, Silk put an extra wiggle in her walk as she sashayed up to the bar. "Scotch and soda," she said to the bartender.

The bartender gave her a long look. "You've never been in here before, have you?"

"Yeah, I've been in here quite a few times."

"That's strange."

"What's strange about it?"

"The fact that I would forget laying eyes on a stone fox like you," he said flirtatiously.

Silk chuckled. "I usually come in during the day when Wally's behind the bar. That's when I put in my number with Tate. Say, have you seen Tate around?"

"Are you talking about Sweet Daddy?"

"Yeah." Anxious to see her lover man, Silk's heart rate sped up.

"He came through earlier tonight, but he left with Arvetta."

"Arvetta?" Silk struggled to keep her voice steady. She'd heard that name before but couldn't remember what she'd heard about the woman. Merely hearing another woman's name associated with Tate's had Silk seeing red. It was a damn shame that she'd left home in a hurry and had forgotten to tuck her switchblade inside her brassiere.

"Arvetta is in apartment number two, over top of the bar. But, listen, you don't have to track down Sweet Daddy." He slid a piece of paper and a pencil in front of Silk. "I work for Sweet Daddy. You can play your number with me." The bartender placed the drink in front of Silk and she guzzled it down quickly. "No, thanks. I like to play my numbers with Tate, personally. Arvetta's in number two, right?"

"Yeah, but it might not be a good idea to go up there and interrupt the card game."

Silk threw two dollars on the bar and said, "Keep the change." She rushed out of the bar and stomped up the metal stairs that led to the apartments over top. She knocked on the door of apartment number two, and when no one responded quickly enough, she began pounding hard, as if she had a warrant for Tate's arrest.

A fair-skinned, mature woman with crinkly, caramel-colored hair cracked open the door. She was attractive if you could look past the crow's feet and the fine lines etched on her face.

"Is Tate here?" Silk inquired.

"Who's asking?" Sounding confrontational, the woman arched a brow and looked Silk up and down. The woman had an air of confidence about her that Silk didn't like one bit. Although she was a fading beauty, the woman was dressed to the nines and wore lots of glittery jewelry. She looked much too high class to be in a dismal joint like this.

"Who do you think you are—Tate's bodyguard or something?" Silk asked with a look of contempt.

"I'm Arvetta Lewis—and you're on my property."

Ah, so this is the former beauty queen that Franny was talking about.

"Do me a favor, *Miss Sepia*," Silk said with a smirk. "Tell Tate that Silk wants to have a word with him."

Arvetta flinched at the verbal jab that Silk had made when referring to a title she'd achieved a few decades ago. Quickly recovering, Arvetta straightened her shoulders and took on a pompous expression. "I can't disturb Sweet Daddy right now." Arvetta wore an amused smile that pissed Silk off so badly, she pushed the door open and shoved the aging beauty queen aside.

"Have you lost your mind? You can't barge in here like that."

"Fuck you, bitch. I can do whatever I want!"

"Get out of here before I'm forced to call the police." Arvetta grasped Silk's arm.

Silk broke free and ran through the tiny living room and toward a short corridor. "Tate!" Silk bellowed.

"What the hell is going on?" Tate came out of a room and closed the door behind him. He was bare-chested, and wearing only a pair of iridescent pants with the fly hanging wide open, revealing a dark forest of pubic hair.

"I thought you were supposed to be playing cards, but obviously your ass is up to no good."

"It's not what it looks like, baby," Tate said in a placating tone. "I was only doing Arvetta a favor."

"What kind of favor?" With a confused expression, Silk looked from Arvetta to Tate. Arvetta was fully clad in her expensive clothes, and Tate was half-dressed. "Who's in that room?" Silk hurriedly opened the door and gasped when she saw a woman with large, beautiful eyes and creamy dark-brown skin sitting up in bed with a sheet wrapped around her waist. Her bare breasts were large and full with jet-black nipples that puckered as if they'd been recently sucked. A shiny, blonde wig flowed past the woman's shoulders, giving her the appearance of a whore.

Silk couldn't make sense of what her eyes beheld. Franny had told her that prostitutes resided in the apartments above the bar, but Silk couldn't understand why a man as confident and good-looking as Tate would stoop so low as to pay for sex with a whore.

CHAPTER 33

"What were you doing with that wig-wearing bitch?" Silk demanded.

"I can explain."

"I can't believe that you were fucking that whore!" Livid, Silk hauled off and slapped the shit out of Tate, and then tried to claw at his face. He grabbed her hands and restrained her.

"That's enough, Silk. If you don't calm your ass down, I'm gonna fuck you up," Tate threatened in a tone that anyone in their right mind would take seriously. But Silk wasn't in her right mind. Insanely jealous, she balled her fists and pounded on Tate's chest, instigating a fight.

Tate grabbed Silk by the shoulders and shook her until her brains rattled, but she kept swinging at him. "Get your hands off of me, you no-good, two-timing motherfucker!"

Although Tate and Silk had been keeping their romance undercover, Silk was so incensed, she had no control over what came out of her mouth. Unable to cause Tate any bodily harm with her fists, she picked up a lamp and tried to knock him upside the head, but he weaved out of the way, and the porcelain base of the lamp shattered against the wall.

"I don't need this kind of trouble!" Arvetta shrieked. "I run a peaceful joint and this kind of ruckus is bad for business. This hussy is gonna scare off my paying customers and bring the cops to my door. Do something, Sweet Daddy! Whip that bitch's ass and drag her off my property." Arvetta spoke as if she had authority over Tate.

"Arvetta, sweetheart, I need you to do me a favor," Tate said while confining Silk in a bear hug. Silk was so irate, she began stomping her feet while screaming and crying.

Arvetta looked at Tate suspiciously. "What sort of favor?"

"Take Peaches to one of the other apartments. All I need is twenty minutes with Silk, and I'll have her under control."

"You better do more than control her. Get her ass out of here," Arvetta spat, narrowing her eyes at Tate.

"I will."

Arvetta beckoned the petrified woman who was shivering in the bed. "Don't bother getting dressed. Cover up with the sheet, Peaches, and let's go."

Peaches wrapped the sheet around her nude body and dashed past Silk as if she were darting away from a caged animal that might break loose and attack her.

The moment Arvetta and Peaches left the apartment, Tate released Silk. "Baby…baby," he said in a pacifying tone as he cupped her face tenderly. "What the hell is your problem? Why'd you come over here starting a bunch of bullshit?" Though using profanity, his voice and facial expression remained tender and caring.

Silk moaned in anguish. In all of her nineteen years, she'd never suffered through the kind of heartache she was experiencing in that moment. "What the fuck is going on, Tate? I thought I was your woman, but you've been playing me for a fool."

"No, that's not true."

"Then why were you in here fucking that whory-looking bitch and calling that ex-beauty queen, sweetheart? I don't know what to make of all this."

"I can explain everything." Tate patted the edge of the bed.

"I'm not sitting on the bed you just got finished fucking on." Silk folded her arms across her chest and remained standing.

"I didn't fuck Peaches. I admit, I was going to, but all that pounding on the door made my dick go soft."

"Why, Tate? Don't I give you all the sex you need? I'm with you damn near every day out of the week, and I'm only with Buddy on the weekend."

Tate laughed derisively. "You have a lot of nerve coming over here wrecking the place and trying to fight me, all because you caught me with another woman. Did it ever occur to you that I might want revenge for having to share you with your husband?"

"But I don't love Buddy. I love you." Silk sat down and put her arms around Tate.

"So you say." He pried her arms from around his neck. The look in his eyes was icy cold. "Look, maybe it's time for me and you to cool it. Arvetta is running a business in these apartments, and I don't need you breaking in here, acting crazy."

"I'm sorry, Tate, but I saw red when I realized you were in bed with that bitch. Are you trying to break up with me over a goddamn whore?"

"It's not what you think."

"Then, what is it?"

"I'll be straight with you. Peaches is a new girl who wants to work for Arvetta. You know, turning tricks. But before Arvetta puts a new whore with any of her valued customers, she likes for me to give the girl a good workout in bed to find out her strengths and weaknesses." Tate spoke in a normal tone as if he were discussing something as mundane as the weather.

"Why do *you* have to be who has to fuck her whores? Why can't she get one of the bartenders or someone else to do it?"

"It's only business, baby. I never told you this, and you have to promise to keep it under your hat." Tate eyed Silk, waiting for her response.

"I promise."

"Mr. Bob is the biggest colored racketeer in the city. He has his hands in a little bit of everything…numbers, narcotics, prostitution, and bootlegging. I've been working for him and his wife, Arvetta, since I was seventeen. The three of us are thick as thieves. I'm like the son they never had."

"Mm-hmm. Is that why you called her sweetheart?" Silk said with envy dripping from every word.

"That didn't mean anything, I call all women sweetheart. I've known Arvetta all my life. I call my own mother sweetheart, and Arvetta is like a second mother to me."

"Any fool can see that there's a lot more than a mother and son relationship between you and that woman."

"If Arvetta was my woman, do you think she'd be willing to share me with her girls?"

Silk shrugged. "All I know is I don't like her uppity ass, and I want you to stick to running numbers, and let her find another stud to fuck her whores."

"It's a deal. After the way you acted, I'll be keeping my dick in my pants unless I'm sharing it with you."

Silk blushed and lifted her mouth up to Tate's luscious lips.

"The way you were fighting and scratching made my dick hard for some reason. You gon' give me some pussy or do I have to fight you for it?" Tate asked with laughter as he pulled down his pants.

His heavy, hanging meat was a delight to Silk's eyes and her hands shook with excitement as she drew his stiffening dick toward her open mouth. She ran her tongue along the underside of his shaft, lathering it up and murmuring, "I love you, Tate," between tongue strokes.

"Shh. Don't talk, baby. Concentrate on sucking this dick."

And Silk sucked it for all she was worth. She moaned and was close to shedding tears of pleasure as she filled her mouth with Tate's hard dick. For some reason, Tate was giving her the rough treatment, pulling her hair and cursing under his breath as he deeply embedded his dick down her throat. As he exploded, he wrapped her long hair around his fists and yanked her head harshly. And for reasons unknown to Silk, she loved the way that Tate was man-handling her. As she swallowed his creamy seed, she smiled dreamily imagining the rough ride of pleasure she was going to have when he climbed on top of her.

Tate's body jerked as Silk sucked out the last drop of goodness. Self-satisfied, she began to undress. Tate watched her with a gleam in his eyes. Once Silk was completely naked, she lay on her back and began enticing Tate by fingering her pussy.

But instead of mounting her, Tate walked over to the closet.

Silk's pussy was clenching up so tightly, it caused her physical pain. "Where you going, baby? Get over here and get some of this."

Tate didn't reply. He took a wire hanger out of the closet and methodically began bending, twisting, and reshaping it into a sinister-looking weapon.

Silk chuckled nervously. "What are you gonna do with that hanger?"

"You came over here and showed your ass, and made me look like a chump in front of one of the new girls. How can I expect my bitches to take me seriously and show me respect if they see you busting in here and slapping me across the face?"

"I'm sorry about hitting you. I lost my temper." Silk looked away briefly and then stared Tate in the eyes. "I thought you said that whore worked for Arvetta."

"It's complicated. Technically, all the girls work for Arvetta, but I get a share of the profits for fucking them and beating their asses when they act up."

Silk flinched. Had Arvetta turned Tate into a pimp? She hated the idea of Tate having sexual relations with anyone other than her, and was desperate to figure out a way to get him away from Arvetta and those whores. Silk's mind was swimming with ideas when she cast a quick glance at the hanger, which Tate was lifting upward in an ominous manner.

"I'd be less than a man if I let you get away with what you did."

"I said I was sorry; what more can I say?"

"It's too late for sorry; you need to be taught a lesson," he said in an icy tone.

Silk suddenly understood his intentions, but before she could spring up from the bed and flee, Tate pounced on her. Wielding a bent hanger, he attacked her, striking her on her thighs, hips, and arms. She struggled to escape to no avail. She kicked and screamed as he forced her onto her belly. Holding her in place, he flogged her ass, her back, and her shoulders. It seemed as if the wire hanger was burning into her flesh, and no amount of tears or pleading could persuade Tate to stop beating her. In the blink of an eye, the man she loved had changed into someone she didn't know—a sadistic stranger without an ounce of compassion.

When the brutal beating was finally over, amazingly, he took her in his arms and kissed her—tenderly. What was even more bizarre was Silk's reaction. She kissed him back with a yearning and desperation she had never known. Licking into his mouth, she whispered his name over and over, but she didn't call him

Tate. The name she murmured with reverence in her voice was, *Sweet Daddy.*

There was a look of triumph in Tate's eyes as he mounted her, covering her welted and bruised body with his own. "Who do you belong to, baby?" he asked in a low, sexy tone.

"I belong to you, Sweet Daddy."

With a satisfied expression, Tate pried her legs open with a bent knee. Both Tate and Silk were panting in lust as he guided his throbbing manhood inside her creamy opening.

Silk's entire body was ravaged and ached from the beating, but she ignored the pain as she wrapped her legs around Tate's waist and encircled her arms around his back.

"I'm sorry for causing a commotion. It won't happen again."

"It better not," he said gruffly.

"I love you, Sweet Daddy. I really do." There was awe in her whispery voice. This man had beaten her like she was one of his whores, and yet she wanted him more than ever.

Slowly moving his hips, he inserted a few more inches of dick.

"Fuck me, Sweet Daddy. Oh, God. Nobody can fuck me the way you do."

"Now that you know I won't hesitate to beat that ass, you better straighten up and fly right," he warned.

"I will," Silk promised in a tiny voice. She realized she sounded stupid and weak, but for the life of her, she couldn't help herself. *He didn't mean to hurt me. And I'm not gonna give him any cause to ever hit me again. We're gonna put this behind us and forget it ever happened, and our relationship is gonna be stronger than ever.*

In the midst of their lovemaking, Silk opened her eyes and noticed Arvetta standing in the bedroom, watching her and Tate. Startled, Silk's body stiffened. Tate glanced up at Arvetta and froze.

"Did you backhand that bitch and show her who's boss?" Arvetta asked.

Tate nudged his head toward the discarded hanger. "Yeah, I got my point across."

"Does she understand who she's messing with?" Arvetta asked as she sat down on the bed next to Tate and Silk's entwined, naked bodies.

"She understands," Tate responded, and then proceeded to deep stroke Silk's pussy.

Silk felt self-conscious with Arvetta watching, but Tate didn't seem to mind her presence. Silk wanted to cuss the bitch out for having the nerve to plop her ass on the bed while she and Tate were busy fucking. But not wanting to rile Tate, Silk kept her mouth shut and didn't speak a word of protest.

She tried to block Arvetta out by closing her eyes, but her eyes popped open when she sensed movement. Silk was outraged. That old bitch was rubbing on Tate's back, kissing and licking his earlobe, and whispering, "I love the way you fuck, Sweet Daddy. Make sure you remember who that dick really belongs to. You hear me?"

"You know who this dick belongs to, sweetheart," Tate said.

"Who?" Arvetta demanded.

"This dick belongs to you, Arvetta," Tate proclaimed, leaning over and giving the former beauty queen a kiss.

Silk's heart dropped. In a panic and fearing that Tate was going to pull his dick out of her, Silk tightened her legs around his back.

Giving Silk a sneering smile, Arvetta rose to her feet and left the bedroom.

CHAPTER 34

Miraculously, Silk was able to crawl back in bed next to Buddy without him realizing she'd been gone for hours. She covered the bruises from the beating with a long sleeved, ankle-length nightgown that had belonged to Ernestine.

While waiting to fall asleep, she thought about the serious conversation she'd had with Tate. After they'd finished making love, Silk broke down in tears, telling Tate that she couldn't bear sharing him with the whores. Most of all, she admitted, she didn't want to share him with Arvetta. Tate confessed that he didn't have genuine feelings for Arvetta, that he was merely stringing her along. Mr. Bob Lewis held the key to Tate's future. As long as Tate treated Arvetta right, she'd make sure that Tate continued to move up the ladder in her husband's illegal operations.

Silk had asked how old Arvetta was, and Tate told her that Arvetta was forty-three. "She looks good for her age," Tate had added, causing Silk to roll her eyes. Though Silk pretended to be twenty-two, she was only nineteen. In her universe, a forty-three-year-old woman was an ancient relic.

Arvetta's husband was sixty-seven and in ill health. It was questionable how long he could continue running his various businesses. Arvetta had convinced Tate that by sticking with her, she would assure that he was next in line to replace her husband.

Silk was none too pleased about any part of the story. She didn't want Tate replacing Mr. Bob if it meant he had to keep kissing Arvetta's old ass. Silk's last conscious thought before sleep claimed her was: *Something has to be done about Arvetta.*

Aside from the horrible Saturday night sex marathons, Buddy was usually too busy for sex. All he had time for was early morning quickies. Silk didn't like being bothered in the morning, and so Buddy usually stole sex from her. Part of his morning routine was to ease up behind Silk and slip his dick inside her while she was sound asleep. She'd wake up and find semen dripping down her thighs long after Buddy had left for work.

On Sundays, he woke up hours before Silk, and would burglarize her poontang two or three times in a row before Silk had even opened her eyes. The moment he noticed her stirring, he would strike again, sliding his dick back into her cum-filled pussy.

But with the kids up and about, Buddy didn't want the mattress squeaking and squealing so he wasn't jumping up and down on her and pounding away. He was taking it easy, sneakily slow-fucking Silk from behind, and whispering dirty talk in her ear.

"Your coochie sure is juicy this morning, sugar. I don't know what it is that's making this thing feel so good this morning." Buddy reached down and lifted up Silk's right leg. She yelped from the pain.

"What's wrong?" Buddy asked, throwing off the sheet and examining his wife's thighs. "What the hell?" He pulled her nightgown up higher and gasped when he saw the bruises that covered her body. He turned her over and covered his mouth in shock when he saw the black and blue lines that crisscrossed her ass and her back. "What happened to you?"

"I…I don't know."

"You're black and blue all over, how could you not know what happened? Talk to me, sugar."

"Well, you see…last night I wanted a cigarette."

"You don't smoke."

"I started smoking after those precious little twins passed away. Not a lot. But I get a hankering for a cigarette every now and then, especially when I think about how those babies both upped and died at the same time."

"Oh, my sweet angel." Buddy enveloped Silk in his arms.

Silk began sniffling. "So, uh, last night while I was mourning the loss, I snuck out of the house to go get a pack of cigarettes to try and calm myself down."

"Where did you think you could get cigarettes from in the middle of the night?"

"I intended to get 'em from the Flower Hill bar, but I never made it. I was attacked from behind. I didn't get any further than Max's store, when somebody jumped out from the shadows and grabbed me. He was strong and he dragged me into the alley and raped me behind those big trash cans. I tried to fight him off, Buddy, but he started beating me with something. He beat me so bad, I just collapsed, and that's when he raped me."

Buddy bit down on his lip, trying to suppress his rage. "Did you get a look at him?"

"No, not really."

"You didn't see anything? Did you notice what he was wearing? Did you hear his voice?"

"He talked kind of funny. He had a slurred voice. Not slurred like a drunk, but it sounded like he might have some kind of speech problem. Oh, and another thing I noticed was that he was wearing sunglasses. I remember thinking it was strange that he had on sunglasses in the middle of the night."

"Sonny Boy! It was that goddamn, retarded Sonny Boy. He raped a white girl down South and his people shipped him up here. It was only a matter of time before he picked up his old habits." Buddy jumped out of bed and began dressing hastily.

"Where are you going?"

"I'm gonna kill that son of a bitch." Buddy punched a wall.

"Buddy, no!" Silk got out of bed and grabbed Buddy's arm. "I can't prove it was Sonny Boy. Just let it go."

"I don't need any proof other than what you told me." Buddy's face was a mask of fury. "Do you think I'd let any man on earth hurt my beautiful wife and not do something about it?"

"Buddy, please…" Silk reached for Buddy, but he stalked off and raced down the stairs. Moments later, she heard his car roaring out of the driveway.

There were soft taps on the bedroom door. "M'dear?" Dallas said softly.

"Come on in, sweetiekins." The door opened and Dallas stood in the entryway with Myron and Bruce beside her.

"Where did Daddy go? He was cursing and he looked real mad," Myron said.

"He's going to beat up a bad man who hurt me," Silk said with a trace of pride.

"Hurt you? Where?" Bruce asked, his eyes searching Silk's face.

Silk pushed up the sleeves of her nightgown and the three children inhaled sharply. Enjoying their reactions, she lifted her nightgown up to her thighs. "Do you see what else the bad man did to me?"

Dallas began crying and Silk beckoned her. Giving Dallas a hug, Silk assured her that she would be all right. "I want you boys to go downstairs and get some ice and wrap it in a dish towel. That should keep the swelling down."

The boys hurried to get ice and when they returned to the bed-room, they each were holding a dish towel filled with ice cubes. Silk shooed Dallas away and welcomed Myron and Bruce on either side of her. Isolated at the foot of the bed, Dallas was treated like an outcast as her two brothers tended to Silk, gingerly applying cold compresses to her wounds.

Two hours later, Buddy arrived home with raw and bloodied knuckles. "I beat out the little bit of sense that bastard had left in him. After the ambulance took him away, his aunt went over to the magistrate's office and tried to press charges. She was crying and carrying on and saying that Sonny Boy wouldn't hurt a fly. I walked right in the office behind her and let Mr. Bowes know why I whooped Sonny Boy the way I did. Mr. Bowes told the woman that I had a right to defend my delicate, young wife. And since Sonny Boy has a history of rape, Mr. Bowes said it would be best to get him off the streets. He offered me the opportunity to press criminal charges against him. But I told Mr. Bowes that my sweet wife who was lovingly caring for my three children couldn't endure the humiliation of court proceedings and newspaper reporting about her being raped. I told him I had handled the situation in the manner I saw fit. So, that's the end of that."

Silk nodded and mustered a faint smile. "Dallas and the boys helped take care of me while you were gone. I'll tell you some-thing, Buddy…"

Buddy gazed at Silk intently.

"I was really looking forward to being a mother to the twins because I figured they'd accept me as their real true mother. And after I lost that chance…" Silk went silent and nervously twisted the sheets. "After we lost the babies, it seemed like I lost the chance to get some love from any of your children. But I want you to know that Myron, Bruce, and Dallas are starting to love me just like I was their natural mother. And it goes without saying that I cherish those children. They're upset enough knowing that a bad man beat me, I don't think they could handle knowing that he raped me, too. The shame of it would be too much for their innocent little hearts to bear."

"The rape is our secret. It stays between you and me. Now, you relax and get comfortable." He plumped up the pillows beneath Silk's head. The kids are gonna help me make you a big country breakfast. You're queen for the day, and me and the children are your loyal subjects."

"Aw, Buddy, that's so sweet."

"I mean it. After what you've been through, we're going to wait on you hand and foot."

"Thank you, Buddy. I'm so lucky to have a strong, loving husband to protect and love me the way you do."

CHAPTER 35

One of the perks of pretending to have been raped and battered was that Silk didn't have to put up with Buddy's early morning sex raids. He kept his dick to himself while she was in the process of healing. He insisted that she remain bedbound and surprised her with a portable TV for the bedroom. If it weren't for her burning desire to see Tate, she would have stayed in bed for the rest of the week, but by the time Thursday rolled around, Silk couldn't take it any longer. She had to see Tate's face. She was desperate to kiss his lips. The bruises had taken on a yellowish tint and she hoped that the unattractive discolorations on her skin wouldn't prevent Tate from making sweet love to her.

Cruising around in her Cadillac, Silk drove from one end of the city to the next, searching for Tate, and making pit stops at the places he was known to frequent. When she spotted his car in front of Womack's Hoagie Shop on Concord Road, Silk broke into a big grin and parked behind Tate's Thunderbird.

But her grin quickly disappeared when Tate stepped out of Womack's flanked by two wig-wearing whores who were decked out in clunky, cheap jewelry, ugly pale lipstick and white eye shadow. Silk's first impulse was to attack the women and yank off their wigs, but remembering how unmercifully Tate had beaten her ass the last time she'd acted up, she wisely controlled herself.

Tate said something to the two women and they walked away and got inside his car. He sauntered over to Silk, looking spiffy in a dark-brown banlon shirt and yellow iridescent pants with razor-sharp creases down the legs. As he approached Silk's Caddy, she couldn't help thinking that Tate was too damn fine for his own good.

"What's the word, Silk?" he greeted with a smile. "I heard you ran into some trouble with that retarded boy. I heard your husband jacked him up so bad, the boy was carted off to the hospital. They said he didn't even recognize his own aunt when she came to visit him." Tate burst into cruel laughter.

"That's not funny, Tate. I had to explain those bruises to Buddy some kind of way, and I feel bad that I had to put the blame on Sonny Boy."

"From what I heard, Sonny Boy swore to God that you were his girlfriend the whole time Buddy was whooping on him." Tate burst out laughing so hard, he doubled over and stamped his feet. "Then Sonny Boy went so far as to claim that you and him have a secret love affair that you sealed with a kiss." Tate could hardly finish the sentence from cracking up with laughter. "I could be bent out of shape and jealous to find out that you've been cheating on me with that retarded, blind boy, but I'm not gonna blow my stack the way you did."

Silk rolled her eyes at Tate for teasing her. "Do you have any idea how Sonny Boy's holding up?"

"Not really. Sonny Boy's condition isn't the kind of information that I'm concerned about. If you really want to know, why don't you go visit your boyfriend at the hospital?"

"Stop calling him my boyfriend! Anyway, I can't visit him; Buddy would have a fit."

"I hope you wouldn't let that husband of yours stand in the way of you coming to see about me if I was ever laid up in the hospital."

"Nothing could keep me away from you, Tate." Silk's anxious eyes darted toward the women sitting in Tate's car. "Who are they? Two of your whores?" She tried to form the question in a casual manner, but couldn't keep the emotion out of her voice.

Tate nodded.

"Do you have to fuck 'em for Arvetta?" Silk asked worriedly.

"I already did that when they were hired a while back. Now, it's strictly business between me and the girls."

Silk let out a sigh of relief and smiled.

Tate leaned to the side and glared at Silk. "You got a lot of nerve interrogating me. Do I ask you how many times you fuck your husband?"

"I don't mean to pry in your personal business, but I get so jealous. I'm sorry, but I can't help myself." She looked at him with a sad expression. "Can you spend some time with me today?"

He scratched the side of his face. "Not right now. Maybe later on tonight."

"But I won't be able to get out later on. Buddy ain't been working his overtime hours this week. He's been coming straight home from work to look after me."

"Look here, baby. I got big plans for you and me. Plans for you to be by my side when I take over the city. But right now, while I'm hustling in these streets, I can't give you all the attention you need. It seems to me that you want a square nigga who comes home at the exact same time every night." He shook his head and turned his mouth down in disgust. "I'm not that kind of cat. That'll never be me."

"I don't want that to be you. I love you just the way you are."

She gazed at Tate pleadingly. "I need to talk to you. Can you sit in the car with me for a minute or two?"

Tate twisted his mouth to the side in annoyance as he glanced down at his watch. "I got shit to do, so make it snappy."

Seeming to move with great reluctance, he slid into the car and closed the door. Silk immediately embraced him, kissing him passionately and telling him how much she missed him. Tate slipped his hand up her skirt and stroked the crotch of her panties. "Make sure you keep this thing hot for me." He put his hand on the door handle. "If you want to get together, then figure out a way to meet me at ten o'clock tonight."

"Where do you want me to meet you?"

"There's a spot on Pennell Street that I use sometimes. Meet me at the corner of Seventh and Pennell tonight." Tate opened the door and had one foot out.

"I won't be able to drive with Buddy's car blocking mine in the driveway. If I walk down to the corner of Ninth and Flower, would you pick me up there?"

"Sure, doll. I'll see you there tonight." Tate got out of the car. With a dip in his walk, he strolled toward his Thunderbird.

Silk didn't pull off right away. She sat in her car observing Tate. He moved like he was gliding. Everything about Tate was so damn smooth. As if transfixed, she remained parked behind his car as he started up the engine. Music blasted from the radio and the two whores instantly began snapping their fingers and bobbing their heads back and forth. Tate said something that made both women burst into laughter. Silk watched enviously as Tate screeched out his parking spot and sped away with the two whores.

Buddy arrived home at four-thirty and was surprised to find Silk out of bed and moving about. "I'm feeling much better," she assured him. "But I'm tired of eating in the bedroom. I want to have dinner with my family tonight." She'd already warned the children not to mention that she'd left the house earlier in the day.

Carrie, the cook, had left an hour ago and had given her daughter, Sharita, instructions to keep an eye on the roast beef that was in the oven. As Sharita set the dining room table for dinner, Buddy and Silk sat in the living watching the news. Buddy kept a protective arm around Silk during the newscast.

The kids were in the backyard playing while they waited for Sharita to call them in for dinner.

"I've been thinking," Buddy said.

"About what?"

"Well, after that close call you had with Sonny Boy, I got to thinking that if something tragic was to happen me, I wouldn't be able to rest in peace if you and the children weren't adequately provided for."

Silk gazed at Buddy with an arched brow. "You already have a life insurance policy, don't you, Buddy?"

"Yeah, but that money wouldn't last more than a year or so." Buddy clasped Silk's hands. "I'd want you to be on easy street if I wasn't able to provide for you. So, I took out an extra insurance policy. And if, God forbid, I have an accidental death, the policy will pay out big."

Silk winced. "Buddy, I don't want to even think about you having an accidental death."

"I'm simply taking every precaution to make sure that you, my beautiful angel, will never have to be concerned about your financial well-being."

Silk shook her head adamantly. "I don't want to talk about an accidental death policy. The subject is too unpleasant."

"I know. But we have to have this conversation one time and then I won't bring it up anymore."

"Okay," Silk said with an unhappy sigh.

"In case of my death, accidental or otherwise, the house will be automatically signed over to you. Now if I lost my life tragically, you'd get a check for seventy-five thousand dollars. That kind of money would take care of you and the kids for a lifetime. All the paperwork is in a safe deposit box at Fidelity Bank. The safe deposit box is in both our names."

Tears filled Silk's eyes. "Oh, Buddy, I can't bear the thought of losing you. Now, you listen to me. I've heard you out, but you have to promise me you won't bring up this awful subject ever again." Silk rested her head on Buddy's chest, sniffling. "I couldn't make it without you, Buddy."

Buddy wiped away her tears and whispered, "Don't worry. I'm not gonna leave you, angel. It's only a precaution, that's all."

During dinner, Silk hardly spoke a word. Her mind raced with thoughts of how she could lure Tate out of Chester and out of the hands of that awful whoremonger, Arvetta, if she had seventy-five thousand dollars cash money in addition to the proceeds she was entitled to collect upon selling Buddy's house.

As far as the kids…well, they could go live in Biloxi, Mississippi with their stupid Aunt Clara. Or she could drop them off at the county orphanage. They weren't her flesh and blood and she surely wasn't going to waste any time worrying about them. But then again, she had a soft spot for Dallas. Maybe she'd get rid of the boys and keep Dallas, as long as Tate didn't mind having a child underfoot.

"Penny for your thoughts?" Buddy asked with a dreamy smile.

"Oh, I'm just feeling a little down in the dumps after what happened to me. I was thinking about how much you and the children mean to me. I know you love me, Buddy. But I'm not sure if the children truly love me."

"I love you, M'dear," Dallas informed with a sweet smile.

Buddy shot a hot look at the boys. "What's wrong with you boys; can't you see that M'dear is brokenhearted? Tell her how much you love her."

"I…um…I love you, M'dear," Myron said quietly, his eyes lowered in embarrassment.

"Me, too," Bruce piped in.

A serious look crossed Buddy's face. "M'dear loves you children as if she were your natural mother. I want each of you to stand up and give her a kiss. Show her how much you love her."

Buddy ordered the three children to line up and take turns giving Silk a kiss on the cheek, and after all the kisses were completed, they were instructed to say in unison, "We love you very much, M'dear."

The love and adoration Silk received at home enabled her to feel good about herself, and it made up for the shabby way Tate had recently started treating her. There wouldn't be any sneaking out of the house tonight, Silk decided. Tonight she was going to stay home and devote herself to her family. Tate would be hot under the collar when he discovered that Silk had stood him up, but he would forgive her when he realized she was putting a plan in motion that would secure their financial future. A plan that would free Tate from the hardship of helping Arvetta pimp a bunch of no-good whores.

CHAPTER 36

After dinner Buddy, Silk, and the kids sat in the living room watching *The Adventures of Ozzie and Harriet*. Dallas stared at the TV screen dreamily while Ozzie and Harriet's teenaged son, Ricky Nelson, strummed a guitar and crooned a love song.

"Do you like the way he sings, Dallas?" Silk asked with a teasing smile.

Dallas blushed and looked downward. "Uh-huh."

"Dallas wants to marry Ricky Nelson," Bruce said tauntingly.

When a commercial interrupted the program, Silk turned down the volume of the TV, got up from the sofa, and opened the wooden cabinet of the hi-fi. She put a stack of 45s on the spindle in the middle of the turntable. When "Twist and Shout" by The Isley Brothers began playing, Silk let out a loud whoop, and began doing a sensual twist in the middle of the living room floor.

"The heck with those slow songs that Ricky Nelson sings; this is the kind of music I like," Silk announced as she sensually lowered her body while twisting from side to side.

Enjoying Silk's impromptu performance, Buddy and the kids began clapping and cheering her on.

"I know you boys ain't gonna let me dance all by myself. Come on here, Myron. You can do the Twist, can't you?" Silk beckoned Myron, but the boy leaned back, looking mortified by the idea of getting up and dancing.

"Go on and dance with M'dear," Buddy encouraged. "Do as you're told, dance with her," Buddy insisted in a stern tone.

Dragging his feet, Myron took forever to join Silk in the middle of the floor. He began moving awkwardly and without any rhythm whatsoever.

"You have to move your hips like this." Silk demonstrated by swiveling her hips and when Myron made a clumsy effort to mimic her moves, Dallas and Bruce giggled behind their hands.

"I don't wanna dance!" Myron stomped back over to the sofa with his lips poked out. Silk made a mental note to pinch Myron when she got him alone. He was showing off in front of his Daddy. If Buddy wasn't home, Myron wouldn't have dreamed of storming off and refusing to do as he was told.

"I'll dance with you, M'dear," Bruce volunteered.

"Come on and join me, handsome," Silk said gaily. The song ended and the next record dropped down on the turntable. "Tossin' and Turnin'" by Bobby Lewis began playing and Silk went from doing the Twist to doing the Pony, a more complicated dance that required bouncy footwork and a great exertion of energy.

Bruce tried to get the steps right, but like his brother, he had two left feet. Silk pulled Bruce in her arms and said, "That's okay, sweetheart. Let's slow drag; it's much easier."

Buddy smiled approving at his pretty wife and young son as they slow-danced to a fast-tempo song. Eventually, Silk had the whole family on the floor while she taught them how to do the Mashed Potatoes, another dance that required at least a modicum rhythm. After Buddy and his children gave up on getting the hang of popular dances, Silk suggested that Dallas put on her ballet outfit and perform the solo she'd been rehearsing for her recital that was scheduled for the end of the summer.

Silk changed records and put on the soundtrack to the movie, *Exodus*, an LP that Dallas' ballet teacher had instructed Silk to purchase so that Dallas could practice her solo at home. Dallas changed into a pink tutu and tights and danced to the theme song by Henry Mancini.

With pointed toes, Dallas waved her arms daintily in the air. She twirled, leapt, and pirouetted to the delight of the family. At the conclusion of her performance, she curtsied, and everyone applauded.

"That's my little ballerina," Buddy exclaimed while clapping enthusiastically. "Those dance lessons are really paying off." Buddy bent down and kissed Dallas on her forehead.

"All right, everyone go change into your pajamas," Silk said.

"Aw, we're not ready to go to bed. It's too early," Myron complained. Silk couldn't wait to get Myron off by himself so that she could pinch him twice.

"I didn't say you had to go to bed." Silk smiled pleasantly. "I want you to get your bedclothes on and come back down and finish watching TV. Hurry up because *The Donna Reed Show* is about to come on. But after Donna Reed and *The Real McCoys* goes off, y'all have to go to bed."

"But it's summertime, and during the summer, Mommy always let us stay up late and watch *My Three Sons*," Myron said in protest.

"Sometimes, she let us stay up real late and watch *The Untouchables*," Bruce chimed in.

Silk was fuming mad at the boys for bringing up their dead mother. She didn't give a damn what that bitch had allowed them to do. But she plastered on a smile, and gazed at Buddy. "Is it okay if the kids stay up past ten o'clock, so they can watch *The Untouchables*?"

"Sure, if it's okay with you."

"I think it'll be all right. Just this once."

Dallas and her brothers smiled with gratitude.

"Buddy, can you make some popcorn for the kids while I help them get into their pajamas?" Silk asked, taking on the demeanor and attitude of the TV mothers she was emulating to impress Buddy.

"Yippee, we're getting popcorn!" Myron exclaimed as he and Bruce bounded up the stairs.

Silk trailed them, holding Dallas' hand. Her pleasant expression showed no signs of the aggravation she felt inside. In Dallas' bedroom, she opened drawers and laid out a tangerine babydoll pajama set. "Take off your dance outfit and put this on while I check on the boys."

When Silk entered the boys' room, they were stripped down to their white briefs. Feeling modest, both brothers tried to conceal themselves, hiding behind furniture as they stepped into their pajamas.

"Y'all ain't got nothing I ain't seen before," she said dismissively, picking up their discarded pants from the floor. "Go in the bathroom and wash your face and hands, and brush your teeth."

When the boys left the bedroom, Silk stuck a book of matches in the pocket of Myron's pants. Looking distressed, she took the pants down to the kitchen where Buddy stood at the stove, popping popcorn in a large pot.

"You need to see something," Silk said solemnly. She handed Buddy Myron's pants. "Look inside the pocket."

Buddy checked the pocket and pulled out the book of matches and gazed at Silk questioningly. "What's Myron doing with matches?"

"This is the second time I've found them in his pocket. I caught him lighting a bunch of newspapers in the backyard last week. He lied through his teeth and told me he didn't know how the fire got started." Silk shook her head. "I hate to give you such bad news, but I think we have a little fire starter on our hands. I didn't want to worry you, with all you've been through, but if you don't nip it in the bud right now, Myron could be headed for a juvenile home."

Buddy stepped away from the stove, sighed, and gripped his forehead.

"He needs a whipping, Buddy. You're gonna have to teach that boy a lesson—for his own good."

Buddy nodded grimly.

"I'll go get Dallas and Bruce and bring them downstairs." She climbed the stairs swiftly. "Dallas and Bruce, come on downstairs with me. You stay in your room, Myron. You're in big trouble with your daddy."

"In trouble for what?" Myron asked with fear in his eyes.

"You'll find out." Silk escorted the two younger children down the stairs.

Buddy unbuckled his leather belt and pulled it off. Carrying Myron's pants, Buddy slowly ascended the stairs.

While Silk filled a large bowl with popcorn, Myron could be heard vehemently denying any knowledge of how the matches ended up in his pocket. The next sounds Silk and the children heard were Myron's wails each time the leather belt cut across his skin.

Carrying the bowl of popcorn, Silk ushered Bruce and Dallas into the living room to catch the last fifteen minutes of *The Donna Reed Show*.

In bed, Buddy was concerned about the kids hearing the squealing mattress springs, but Silk was so aroused by the fact that she had conned Buddy into beating Myron, she convinced him to disregard the sounds.

"We're married and it ain't nobody's business how much noise we make in our bedroom. The kids are sound asleep, so stop worrying." Silk was tickled that Buddy was so love-struck, he was willing to believe any lie that came out of her mouth.

The sense of power she felt made her horny. She pushed Buddy on his back and straddled him. Reaching for his manhood, she hissed, "Fuck me, goddammit. Don't you know how hot I am for you?"

"How hot are you, sugar?"

"It feels like a furnace is burning inside me, and only you can cool me down." She grinded on his shaft, but wouldn't let him insert it.

"Come on, sugar, let me get in there," Buddy pleaded.

"Not yet."

"Why not?"

"I don't think you really want me."

"I want you more than I ever wanted anyone."

"It don't seem that way."

"How can you say that? I treat you like a queen."

"Sometimes, you do. But you don't always take care of my needs in the bedroom."

Buddy propped himself up on an elbow and squinted at Silk in disbelief. "I gave it to you for two or three hours last Saturday."

"I know you did, Buddy, but a delicate girl like me don't always want to be pounded like a piece of meat."

"I'm sorry, sugar. I thought you liked it like that."

"Don't get me wrong, you're real good in bed, but it would be nice if you spent a little more time getting me in the mood. It's been a long time since you took a trip downtown, I'm starting to get the impression that you don't like putting your tongue inside my poontang."

"I, uh, I don't mind doing that every now and then. But it's not something that I'm used to doing. You're the first woman I ever put my mouth on...down there."

Buddy looked and sounded embarrassed by the topic of oral sex, and Silk's expression turned sour.

"What's wrong, sweetheart?"

Silk shrugged. "When I fell in love with you, I gave you my all. I never held anything back from you, Buddy. But if you can't do the same, then it makes me wonder what kind of marriage we have."

"We have a beautiful marriage, and I don't want you to ever doubt my love."

"Hmph. You can't prove that by me," Silk said, sulking. "Does my poontang stink? Does it taste nasty or something?"

"No, angel. Everything about you is perfect."

"The halfhearted way you go down on me makes me feel self-conscious about myself."

"Be patient with me, sugar. I'll get better at it—I promise."

"Practice makes perfect," Silk said, sliding off Buddy. Lying on her back, she opened her legs and waggled her finger.

Responding to her signal, Buddy hovered over Silk's vagina and moistened his lips.

"I want you to pretend like you're French kissing my mouth. Use your tongue and explore. Take your time and search up and down—search everywhere. And then, when you get me all gushy and worked up, I want you to pucker up and suck all the cream out of me. Can you do that for me, Buddy?"

"Yeah, sugar. I can do that. I'll do whatever it takes to keep you satisfied."

Wearing a soft smile, Silk closed her eyes while Buddy catered to her desires.

CHAPTER 37

Having been unattended since Ernestine's death, the greenery and flowers in the backyard had turned into a jungle, attracting all sorts of insects. The children each had a jar filled with leaves and dandelions in one hand and held the lid of the jar in the other as they crept up on bumblebees, attempting to capture them. Silk had no idea what the silly kids planned on doing with the bees, but they damn sure weren't going to bring them in the house.

"Y'all better be careful. I don't feel like driving anyone to the hospital with a bunch of bee stings," Silk called out from the glider where she was relaxing and drinking lemonade while Sharita scrubbed the kitchen floor.

The children were so absorbed in their activity, they didn't bother to respond. Silk rested her head on the back of the glider, closing her eyes. As she ruminated about ways to get her hands on Buddy's accidental death insurance policy, Sharita appeared at the back door and noisily swung the screen door open.

"What's your problem, girl? Can't you see I'm resting my eyes? Why you gotta be so loud all the time?"

"Excuse me. I came out to tell you that somebody's at the front door asking for you."

Silk scowled at Sharita. "I ain't buying nothing. And I don't want a pile of pamphlets from any Jehovah's Witness, so whoever it is, tell 'em to scram."

"It's not a salesman or a Jehovah's Witness."

"Well, who is it, then?"

"It's the numbers man—Mr. Sweet Daddy," Sharita announced, moon-eyed with infatuation.

Stunned, Silk nearly fell off the glider. "Sweet Daddy's at the front door?"

"Uh-huh."

Silk glanced over at the kids, who were still having fun catching bees. "Listen, Sharita. I need you to sit out here and keep an eye on the kids while I go play my numbers with Sweet Daddy." She whispered conspiratorially, "Between you and me, Buddy don't approve of gambling, so don't you dare mention to anybody that Sweet Daddy stopped by to see me."

"I won't say anything," Sharita assured her.

"If you value your job, you'd better keep your mouth shut."

"I will."

"And don't let the kids in the house for any reason."

"No, ma'am, I won't."

Silk stood up and Sharita took her place on the glider. "Can I drink the rest of your lemonade, Miss Silk?"

"Yeah, go ahead," Silk said irritably. Sharita was greedy as all get-out. She was always asking for something to eat or drink. The big oaf of a girl got on Silk's last nerve.

Smoothing down her hair that tended to curl at the edges in humid weather, Silk made her way into the house. She glanced at her reflection in the dining room mirror, and noticed that her complexion seemed a little flushed.

The front door was open and she could see Tate standing on the porch. Silk's heart pounded in her chest. Even from a distance, Tate oozed sex appeal. Always dressed to the nines, he looked extra fine today. He had on a navy-blue shirt and powder-blue pants. The jewelry around his neck, wrist, and fingers, sparkled in the sunlight. Woo-wee, that man could dress like nobody's business.

Silk stood at the locked screen door. "Hello, Tate."

He gazed at her with anger sparkling in his light-brown eyes. "Are you gonna invite me in or what?"

"You know I can't do that."

"Why not? Your husband won't be home for hours, and I can hear the kids playing in the backyard. That girl, Sharita won't say anything if I slip her a couple dollars."

"I don't know."

"All I wanna do is talk to you in private for a few minutes. Come on, Silk. Open the door, baby."

Persuaded by the words that emerged from Tate's mouth, which sounded as sweet as honey, Silk unlocked the screen door. She pushed it open, and welcomed her lover inside.

Tate entered slowly, but in a sudden flurry of movements, he gripped Silk by the collar with one hand and smacked her across the face with the other. "You thought it was cute standing me up last night, didn't you?"

"No! I can explain."

"Do you think I'm a joke?" He smacked her again; this time the blow landed on her ear, and Silk heard bells ringing.

"Tate, please!" She pulled away and fled toward the stairs. She made it to the middle of the staircase before he caught her by the hem of her dress and dragged her back down.

"You must love getting your ass beat," he exclaimed as he roughed her up.

"Listen to me, Tate. It's not what you think."

"Then, what is it?" he asked sneeringly, clutching her jaw and forcing her to look him in the eyes.

"I got a plan that'll put us on easy street. I got a way to get my hands on a lot of money. Way more money than Arvetta has."

"How much are you talking?" Suddenly interested, Tate released his grip on Silk's jawline.

"Seventy-five thousand dollars," Silk said with a wide grin.

Tate let out a whistle. "With that kind of scratch I could get out of Mr. Bob's shadow, and be my own man."

"And you could cut Arvetta and those whores loose, too."

"Yeah," Tate muttered, running a hand down the side of his face. "How do you plan on getting that kind of dough? What's your angle?"

Silk smirked. "Buddy took out an accidental death insurance policy."

Tate held up his hands. "Whoa. I know you're not thinking about going so far as to murder your husband."

Silk nodded.

"Are you nuts? I'm a hustler, not a gun for hire."

"You don't have to get involved. I got a plan all worked out in my head. I'm gonna set it up where Buddy becomes a victim of a tragic accident, and after I collect the money, I'm gonna sell the house and skip town." She gazed at Tate. "I wanna move to Chicago and open up a nightclub. I'm hoping you'll join me."

"What's in it for me?"

"As my husband, I'll share everything I own with you."

"I'm not the marrying kind, baby. No woman is gonna tie me down."

A superior smile spread across Silk's face. "Maybe you'll have a change of heart after you have a look at all those greenbacks I'm gonna inherit from Buddy's demise."

"What about his kids?"

"What about 'em?"

"Do you plan on dragging a bunch of kids to Chicago with us?"

"Hell, no. Most likely, I'll ship 'em to Buddy's family in Mississippi."

Tate grew pensive. "Seventy-five thousand will go a long way."

"It sure will. We could sell our cars, fly out to Chicago, and buy ourselves a Rolls-Royce when we get there."

"A Rolls-Royce! Hot damn, you're talking my language, now. But you sound like a fool suggesting that I get inside an airplane. That ain't gonna happen. No way, no how. When I travel, I like to be close to the ground," Tate said with a nervous chuckle.

Tate's mood had lightened, and Silk could tell that he had begun to take a shine to her idea. Deciding to butter him up a little more, she caressed his clean-shaven face. "I missed you like crazy, Tate."

Tate put an arm around her waist. "How much did you miss me, baby?" His voice was a low, sensual growl.

"Why don't you come on upstairs with me and find out."

Without hesitation, Tate followed Silk up the stairs. When they reached the top, he scooped her up in his arms and carried her across the threshold of her marital bedroom.

CHAPTER 38

Although it was a weeknight, Silk strayed from their normal routine and enticed Buddy into having sex. And she really whipped it on him. She fucked and sucked him dry, and now he was sleeping so hard, he seemed dead to the world. Unable to fall asleep with Buddy's loud snores rattling the windows, Silk sat on the edge of the bed, trying to decide if tonight should be the night to put her plan in motion.

I want to, but I'm not sure if it'll work. I should have asked Franny to let me hold a couple of those sedatives she uses to calm herself down when her little brats get on her nerves.

Silk's friend Franny had mentioned that whenever she took a sedative, she could sleep through a hurricane or even an earthquake. Silk didn't want the medication for herself; she wanted to slip a couple pills into Buddy's whiskey to make sure he stayed asleep through the night, allowing her the freedom to chase behind Tate.

Silk glanced at Buddy and rolled her eyes at the way he was sleeping with his mouth wide open. She couldn't wait until the day came when she could lie in bed next to Tate and wake up in his arms in the morning light. The more Silk imagined sharing her life with Tate, the more irritated with Buddy she became.

Franny had been throwing hints trying to find out if Silk had a thing going on with Tate, but Silk refused to satisfy the nosey woman's curiosity. But earlier today, when Silk had stopped by the bar, pretending she wanted a drink, while actually looking for Tate, Franny had made several remarks that Silk found upsetting.

"Honey chile, did you hear about Mr. Bob Lewis?" Franny had said while wearing a shit-eating grin.

"What about him?" Silk responded with her face contorted in aggravation.

"The ambulance took him away a couple of days ago—in the wee hours of the morning. He's over at Chester Hospital in grave condition. They say he might not make it."

"What's wrong with him?"

"Some kind of respiratory infection. Pneumonia, I think. Whatever it is, it's serious enough that Sweet Daddy done moved in with Miss Arvetta over there in the big house."

"What big house?"

"Didn't you know that Mr. Bob and Miss Arvetta have a beautiful, split-level home with a pool and everything out in the suburbs?" Franny continued without waiting for Silk's response, "Yeah, honey chile, they got a nice place over there in Ridley Park. You gotta drive along the Conchester Highway to get to where they live. Folks say that Sweet Daddy and Miss Arvetta ain't bothering to sneak around no more. They done brought their love affair out in the open now that Mr. Bob is almost dead. I heard that Miss Arvetta took Sweet Daddy to Philly and bought him all kinds of expensive menswear. She bought him a bunch of suits from Krass Brothers on South Street and then she took him somewhere on Market Street in downtown Philly, and paid big money for some tailor-made suits. You know how Sweet Daddy is—that man stays sharp, and Miss Arvetta doesn't mind spending her husband's money to keep him dressed to kill."

A streak of pain shot through Silk's heart as she recalled how

Franny had insinuated that Arvetta had stolen her lover man. With Tate being busy, going on shopping sprees with Arvetta, there wasn't any wonder that Silk hadn't been able to catch up with him lately.

She looked over at Buddy and sucked her teeth in disgust. Buddy was suffocating her by keeping her holed up in the house. She needed to be out and about, tracking down Tate. She wondered if Tate was out in the suburbs in bed with Arvetta at that very moment. A sudden ache in the center of her chest caused Silk to wince. It was painful to think of him kissing and making sweet love to another woman.

Sedatives or not, tonight was the night she had to make her move and get her man away from that ol', wrinkly-faced Miss Sepia.

Fueled by envy, greed, and passion, Silk threw a bathrobe over her nightgown, and tucked a cigarette lighter in one pocket and her switchblade in the other. Fondling her knife, she approached Buddy and stood over his sleeping form. She took a few deep breaths and then said softly, "It was nice knowing you, but it's time to say goodbye." She bent over and before second thoughts seeped into her mind, she quickly slit his throat. As Buddy gasped and made gurgling sounds, Silk left the bedroom, and closed the door behind her.

Killing felt so good, she wanted to dance and sing. She had to force herself to step quietly down the hallway. Elated, she eased inside the bathroom. *Everybody knows that Myron loves to play with fire,* she thought to herself as she withdrew the cigarette lighter from the pocket of her robe. She glided up to the bathroom window, flicked the lighter, and set the curtains afire. Mesmerized, she watched the curtains go up in flames. A few moments later, she snapped out of her trance and quickly exited the bathroom.

Silk was about to go inside the boys' room and rouse them out their sleep, but she made a snap decision. Those two big-headed brats weren't worth saving. They could burn up with their father for all Silk cared. Swiftly, she moved along the hallway to Dallas' room.

"Wake up, sweetiekins, we have to get out of here," Silk said urgently. But Dallas didn't stir. "Get the hell up, Dallas. Your brother was playing with matches, again, and this time he set the damn house on fire."

"What?" Dallas asked, sluggishly rubbing her eyes.

"We have to get out of here before the house burns down."

"Where's Daddy? And what about Bruce and Myron?"

"Ain't no time for Twenty Questions. Let's go!" Silk yanked Dallas by the arm and nearly dragged the child toward the direction of the stairs. When flames burst from the bathroom and into the hall, Silk watched the raging fire in fascination. The flames writhed and danced like gleeful demons, eager to cause chaos and claim lives.

Silk tore her eyes away, and with Dallas in tow, she scrambled down the stairs.

By the time they made it to the back porch, Dallas was fully alert and hysterical. "What happened to my daddy and my brothers?"

"They're safe. They made it out ahead of us, and the three of 'em got in the car and rode to the fire department. When this is all over, I hope your daddy whips Myron's tail for playing with matches again."

"Myron doesn't play with matches."

"Yes, he does, but he's real sneaky about it. Your daddy had to whip his butt the other night when he found matches in his pocket. Now, look what that bad boy has done."

Hugging herself, Dallas looked around uncertainly. Out of view, Buddy's car was parked in the driveway in the front of the house, and Dallas had no way of knowing that her father and brothers were inside the burning house.

"I'm sure they'll be back real soon. I bet the boys are having fun riding in that fire engine," Silk added, trying to lift Dallas' spirits.

Dallas cracked a slight smile while picturing her brothers riding in a fire truck, but a few moments later, tears began to pool in her eyes. "My ballet outfit for the recital is in my room. We have to get it, M'dear." Dallas reached for the door handle.

"Are you nuts? You can't go back in the house. I'll get you a brand-new outfit. Now stand here like a good girl and wait for the firemen to get here."

Silk stood with an arm around Dallas' shoulders. The house was eerily silent. There were no shouts and no sounds of either of the boys struggling to get out. Silk concluded that Myron and Bruce had succumbed to smoke inhalation while they slept. She decided to stand around for another ten minutes or so and allow the fire to burn out of control before she ran screaming into the night, pleading to use a neighbor's telephone.

Suddenly, the back door opened and there was Bruce, standing between the main door and the screen door. He looked traumatized with eyes that were large circles of fear.

Seeing Bruce was like looking at a phantom, and Silk nearly jumped out of her skin. *That boy is supposed to be dead, goddammit. Now what am I supposed to do?*

Bruce pushed the door open and rushed toward Silk. Crying hysterically, he wrapped his arms around her waist. "Myron is trapped upstairs. I think Daddy is too."

"I didn't know you all were trapped up there. I thought you boys and your daddy drove to the firehouse," Silk said for Dallas' benefit. She was stumped for a few moments, wondering about her next move. When a good idea came to mind, she gave Dallas a stern look and said, "You stay out here on the porch and don't you move. I gotta take Bruce back inside to help me save your daddy and Myron."

"I won't move," Dallas murmured in a frightened voice.

"But…but…how can we save them? All the bedrooms upstairs are on fire," Bruce whined.

"We have to be brave, son. Come on, let's go."

Clutching Bruce by the hand, Silk pulled the terrified child through the kitchen and dining room. "Don't be scared. Everything is gonna be all right," Silk said in a croaking voice as smoke clogged her lungs. Through the thick smoke, she journeyed to the living room with a reluctant Bruce by her side. The boy was coughing and choking as she determinedly tugged him along.

In the living room she could hear Myron yelling for help at the top of the stairs. She couldn't save Myron if she wanted to, not with vicious flames dancing wildly up and down the wooden staircase.

"What are we gonna do, M'dear?" Bruce asked with a petrified look on his face.

"One thing is for sure, we can't fight our way through that fire. All we can do is pray that the firemen hurry up and get here. While we're waiting, I want you to say a special prayer and ask the Lord to please spare your daddy and your brother," Silk advised while stealthily sticking her hand inside the pocket of her robe. She glanced up at the top of the stairs. Myron was no longer standing upright, but his screams hadn't died down. In fact, his plaintive wail had gone up several pitches higher. From what she could tell, the boy seemed to be curled up in a fiery ball on the floor, rolling around and screaming.

Beside her, Bruce had his head bowed and his eyes squeezed

tight. His lips moved swiftly as he prayed on behalf of his father and brother. But his prayer was halted when Silk drew her knife from her pocket and suddenly lunged for Bruce and plunged the switchblade into his stomach.

Reflexively, Bruce doubled over and grabbed his stomach. In shock, he was oddly silent as Silk yanked and dragged him over to the burning staircase. With a forceful shove, she pushed the injured child into the inferno that had once served as the family's staircase. Fascinated, she watched him burn and listened to his high-pitched screams that suddenly went silent when the staircase collapsed on top of him.

CHAPTER 39

The front page article in the *Chester Times* depicted Silk as a heroine who had managed to save Dallas Dixon from a house fire that claimed the lives of her father, Richard Dixon and her two brothers, Myron and Bruce Dixon. The fatal fire was the latest misfortune of a family that had been plagued by one tragedy after another, all in the course of one summer.

Red Cross workers assisted Silk and Dallas with temporary lodging at a motel outside of Chester. Tate never left Silk's side, surprising her with his attentiveness and support. Being the sole beneficiary of Buddy's and the boys' insurance policies as well as being the new owner of the fire-damaged home, Silk was required to sign mountains of paperwork, and Tate dutifully accompanied her from one end of the city to the next as she filed insurance claims and made funeral arrangements.

Waking up in Tate's arms in the morning was a dream come true for Silk. But it was a shame that Dallas' presence deprived them of the privacy they deserved. All in good time, she told herself. As soon as she received the checks she was expecting, she, Tate, and Dallas would be moving to Chicago.

Dallas didn't warm up to Tate at first, but after a while, he won her over when he exposed his playful side. He tirelessly gave Dallas piggyback rides, played hide-and-seek with her, and brought her shopping bags filled with coloring books, crayons, paper dolls, and an assortment of board games that he patiently played with her.

Silk was happy to see him and Dallas getting along. After all, Tate was going to be Dallas' new daddy, and Silk didn't want any friction between the two of them.

Mr. Bob Lewis had miraculously pulled through his bout with pneumonia, and although he continued to battle ill health, the stubborn old man insisted on continuing to run his businesses. Eager to be his own man, Tate assured Silk that running numbers for Mr. Bob and assisting Arvetta with the whores was a thing of the past. He was Silk's man now—body and soul. He admitted to warming up to the idea of getting married once they settled down in Chicago.

Silk knew shit-talk when she heard it, and she was certain that Tate was speaking truth. Now that he no longer had to carry himself like a hard-core pimp, he was free to express his inner feelings. At night after Dallas fell asleep, he made love to Silk with such love and tenderness, Silk was moved to tears. She could feel his love with every stroke, and concluded that a man couldn't fake the kind of feelings that Tate revealed.

Early one morning after Tate had left to go to his mother's house to change his clothes, there was an unexpected knock at the door of Silk's motel room. She peeked through the peephole and was stunned to see Deacon Whiteside accompanied by Sister Beverly.

Silk held up a finger to her lips, informing Dallas to be quiet. She knew what those two pests wanted. They'd heard the news that she was having a private service for Buddy and the boys at Hunt's Funeral Home, and they had come by the motel to try to talk her into having the triple funeral at the church. But Silk's mind was made up. She planned to get her family's charred bones in the ground as soon as possible and without any fuss.

"It's about time," Silk muttered after the deacon and Sister Beverly finally gave up and left.

Feeling even more in a rush to get the funeral business over and done with, Silk made phone calls to both insurance companies and was delighted to learn that her checks had been cut. "I'll pick the checks up, personally," she volunteered when she was told that the checks would be put in the mail.

Silk was giddy with the knowledge that she had struck it rich. Booze, good food, and lots of sex were perfect ways to celebrate her windfall with Tate. But there was one problem—Dallas was in the way. Silk regretted the bad blood between her and Mrs. Sudler. The woman was a good babysitter, always available with little advance notice.

After collecting the insurance checks, Silk drove straight to Fidelity Bank. She thought the bank manager's eyes would pop out of his head when he saw the amount of money she planned to deposit into her account.

If they could see me now, she said to herself, thinking of all the pampered white women whose homes she often visited while dropping off Big Mama's potions. Those bitches thought they were so much better than she was. It didn't matter that her skin was damn near as pale as theirs, they still turned their noses up at her while urgently snatching the bottles of potion out of her hands.

Back then, Silk had her own unique way of dealing with those uppity bitches. She fucked all their husbands and made sure that she was receiving the special treatment as well as backdoor tongue licking from every one of them before sending them back to their snotty wives. Now Silk had just as much money as the cracker bitches who looked down on her.

As it turned out, she hadn't needed Nathan Lee or any other white man to give her the luxury lifestyle she craved. She'd gotten it for herself and she couldn't be prouder of her accomplishments.

After leaving the bank, Silk got the bright idea to ask Franny to babysit for Dallas. Franny had a houseful of crumb snatchers, and one more wouldn't hurt. She pulled up to Franny's house in the projects and got out of the car. In an instant, Franny shot out the house, yelling and waving her arms around like she'd been stricken by the Holy Ghost.

"What the hell is your problem?" Silk asked, annoyed.

Franny gave Silk a bear hug. "I wasn't sure if I was ever gonna see you again. Nobody knew how to get in touch with you. Oh, my heart aches for you, Silk. I'm so glad you came around so I can give you my condolences."

Reminded that she was supposed to be in mourning, Silk assumed a sorrowful expression. "These tragedies have beat me down, Franny. I can't take any more," she said in a weak voice.

Franny patted Silk on the back. "The Lord won't give you more than you can bear."

"That's what they say, but I'm lost without my dear husband and those sweet little boys."

"I know, I know," Franny said, cutting her eyes at the neighbors who were watching like hawks and wondering what kind of information Silk was sharing with Franny. Being Silk's only friend, Franny intended to get firsthand knowledge regarding the terrible fire that had wiped out most of the remaining members of the ill-fated Dixon family.

"Come on inside," Franny offered, beckoning Dallas and leading Silk toward her front door. Once inside, Franny offered Silk a seat at the kitchen table, and encouraged Dallas to join her four kids who were watching TV in the living room.

"Everyone is grief-stricken over your tragedy, and the whole town is going to show up for the funeral. Well, that is everyone except Sonny Boy's aunt. She's still holding a grudge for the unmerciful way Buddy beat Sonny Boy and broke his jaw. She swears that you falsely accused her nephew. Sonny Boy's jaw is wired up, and his aunt said that he's in so much pain, he cries out in the night." Franny's protruding eyes were fixed on Silk, watching her reaction.

"For all the pain Sonny Boy put me through, he's lucky Buddy didn't kill him."

"With his poor vision, bashed-in head, and his afflicted way of walking, Sonny Boy was messed up bad enough. Now, he can't even open his mouth to talk. I don't know what else can happen to the poor man. But I suppose he got what he deserved for beating you so savagely." Franny gave Silk a searching look. "Did he rape you, too?"

"He did unspeakable things to me," Silk said in a whisper.

"Like what?"

Silk shook her head and glanced away. "I don't want to talk about it."

"So, what happened the night of the fire?" Franny asked, leaning forward as she changed the subject. "The papers said Myron was playing with matches and he started the fire. Is that true?"

Silk nodded and dabbed at imaginary tears at the corners of her eyes. "I can't talk about it, Franny. It's too soon. I'm still in shock. I dropped by to ask if you could keep Dallas overnight so I can spend some time alone and deal with my grief. I've had to be strong for Dallas' sake, but now I'm at my breaking point, and I can't hold my tears in much longer."

Franny nodded in understanding. "It's not good to hold grief inside. You have to get it out. Dallas is always welcome here. I'm your friend, and don't you forget it. When you're ready to talk, I'll be right here, ready to listen."

"That's good to know," Silk said, standing up.

"You leaving already?"

"Yeah, I feel so empty and weak. I need to go lie down."

"Where're you staying at?"

"A motel on Baltimore Pike."

"I see." Franny furrowed her brows. "A word to the wise…"

Silk inhaled deeply, preparing for more unwelcome gossip.

"As your only friend, I want to pull your coat."

"Speak your mind."

"Well, Sister Beverly from the church—"

"What about that ol' meddling heifer?"

"Sister Beverly and Deacon Whiteside have been coming to the projects quite frequently since the fire. They've been having secret conversations with that gal that you had cleaning your house."

Silk's heart dropped. "Sharita?"

"Uh-huh. Sharita and her mother are members of Sister Beverly's church. Rumor has it Sharita's been crying nonstop since the fire, and mumbling that she knows the truth about what happened. But she wouldn't tell Carrie what she knew. So Carrie forced Sharita to go talk to the pastor, and that's how it all got started.

"Now I don't know what all Sharita told the pastor, but this morning, the deacon and Sister Beverly went over to the magistrate's office and a little while later, the police came and carted Sharita off in a squad car."

"They arrested Sharita for starting the fire?" Gleeful, Silk's voice climbed several octaves.

"Not exactly. When the cops brought Sharita out of the house, I thought she had something to do with the fire, too."

"Well, she probably did." Silk was ready to serve up Sharita to law enforcement on a silver platter.

"As it turned out, they only took Sharita down to the station to get an official statement from her. And then they brought her back."

"Do you have any idea what Sharita told them?"

"No idea whatsoever. Her mother's being extremely tight-lipped about the situation. But maybe she'll talk to you."

Silk shook her head vehemently. "No, I'm too busy grieving to go around trying to dig up the truth. Listen, Franny, with Sharita being slow and all, it shouldn't be too hard to get some information out of her. The next time you see her walking to the store or running an errand for her mama, I want you to pull her to the side and make her tell you what she knows."

"I'll try," Franny said doubtfully.

"Okay, well, it's time for me to get going. I'll be back for Dallas first thing in the morning."

"Alrighty. I'll take good care of her."

"Thanks, Franny." Deep in thought, Silk walked slowly to her car.

"Oh, by the way," Franny called out. "Sister Beverly and the deacon said you came to Chester pretending to be a teacher working for a Christian school, but they investigated and there's no such school. Is it true that you told folks you were a schoolteacher?"

"They're lying on me. And whatever Sharita said about me is a lie, too."

I should have cut that hare-lipped bitch's throat when I had the chance.

That butt-ugly Sharita better not be trying to point the finger at me. I know damn well she doesn't have any useful information that could build a case against me. I didn't tell a soul—not even Tate—that I was going to start a fire. That bitch is lying on me, and I've got to figure out a way to shut her up. But if the police are on my trail, then I'm going to have to withdraw that money I put in the bank and hightail it out of Chester first thing tomorrow. I'm not paying that mortician a goddamn cent. Fuck a funeral; I ain't got time for all that! I gots to get out of Dodge before the lawmen try to catch up with me.

CHAPTER 40

Sitting on the bed in her motel room, Silk took a swig out of a bottle of Johnnie Walker that she'd been nipping on for the past few days. She had planned on restocking her liquor supply, and also picking up some fried butterfly shrimp and coleslaw to celebrate with Tate. But after getting hit with the news that Franny had divulged, Silk was no longer in the mood to celebrate her windfall. It had taken all of her willpower not to get in her car and drive herself clear out of Chester after learning that Sharita was running her mouth to the police.

If it weren't for the fact that the insurance money was sitting in the bank, Silk and Dallas would be on the highway, speeding out of Chester.

The liquor she was drinking provided little comfort, and she wished Tate would soon arrive at the motel and take her mind off her troubles by making sweet love to her.

Finally, she heard a car engine and a loud radio. *Tate!* Silk rushed to the window and gazed out. It was Tate all right, but judging from his somber expression, he had something serious on his mind. Silk swung the door open before Tate raised his fist to knock.

"What's wrong, Tate?"

"We got troubles, baby. That girl you had cleaning for you went to the police station and gave them a story."

"What did she tell the cops?"

Tate let out a long sigh. "Apparently, she was being nosey that day I stopped by your house to see you. She told them that she heard you telling a man that you were going to give your husband an accidental death so that you could collect his insurance money."

"Did she name you as the man I supposedly told this to?"

"No. For some strange reason, she pretended that she'd never seen the man before. Sharita may have wanted to protect me. I think she has a little crush on me. She's always blushing and grinning whenever she sees me."

Silk covered her face with both hands, and then looked up. "What are we gonna do, Tate?"

"I spoke to Mr. Bob Lewis, and he used his connections to slow things down. The magistrate of Chester, Mr. Bowes, was going to issue a warrant for your arrest, but Mr. Bob gave him a call and convinced him to hold off on the warrant."

Silk wobbled when she heard the devastating news. Tate steadied her and assured her that he had everything under control.

"I can't go to jail, Tate. That's out of the question. I'll die if I was cooped up in a cell."

"You won't be cooped up for long. Mr. Bob doesn't think the charges are gonna stick. Baby, listen…no jury in their right mind is to believe that dim-witted girl."

Silk made a scornful sound. "I can't take the risk of standing before a jury. With all the money I put in the bank, we can get out of town right after the bank opens tomorrow."

"I didn't know you got the insurance checks already."

"Yeah, I picked them up today. I was gonna surprise you with the news."

"Checks don't clear overnight; you know that, don't you?"

"No, I didn't know that." Silk didn't have any banking experience. She'd never walked into a bank until today.

"It could take up to three or more business days for those checks to clear."

"Shit. What am I gonna do?"

"I have an idea. We can go see Mr. Bowes, fill out some forms and have him notarize them."

"Are you crazy? I don't want to walk into the office of the man who's planning to issue a warrant for my arrest."

"I told you Mr. Bowes is holding off on that warrant until you get your affairs in order."

"What kind of forms are you talking about?"

"Forms that will give me access to your bank account. Listen, baby, if you get picked up by the cops while you're waiting for that money to clear, there won't be a thing I can do to help you. But if you give me permission to make withdrawals from your account, I can act on your behalf in a swift manner. I'll use some of the money to get you out on bail and also to get you a good lawyer…" Tate paused and gazed at Silk intently. "Or you can run away tonight and let the state have all that money." With those ominous words, Tate raised an eyebrow as he waited for Silk's response.

"Fuck that. I went through too much trouble to get that money, and I'll be damned if I'd be stupid enough to let the state bamboozle me out of what's mine," Silk said, expressing her usual fiery temperament.

"That's my girl. Now you're talking." Wearing a satisfied smile, Tate embraced Silk. "Don't worry, everything's gonna be all right, baby. We're going through a rough patch, but it won't last long. I'll be sticking by your side through thick and thin."

Silk buried her head in Tate's chest. "Oh, Tate, I hope you know what you're talking about. I don't know what I'd do if I got jammed up with murder charges."

"Put your faith in me, baby. You won't have to sit for more than a few hours before I bail you out. I've bailed quite a few of Arvetta's girls out of jail, and I know how the system works. Once you're out on bail, we'll skip town. But we can't leave until we have that cash money in our hands, Silk."

Silk bit down on her lip nervously. "I'm scared, Tate."

"There's nothing to be afraid of." He caressed the side of Silk's face and softly kissed her lips. "Do you believe in love at first sight?" he asked, taking the conversation in a different direction.

Silk shrugged.

"I know you have a lot on your mind, but I need you to hear me out. I want you to understand how strong my love is for you. I fell for you the first time I saw you at The Melody Lounge," Tate confessed. "I've never chased after a girl the way I chased after you. You kept shooting me down and I kept coming back for more until I finally won your heart. As hard as it was to get you, do you think I'd ever let you get away from me again? I'm the man that risked his life coming to your house and making love to you in the same bed you shared with your husband. That's love, baby. Niggas have been shot and killed for less.

"Think about Chicago," Tate continued. "Think about you, and me, and Dallas starting a new life together. We'll open our classy nightclub and get ourselves a new Rolls-Royce." His eyes suddenly lit up. "Hey, I have an idea! Why don't we name our nightclub, The Rolls-Royce?"

Silk smiled through the tears that were brimming in her eyes. She didn't want to go to jail—not even for a minute. But with Tate using his street smarts and his connections to get her out of the jam she was in, she was certain she'd come out smelling like a rose.

Mr. Bowes was a white-haired, elderly gentleman who wore wire-rimmed eyeglasses. He spoke slowly and deliberately, and sounded like an educated man. But the stoop in his back, his sluggish movements, and the way his false teeth clattered up and down, made it difficult for Silk to take him seriously.

Using a hand that trembled from some sort of old folks' infirmity, it was with great effort that Mr. Bowes slid three documents across his desk for Silk to sign.

"This gives Mr. Tate Simmons access to your bank account," Mr. Bowes informed in his crisp, scholarly tone.

Frowning, Silk glanced at Tate and whispered, "Are you sure this is a good idea?"

"We don't have any other options, baby. Go on and sign." The irritation in Tate's voice prompted Silk to affix her signature on the lines marked with an *X*. After Silk signed the documents, slow-moving Mr. Bowes took forever to stamp the papers with his notary public seal.

Unsure if she'd made the right decision, Silk began rubbing her chest, trying to slow down her fast-beating heart. Tate placed a protective arm around her shoulder and kissed her forehead.

"Thanks, Mr. Bowes," Tate said, clutching the signed documents as he escorted Silk out of the magistrate's office.

No sooner had they stepped outside, when suddenly sirens blared, and two squad cars sped into the parking lot that was shared by Max's store, Fred's barbershop, The Flower Hill bar, and the Office of the Magistrate.

"Silk Dixon, we have a warrant for your arrest," one of the offi-
cers said, immediately handcuffing her as he read Silk her rights.

"Don't worry, baby. I'm gonna have you out in a few hours,"
Tate promised as Silk was put into the patrol car.

Residents of the projects swarmed the area to get a closer look.
Patrons from the barbershop and the Flower Hill bar streamed
out of the establishments, chattering excitedly as they witnessed
Silk's arrest. Above the bar, Arvetta, joined by the prostitute named
Peaches, leaned over the railing, looking down at Silk with eyes
alit with triumph.

CHAPTER 41

When one day stretched into two, and then three, Silk began to panic as she sat behind bars. Had Tate run into problems when he tried to withdraw her money from the bank? Perhaps the bank manager had refused to accept the papers that Mr. Bowes had drawn up. Where she came from, a colored man who presided over the affairs of Negroes didn't have much clout with white bankers. Most likely those documents Mr. Bowes had notarized were worthless.

Silk charmed her jailer into allowing her to make numerous phone calls. Looking for Tate, she called the hoagie shop, the pool hall, and several bars that Tate was known to frequent. But no one had seen him in days.

She stood by the pay phone racking her brain, trying to figure out whom to call on for help. She thought of Buddy's coworker, Cephus. *No, Cephus is probably holding a grudge over the way I rejected him.* Scratching her head, she thought some more, and then remembered Ed, her part-time lover and former driving instructor. Ed's family owned the driving school and a dry-cleaning business. Surely Ed would loan her the bail money she desperately needed.

Ed would drink my dirty bathwater and do anything in the world for me, she reminded herself as she dialed his number. "Hello, Ed?" she said when he picked up. "I'm in a jam, sweetheart. You read about the fire and the deaths of my family members in the paper, didn't you? Well, they got me locked up—they're trying to pin the blame on me, which is ridiculous because everybody knows that Buddy's son, Myron—may he rest in peace—wasn't nothing but a little fire bug.

"Anyway, Ed, I'm over here at the police station, and I need you to gather up seven hundred dollars to bail me out."

Ed balked at the amount of money, but after Silk assured him that she would pay him back first thing in the morning, he agreed to come to her rescue.

Putting on an act to garner sympathy from Ed, Silk emerged from her cell appearing extremely shaken. Her flushed face and watery, red-rimmed eyes announced that she'd been through hell and back. Inside the driving school car, Silk pretended to sob into her hands while giving Ed directions to her motel.

In the lot of the motel, her Caddy appeared to be in pristine condition despite the fact that the convertible top had been down, exposing her car to the elements for three days. Silk thanked her lucky stars that it hadn't rained during her confinement.

She opened the passenger door and Ed grabbed her by the shoulder. "Is it okay if I come inside and spend some time with you?"

"Not today, Ed," she said, sniffling and pretending to cry. "Can't you see I'm in bad shape? I know you'd like a roll in the hay, but that's gonna have to wait until tomorrow when you come by to pick up the money I owe you."

Disappointment crumpled the features of Ed's handsome face. "What time should I stop by?"

"Around-about eleven in the morning, I suppose." Anxious to get rid of Ed, she said with finality as she hopped out of the car, "I'll see you in the morning."

In the motel room, she took a big gulp of Scotch before shedding the clothing she'd been forced to wear for three days in a row. After a quick shower, she changed into the only other outfit she possessed: a pair of pink Wrangler jeans, a pink ruffle blouse, and white tennis shoes. On her way out of the room, she grabbed the bottle of Johnnie Walker, taking it along to keep her nerves steady while she tracked down Tate.

Cruising in her Caddy with a scowl on her face, Silk made stops at all of Tate's known hangouts. But she was repeatedly told that he hadn't been around in days. It appeared that Tate had fallen off the face of the earth. *I know one thing: every penny of my goddamn money better still be in my bank account.*

The thought that Tate may have swindled her, made her nauseous. After leaving the pool hall, Silk swung by Franny's place to pick up Dallas before heading to the bank to find out the status of her account. *I'm gonna kill that bastard if he withdrew even one lousy dollar of my insurance money.*

Franny was sitting outside her house on the stoop, combing her youngest daughter, Tootsie's hair with a jumbo-sized, wide-tooth comb. "Goodness, gracious, you're a sight for sore eyes. I've been praying for you night and day. The word around town is that you were underneath the jail and facing the electric chair."

Silk winced.

"People love to spread rumors, honey chile. But I knew in my heart that you was gonna clear your good name and get out of the slammer," Franny exclaimed, grinning like a Cheshire cat. Her hands never stopped moving as she worked on her daughter's hair.

Briefly distracted by the orchestration of Franny's dancing fingers as she rhythmically combed, parted, and plaited hair, Silk watched with curiosity. Franny stuck her middle finger into a jar of Royal Crown hair pomade, rubbed the glob of greasy substance onto Tootsie's coarse hair, and then swiftly wove and intertwined sections of hair into a style that Silk considered frightful.

Silk would never let Dallas be caught dead with a bunch of pickaninny-plaits all over her head. She paid Carmalee good money to keep Dallas' hair hard-pressed and glossy. It was on the tip of Silk's tongue to tell Franny that she had Tootsie looking like she belonged on a slave plantation, but she kept the thought to herself.

"Where's Dallas?" Silk asked, feeling irritated by the summer heat, Tootsie's awful hairdo, and Franny's shit-eating grin.

A look of surprise came over Franny's face, and her poppy eyes bulged worse than ever. "You didn't hear what happened to Dallas?"

Silk's heart plummeted. "What about her? Where's my child?"

"Miss Arvetta and Mr. Bob came and picked her up the other day. Before coming here, they went over to Mr. Bowes and had him draw up some paperwork, naming them as her foster parents."

"They can't steal Dallas from me!" It seemed as if bombs were detonating inside Silk's head. As her world exploded, she took a few steps forward and steadied herself by pressing her palm against the brick structure of Franny's house. "No, no, no," Silk moaned, holding her head with both hands.

"You got a headache, Silk? I got a few Anacin tablets if you need one."

"I don't need any fucking Anacin. I left Dallas in your care. How could you turn her over to that whoremonger, Arvetta?"

"Looky here, Silk. You need to simmer down. What was I supposed to say when they stuck those official documents that were stamped with the county seal in my face? Now, if you want to get Dallas back, then you need to go see Mr. Bowes and file your own paperwork."

"Fuck Mr. Bowes. That man's corrupt, and so are Mr. Bob Lewis and Arvetta. They're all snakes. Every one of them."

"I don't consider Mr. Bob a snake. That man got out of his sick bed, pushing an oxygen tank, just so he could ensure that Dallas would have a good home. Quiet is as kept, Mr. Bob looked like death eating soda crackers. I doubt if he'll make it 'til Christmas. I wonder if Miss Arvetta plans on raising Dallas by herself or if she's gonna get Tate to help her? I hope she doesn't raise sweet, little Dallas around all that prostitution she's involved in." Franny scratched her head in thought. "Anyway, Miss Arvetta said they're going to legally adopt the poor little orphaned child as soon as possible."

"Dallas is not an orphan." Silk jabbed a finger in her chest. "I'm her mother!"

"What I heard is that Sister Beverly got ahold of one of Dallas' blood relatives. An aunt who lives in Mississippi. The aunt told Sister Beverly that she'd fallen on hard times and wasn't able to take her niece in at this time. She said her husband is out of work and they can barely feed their own three kids. Sister Beverly put in a good word for Arvetta, and the aunt said she wouldn't fight the adoption." Franny paused briefly and gave Silk a sidelong glance. "By the way, I was told the aunt took it real hard when she was informed that you had killed her brother and her nephews."

"I didn't kill anybody," Silk shouted. "How many times do I have to tell folks that Myron had a bad habit of playing with matches?"

Franny shrugged. "I'm only repeating what I heard."

"I have to go," Silk said abruptly, whirling around.

"Where are you running off to? You gonna drive to Ridley Park and give Miss Arvetta and Mr. Bob a piece of your mind? You better be careful because Miss Arvetta is known to carry a gun. I'd think twice before I stepped foot on her property."

Silk kept walking without bothering to respond. She wanted so badly to ask Franny if she had seen or heard from Tate, but at this point, Silk couldn't take any more bad news.

While driving to the bank, she silently prayed that the man she loved and intended to marry hadn't wiped out her account. *Please, Tate. Don't make me have to kill you, too.*

CHAPTER 42

Silk almost collapsed when the bank manager informed her that there was only one dollar left in her account—the exact amount required to keep the account open. Instead of falling out on the floor, kicking and screaming, Silk did her best to maintain her composure. She pretended to be aware of the withdrawal, telling the manager that she had merely stopped by the bank to make sure Mr. Simmons, her trusted friend, hadn't mistakenly closed her account.

"I plan on making another large deposit," she said, wishing her words were true. But the fact was, Silk was flat broke.

Having read about Silk's notoriety, the bank manager stood there for a few awkward moments, and then, unwilling to continue conversing with an accused murderer, he began backing away.

Somehow she managed to exit the bank without showing signs of deep distress. Outside the building, her footfalls were heavy, her feet felt like cement blocks. Unable to take another step, she slumped against the building next to the bank—gasping and sobbing. Completely defeated, Silk hung her head and allowed a stream of tears to run down her face.

That pimp-bastard stole all of my fucking money and left me in jail to rot. Silk was certain that Tate and Arvetta had plotted against her together, and she'd fallen for their scheme hook, line, and sinker.

Gathering her wits about her, Silk straightened her shoulders and began plotting her revenge. Tate couldn't hide from her forever, and he was going to have to answer for what he'd done. She supposed that Arvetta was tired of waiting for Mr. Bob to die. She and Tate probably had big plans to use Silk's money to run off somewhere together.

But what was the purpose in snatching Dallas? Did Arvetta actually want a little girl of her own or had she taken Dallas as a way of twisting the knife in Silk's back?

It was difficult to fight for Dallas when Silk had to fight to save her own neck. The whole town had turned against her, labeling her a murderer without any evidence. There was no doubt in Silk's mind that Arvetta would utilize her husband's political power to make sure that Silk was convicted and sent to the electric chair.

Facing the sorrowful facts, Silk came to the realization that she had to leave Dallas behind and get out of Chester while the getting was good.

But before she left town, she was going to hunt down Tate and make him pay for what he'd done. The overwhelming feeling of love she'd once felt for him had turned into a seething hatred that consumed her. Tate Simmons deserved nothing less than a slow, painful death.

Silk parked her Cadillac in a deserted area behind Rainey Street, about a quarter-mile from the Flower Hill bar. In the dark of night, she took off on foot. Lurking in the shadows, Silk tiptoed up the steps that led to the whores' apartments over top of the bar. She tapped softly on the door of apartment number two, and when the door cracked open, Silk forced her way in. She put her switchblade up to the neck of Peaches, the whore that she'd caught in bed with Tate.

"Where's Tate?" Silk hissed.

"I don't know." Peaches trembled in terror.

"You better act like you got some sense." Silk put Peaches in a chokehold and brought the knife downward, resting the tip of the blade against the prostitute's crotch. "Don't make me cut out your whoring pussy. You won't make it very far in your profession with your shit all sliced up."

Peaches murmured prayers and shuddered in fear.

"If you want to keep your pussy in one piece, you better get on the phone and call Tate. Tell him that a trick is getting rough with you and refuses to pay for the goods. Say whatever it takes to get Tate over here as quick as possible."

She brought the knife up to the prostitute's throat, and walked her over to a rotary phone that was set on a table near the couch.

Peaches made the call, and there was genuine terror in her voice when she whispered into the phone that a drunken John had beaten her and stolen the money from her purse. "He's in the bathroom, but I think he's planning to beat and rob all the other girls." Peaches paused, listening to Tate and then nodded her head. "You want me to trick him into staying a little longer? Okay…I'll try."

Silk could hear Tate yelling at Peaches on the other end of the phone.

"All right, Sweet Daddy. I won't *try*, I'll do it!"

Peaches hung up the phone and said in a somber tone, "He's on his way."

Having no more use for Peaches, Silk took great pleasure in walking her into the bedroom at knifepoint. "This is for Arvetta," Silk said quietly.

"What's for Arvetta?" Peaches asked.

Wearing a smile, Silk calmly slit the prostitute's throat. When she toppled to the floor, Silk used her foot to push her body out of sight, sliding it under the bed. She closed the door and waited for Tate in the front room.

It seemed to take an eternity for Take to arrive, but finally she heard his pounding footsteps climbing the metal stairs. Silk rose from her seat. Bracing herself, she pressed her back against the wall next to the door. She heard the jangle of keys, and took a deep breath as Tate turned the lock and opened the door.

"Peach—" was all he managed to get out before Silk lunged at him, driving her switchblade deeply into his gut. She twisted it several times, inciting him to cry out in pain.

"I cried worse than that when I discovered you'd wiped out my bank account," Silk hissed, giving him a scathing look as she took in his fashionable attire. The black silk shirt with white trim around the collar and the crisp white slacks he wore was a painful revelation that Tate and Arvetta had used Silk's money to go on a shopping spree.

"I love you, baby, I never meant to hurt you," Tate said in an anguished voice.

"Liar!" Silk twisted the knife again, causing Tate such excruciating pain, he let out a long groan as his legs gave out.

"It was Arvetta's idea, not mine," he said, choking out the words.

Silk kneeled down next to him. "Where's my money, mother-fucker?"

"Arvetta has it."

"Yeah, well, since I can't get to Arvetta, I suppose you're gonna have to pay the price for both of y'all." Silk pulled the knife from his gut and Tate promptly clutched the gaping wound, all the while pleading for Silk to call an ambulance.

"It's like they say, baby…an eye for an eye," she snarled as she viciously jammed the knife into his right eyeball.

Tate's right hand flew up to his injured eye while his left hand continued to shield the wound in his gut. Silk smiled in satisfaction as she listened to Tate's cries of pain and watched blood trickling down his hand.

"That was for you cheating on me and this is for stealing my money," she said before spearing his other eye.

With a tortured groan, Tate yanked his hand away from his belly and slapped it over his left eye. "I'm gonna fuck you up for this. I swear to God I'm gonna fuck you up," he wailed.

"Are you threatening me, you blind motherfucker?" Silk tightly gripped the handle of the switchblade and raised it high above her head before driving it into his crotch and savagely mutilating his genitals.

She gazed sneeringly at the circle of red that rapidly spread in the front of his white pants. "You look like you're on the rag," she said scornfully. She rose to her feet and went to the bathroom and carefully washed blood splatter from her face, neck, and arms. Throughout the cleanup process, she could hear Tate moaning and whimpering. She came out of the bathroom and stepped over his twitching body. It didn't matter to her if he was dead or alive. Even if he survived the brutal attack, he wouldn't be worth a damn anymore. Tate would be worse off than Sonny Boy, Silk thought with a snicker. And without a dick, he'd be completely useless to Arvetta and the whores.

Covered by darkness, Silk made it back to her car. She had only the clothes on her back, a quarter of a tank of gas, a few dollars, and some small change in her purse. But despite her desperate circumstances, she felt on top of the world. She turned on the radio and hummed along with "Playboy" by the Marvelettes. She laughed out loud, thinking about Tate and how his playing days were officially over.

Heading south, she drove down Engle Street and made a right on Ninth Street. She kept going straight until she ended up in Claymont, Delaware. In Claymont, she pulled off on the side of the road and slept in the car. In the morning, she followed the signs that took her to Wilmington where she found a pawn shop and hawked her diamond engagement ring and her gold wedding band. Next she located a car dealership and sold her beloved Cadillac. Although the car hardly had any miles on it, the salesman sensed that Silk was in a bind and paid her only a fraction of what the car was worth.

Such is life, she told herself with a shrug of her shoulders as she made her way on foot to the Greyhound bus terminal. Getting gypped by a car salesman was better than going to jail and standing trial for a triple murder, she told herself.

Silk thought about catching a bus to New York or Chicago, but hit with a sudden flash of memory, she believed she knew exactly where Big Mama had hidden the ten thousand dollars that technically belonged to Silk now that Big Mama was dead.

Going home to collect her inheritance was a risk she was willing to take. She was a cunning girl and had no doubt that she could slip in and out of Devil's Swamp, undetected.

I can pull it off. I know I can. All I have to do is cover my hair with a scarf that's tied Aunt Jemima-style and put on a pair of dark sunglasses, and no one will recognize me when I get off the bus in Baton Rouge. From Baton Rouge, I'll hitch a ride to Devil's Swamp and slip off into the woods until I get to Big Mama's hiding place.

Ten thousand dollars is peanuts compared to all that money Tate and Arvetta stole from me, but it's better than nothing. At least I have the satisfaction of knowing I got revenge on Tate, and one of these days, I'll get revenge on Arvetta.

After I get my hands on those greenbacks that Big Mama hid, I'm leaving for Hollywood, California. I probably could become a movie star if I put my mind to it. But being a wanted criminal in two states, it would be wise if I kept a low profile. My best bet would be to marry a rich man and live a quiet, pampered life. I'll use my rich husband's money to hire someone to knock off Arvetta and bring me my daughter. With Dallas around, I'll have someone to comfort me whenever I get upset or agitated. It'll be mighty nice to have things back the way they used to be between my sweet child and me. She was really looking forward to dancing in that ballet recital, and somehow I've gotta make it up to her. I know what I'll do! I'll put her in another dancing class in California. I bet that'll make her smile.

CHAPTER 43

S ilk had to make two separate bus connections to get to Baton Rouge, but despite the long, exhausting journey, the moment she stepped foot on Louisiana soil, she felt all warm and fuzzy inside. It was good to be home. If it weren't for the fact that Sheriff Thompson would most likely have a lynch mob after her, Silk would have gladly used a portion of her ten-thousand-dollar inheritance to put down roots in Baton Rouge or maybe New Orleans.

Outside the bus terminal, Silk began walking in the direction of Devil's Swamp. Within two minutes of sticking out her thumb, a white woman driving a Ford Cutlass stopped and gave Silk a lift. The woman was very chatty and nosey as hell, asking Silk a million different questions. Miss Motor Mouth was lucky Silk was more interested in getting her hands on Big Mama's savings than in killing, otherwise the white woman would be slumped over the steering wheel with blood pouring from a slash in her neck.

"You be careful now, young lady," the woman warned when Silk arrived at her destination on the highway. "I've heard Devil's Swamp is populated with a lot of unsavory characters."

"I'll be careful," Silk said with a wave of her hand. She waited until the Cutlass was out of sight before darting into the familiar woods that she'd used as her personal playground during her youth and as a killing ground when at the age of fourteen she murdered Mr. Perry, the ice man. As she matured and became much more sexually active, these woods had served as a love nest for her and her many paramours.

Silk treaded lightly, in case someone was lurking about. With the stealth of a big-game hunter, she was careful not to disturb the forest creatures and cautious about stepping on twigs and crunching dried leaves. She yearned to see the old shack one last time. It would be nice to pay her respects by putting some flowers on Big Mama's grave.

Big Mama had always said she wanted to be buried right there in her garden, and the folks of Devil's Swamp would have been too afraid of an after-death hex to put her anywhere else. After all the dreadful misfortune that Silk had experienced up North, she was living proof that Big Mama's after-death hex was indeed powerful.

As badly as she wanted to, Silk couldn't risk going near the shack. The place was most likely occupied by new residents who'd surely recognize her, and run off to tattle to Sheriff Thompson.

When she passed the old hickory tree, she realized she was about ten minutes away from Big Mama's stash. A shovel would have come in handy, but she'd have to make do and dig up the money with a tree branch or a stick.

Silk's head was hot beneath the scarf, and perspiration poured down the sides of her face, but she was too excited to care about an inundation of sweat. Within eyesight, she could see the big gray rock that Big Mama used to sit on when she went fishing in the lake.

Without any doubt in her mind, she knew that Big Mama's savings were buried under that rock!

Silk recalled being a little girl, no more than three or four years old, playing in the water while Big Mama unearthed a box that was filled with paper money and silver dollars. After adding more greenbacks to her stash, Big Mama put the box back in the ground and buried it. Huffing and puffing, she pushed the rock back into place, ensuring that it covered the secret spot.

Grunting, Silk pushed against the rock with both hands, but it didn't budge. She tried pushing it with the sole of her tennis shoe, but still couldn't move it. "Shit," she muttered, taking a seat on the rock as she caught her breath and wiped sweat from her face. *I knew Big Mama was strong, but damn! How in the hell am I gonna move this big ol' stubborn thing?*

While contemplating her dilemma, she heard the rustle of leaves. Danger alarms immediately went off inside her head. But before her body could respond to what her brain already knew, Silk felt a powerful blow to the back of her head, and the lights suddenly went out.

She awoke to a throbbing pain in the back of her head, and when she attempted to touch it, she realized that her hands were bound. Something was covering her eyes, preventing her from seeing her captor. She tried to cry out but discovered the sounds were muffled by duct tape that sealed her mouth. Silk shuddered as she became aware of the unmistakable sounds of a shovel digging into the earth and the thud of the excavated dirt as it hit the ground. The sunshine beaming on her face informed her that she was outdoors, lying on a bed of grass that tickled her back. Feeling the sun on her breasts, Silk realized she'd been stripped of her clothes and was lying outside, butt naked.

She wondered if there was a reward on her head, which had prompted one of the locals to knock her unconscious and hold her as a naked hostage until Sheriff Thompson came to collect her. Though terrified of learning the truth, she wanted answers, and began moaning and wiggling around.

"Well, looky who decided to wake up from her nap."

Silk's body stiffened in fear and utter shock. Beneath the blindfold, her eyes widened and practically bulged out of her head. She gasped so sharply, she began to choke and gag. That voice! She'd recognize it anywhere. *Oh, my God, Big Mama has returned from the dead!*

Chills of terror ran up Silk's spine as she heard Big Mama's footsteps coming toward her. "Welcome home, Silk. I always knew you'd come running back when times got too rough for you out there. Plus, I put a come-back-home hex on you that would force you to return to me no matter how far you ran."

A come-back-home hex! So, that's the spell Big Mama put on me. Instead of chasing behind Tate, I should have been searching for a voodoo woman to take her goddamn curse off of me.

"Last night I had a vision that today was the day you'd come on home, and damn if I wasn't right," Big Mama said delightedly. "Good thing I started digging this here hole as soon as the sun started to shine, otherwise I'd be digging 'til midnight, and I have other things to do with my time besides putting you in the ground."

"Oaahhh. Mmmmf!" Silk made a variety of unintelligible sounds as she attempted to ask Big Mama why she wanted to put her in the ground. Did she plan on killing her and then burying her in the plot of land that Big Mama had picked out as her own final resting place?

Big Mama untied the blindfold and Silk blinked back the brightness of the sun, wishing desperately that she could shield her eyes with a hand. Big Mama hovered over Silk's face, tapping on the thick scar on her neck that Silk had inflicted with her switchblade.

"I sewed it up myself with cat gut, and covered the wound with maggots and mud. I used the same remedy on that stab wound you put on my belly, and the healing took hold swiftly. Although these scars you left on me tend to itch like the devil, I'm still here, so I suppose I shouldn't complain." Big Mama's face was so close to Silk's, Silk could smell the tobacco on her breath.

Silk struggled to form the words, *I'm sorry*, but the sounds that emerged from her taped-up mouth sounded like gibberish.

"Did you hear about your old beau, Duke Durnell? He was accused of the crime you committed. That poor boy never made it inside a courtroom. The lynch mob got to him. Beat him something terrible and then strung him up. Left him hanging from that ol' hickory tree in the woods 'til his stinking body separated from his rotting neck." Big Mama's mouth turned down in dismay. "I made a strong potion for Duke's mama, to help her sleep at night. But she took it upon herself to mix my potion with moonshine, and now she's crazy as a bedbug."

Silk tried to muster some sympathy for Duke Durnell and his mama, but it was hard to feel sorry for others while she was in such a precarious position.

Big Mama gazed in Silk's direction, staring at her as if she could actually see out of her opaque-colored eyes. "I heard about that exterminator-fella that was found with his throat slashed in his car. White folks called it a random, unsolved murder, but I knew right away that you was the one responsible for that devilment."

Big Mama gazed up at the sky. "Welp, it's time to get you in the ground."

No, no. Please, Big Mama. I'm sorry for what I did to everyone I hurt. And I'm real sorry for what I did to you. I'm begging you, Big Mama, please don't bury me alive, Silk shouted in her head.

Big Mama ignored Silk's grunting sounds and her pleading eyes. She grabbed Silk by the ankles and pulled her several feet and then dumped her in a deep hole. Silk was curled lopsided, so Big Mama eased down in the hole and straightened her out, positioning her body and legs to sit in the hole, Indian-style.

Then Big Mama clawed her way out of the hole and began tirelessly dumping shovelfuls of dirt onto Silk's body. She didn't stop packing dirt around Silk, until she was covered up to her neck.

Using her hands to see, Big Mama's fingers roamed over Silk's face and head. Pleased with her handiwork, she showed off her brown-stained teeth by offering a big smile. "Look at you, I bet you look just like a pumpkin with your head sticking out the ground." Big Mama went into a bout of choking laughter while tears streamed from Silk's eyes.

How could Big Mama put her in such a humiliating and vulnerable position? She was supposed to love and forgive Silk no matter what. Forgiveness was a big part of a mother's love, wasn't it?

Big Mama walked away, leaving Silk with the hot sun burning down on her face. After a few moments, Big Mama returned and revealed that she was carrying Silk's switchblade. "I found this tucked down in your bosom when I undressed you. It was dull, but I sharpened it up real good."

God help me, what is Big Mama gonna do with my knife?

As if reading Silk's mind, Big Mama responded by dropping down to her knees while wielding the knife. Silk tried to lean away, she tried to jerk her head back and forth, but the dirt that was packed around her body only allowed her to turn her head slowly to the left and right.

In one quick motion, Big Mama grabbed Silk's hair and wrapped it firmly around her hand. She snatched Silk's head back to expose her young, unblemished neck. "Be still, gal. If you keep moving all about, Big Mama might do more damage than I intend to. I can't see for shit so I gotta do this by feel. You best heed what I say unless you wanna end up dead." As Big Mama drew the knife toward Silk's neck, Silk became wild-eyed and frantic. She tried to scream but only managed more muffled sounds.

With the expertise of a surgeon, Big Mama sliced through a few layers of flesh, soft tissue, and tendons. Silk shrieked from the pain, but of course the tape around her mouth muted the sound. Big Mama cut deeper until she had successfully severed Silk's larynx. "There you go," she said with a proud twist to her lips. Admiration of her surgical skill was evident in her tone.

Big Mama ripped the tape from Silk's lips, and when Silk opened her mouth to emit a loud scream, no sound emerged from her throat; there was only the soft hiss of air. "I can't have you screaming out here and having folks wondering what I'm up to," Big Mama explained.

Realizing that her vocal cord had been cut, Silk began pleading with her eyes.

"Ain't no point in begging because it won't do you any good. Besides, I'm not finished working on you, gal—I'm only jest getting started."

It was unbelievable that her own mama had turned her permanently mute, and she couldn't imagine what else Big Mama had in store for her.

"Get on away from here," Big Mama fussed as she shooed away the big horse flies that had begun to buzz around the bloody incision in the front of Silk's neck. She didn't want flies laying eggs on the cut. Not yet anyway. But if the wound became infected, then she'd let the flies have at it.

"I bet you couldn't give two shits that my remedy business went completely downhill after you cut out on me. My balms and tonics and what have you ain't have the same kick without the special ingredients I got from you." Big Mama paused and added, "I supposed you didn't realize that you was my most valuable secret ingredient, which is why I was gonna give you a generous amount of money when you came of age. But all that changed when you stabbed me and left me for dead."

Big Mama grabbed a hank of Silk's hair and crudely sawed it off with the switchblade. "I'm back in business now," she said, cackling with glee. "I need to soak this silky hair of yours in some frog's blood and coon piss to make up a batch of my quick hair-growing potion that the colored folks around here swear by. They be spending real good money for it, too." She went silent for a few moments and concentrated on cutting off Silk's hair.

"By the way, according to my calculations, your menstrual cycle should be starting in a day or so, shouldn't it? From the day I pulled your infant body out the ground, I been using your urine and feces to make my remedies more potent. Guess it had something to do with you coming back from the dead after you was born. But after you started your menses at age twelve, I added your menstrual blood to my passion potions and they started selling like nobody's business. Your selfish ass probably don't give a goddamn, but ever since you took off the way you did, my customers been complaining about the quality of my products. I bet they'll shut their traps now that I got my cash cow back. Ain't gon' be no more collecting and lugging fertilizer for my garden. Nosiree. Not with you shitting and pissing right into the ground. Yes, gawd, I'm gon' be bringing in plenty of money from now on."

Big Mama was talking up a blue streak and unconcerned that she was slicing chunks of Silk's scalp as she hacked off her hair. Silk flinched and expelled another burst of air when she tried to yell after the knife penetrated her flesh. After hacking off most of

Silk's once luxurious hair, Big Mama reached in her shirt pocket and brought out the hand clippers to cut off the rest.

It was bad enough that the sun was beating down on Silk's ravaged head, but she also had to endure Big Mama sewing up the gash she'd made in her neck with cat gut and a dull, old sewing needle.

After Big Mama finished collecting Silk's hair, she covered Silk's head with a burlap sack and made her way toward the shack. Whistling a tune, Big Mama was happy as a lark and anxious to start prepping for her new and improved batch of potions.

At dusk Big Mama returned, and yanked the sack off Silk's head and began spoon-feeding her applesauce that she'd handmade by pulverizing an apple with a jagged stone.

"Welp, I guess it's time to say goodnight. Wish you could sleep in the iron bed with me like old times," Big Mama teased. "But since I can't trust you as far as I can throw you, you'll have to try and get comfortable right where you are." Once again, she covered Silk's head with the burlap sack and then placed a wooden, apple barrel over her head for extra protection.

"This here barrel will have to do until I can get my hands on something sturdier that'll keep the night creatures from getting at you."

Tears ran down Silk's face as she silently pleaded, *Please, Big Mama. Don't leave me out here.*

In the pitch-dark, Silk itched from head to toe. Being planted like a crop in the earth with biting ants and wiggling worms was driving her to the brink of madness. Her predicament was certainly bad enough, but now she had to worry about bigger creatures such as opossums, raccoons, and alligators coming around to forage for a bite to eat. Terrified by the thought, Silk squeezed her eyes shut.

She imagined a hungry pack of dogs or wolves chewing off her face, and then digging around her, desperately trying to get at the rest of her body that was planted in the ground. She dreaded being ripped to shreds by ravenous animals, but a bite to her jugular vein would quickly end her suffering. If she was lucky, she wouldn't last through the night. With the torturous life that Big Mama had planned for her, a quick death was the only thing Silk had to look forward to.

EPILOGUE

S ilk lost track of time. Day turned into night—over and over again. The movement of the sun was her only way of judging the passing of time. Her mornings always started with Big Mama plopping down and scooting up to Silk's face and nearly smothering her by wrapping her stout legs around Silk's neck while demanding the special treatment from her favorite gal.

Nights ended the same way, with Big Mama getting pleasured before she slapped the sack and barrel on top of Silk's head and calling it a night.

Sick of catering to Big Mama's desires, Silk began stubbornly refusing to give Big Mama the special treatment. She clenched her teeth and defiantly squeezed her eyes closed. But when Big Mama had finally had enough of Silk's willful behavior, she smashed her in the mouth with a ball-peen hammer, busting her lips, and knocking out her front teeth. She threatened to cut out Silk's tongue if she didn't take care of her needs and treat her right.

Silk had always been told that she was born bad, but with so many thoughts running through her mind, she came to realize that no child was born that way. Her wicked ways had been taught to her by Big Mama and shown by example. Big Mama had to be the most deranged woman in Louisiana, and it was unfortunate that Silk had been raised from infancy by such a vengeful madwoman.

It was ironic that those greenbacks that Silk had yearned for so badly now had no meaning whatsoever. The one thing she wanted more than anything in life, stubbornly eluded her.

When I dream, I dream about the people I killed. Mostly I dream about the innocent ones that didn't deserve to die. Although Sonny Boy's not dead as far as I know, I dream about him, too. They're all up in heaven, waving and smiling down at me, and saying that they forgive me. Well, if that was true, why don't they send one of God's angels down here to rescue me from this hole in the ground and take me up to heaven with them?

Having nothing but time on her hands, Silk's mind chatter never turned off. She'd done some awful things in her life; there was no denying that. The way she methodically destroyed the entire Dixon family was the most vicious and despicable of all her sinful actions. Because of her, sweet little Dallas was orphaned and left in the hands of that wicked Arvetta. Silk deeply regretted having abused Dallas in the same manner that Big Mama had abused her. Though she doubted it, she held on to the hope that Arvetta had a shred of decency and would provide Dallas with a good home life.

Despite all her wrongdoing, Silk found it hard to accept that her misdeeds warranted existing in the hell-on-earth conditions that Big Mama had assigned her to.

A lone tear of regret trickled out of Silk's eye, weaving a trail through the filth on her face. Nearby she heard Big Mama pulverizing a piece of fruit with a rock, making it soft enough to pass through Silk's mutilated throat.

Big Mama was determined to do everything in her power to keep Silk nourished and alive. But Silk was determined, also. Yearning for release from this mortal coil, she sent up fervent prayers for death—the one thing she truly desired.

The harsh sound of Big Mama pounding and pulverizing her meal gradually became a distant, muffled sound. Though Big Mama was close by, it was as if they were separated by many miles. Much more clearly, Silk could hear the voices of a celestial choir, and she suddenly felt herself surrounded by a bright, glorious light that emanated the purest love she'd ever known.

Even Big Mama's blind eyes saw the overpowering glow of light, too. "What the heck is going on?" she asked gruffly, stomping toward Silk and prepared to ward off the invisible intruders with the jagged rock she held in her hand.

A smile came over Silk's face as she realized that her prayers had finally been answered. She could feel her life ebbing and fading away. Indiscernible hands gave her a forceful jerk, mercifully liberating her soul from her lifeless body that was neck-deep in soil.

Desperate to bring her cash cow back to life, Mama smacked both sides of Silk's face as she tried to revive her.

But Silk was gone, and Big Mama howled in fury, left with nothing but the empty shell of the young woman whose life she'd stolen many years ago.

ABOUT THE AUTHOR

Allison Hobbs is a national bestselling author of twenty-four novels and has been featured in such publications as *Romantic Times* and *The Philadelphia Inquirer*. She lives in Philadelphia, Pennsylvania. Visit the author at www.allisonhobbs.com and Facebook.com/Allison Hobbs.

CHAPTER 1

Brick paused in the doorway of Misty's hospital room, frowning in confusion.

Hovering over Misty was a woman dressed in a business suit; she was writing something in a notebook. At the foot of the bed, a man held a camera, snapping pictures of her.

Noticing Brick, Misty impulsively tried to sit up straighter, momentarily forgetting about the paralysis that restricted her movement. Helpless to shift her position, she feebly gestured for Brick to have a seat next to her.

Brick crossed the room. "What's going on, Misty?"

"This is Sharon Trent, a reporter from the *Philadelphia Daily News*. She's writing a story on me." Misty nodded toward the man with the camera. "That's Jack, a photographer for the paper." She smiled at the reporter and the photographer and said, "Sharon and Jack, meet Brick."

"Hello," Sharon greeted, looking Brick over with a curious gleam in her eyes.

Jack grunted a salutation as he continued snapping pictures of Misty.

"Pardon me for being a nosey reporter, but I'm curious about the connection between you and Misty. Are you a relative…a boyfriend? And how do you feel about Misty's new ability?"

Brick ignored the reporter's questions and asked Misty, "What kind of story is she writing?" He glared at the photographer, who had resumed taking pictures of Misty. "Chill, man. Put that camera away for a minute."

Not sure if he should listen to Brick, the photographer looked at the reporter, waiting for her instructions.

Sharon held up a hand. "We probably have enough pictures, Jack. Let's pack it up."

"You want to tell me what's going on, Misty?" Brick pulled up a chair next to Misty's bed.

"Something big. We'll talk after they leave, okay?"

Sharon stuffed her recorder and notepad inside her handbag. "The story should be featured in Friday's edition. I'll be in touch if I need more information."

"Cool. I'm excited about sharing my experiences," Misty said and then turned her attention to Jack. "Are you sure it's a good idea to use my photo in the piece? My face is so damaged; I'm not comfortable being seen like this. Can't you use one of the old pictures I gave you? You know, to let people see how I looked before my face got jacked up?"

"The plan is to put an old photo next to a current one, to garner sympathy, and get some donations pouring in," Sharon said. "The way you've triumphed over tragedy and then survived a coma after trying to end your life is a great, human interest piece. The psychic aspect of the story will fascinate readers."

Brick groaned in frustration. "What psychic aspect? Will somebody tell me what's going on?"

"I'll let Misty fill you in; I have to get back to my desk and start working on the story," Sharon said. With a sense of purpose, she made her way to the door with the photographer lugging his equipment as he trailed behind her.

Alone with Misty, Brick asked, "How'd you turn into a media sensation, overnight?"

"You'll never guess." Misty grinned mischievously.

"I don't feel like playing guessing games. Are you gonna shed some light on the subject? When I left last night, you were feeling sorry for yourself. Now you're grinning like a Cheshire cat. What are you up to?"

"Why do I have to be up to something?"

"Because that's how you do. After all you've been through, please don't tell me you're back to your old tricks."

"Don't be so quick to judge until you hear what happened."

"I'm listening."

"Early this morning, when the nurse woke me up to give me my meds and to take my vital signs, something weird happened."

"Weird, like what?"

"Her palm accidentally brushed against mine, and there was a strange, stinging sensation—popping and crackling—like static when two pieces of fabric connect."

Brick frowned in bewilderment.

"It's hard to explain. It's like, we both felt it, but didn't understand what had happened. The nurse gawked at the blood pressure cuff, as if it had caused the shock. Then she started fiddling with it, and that's when I started seeing this fast-moving video slideshow of her life."

"Where'd you see it—on the wall?"

Misty shook her head. "Images from her life were playing inside my mind. I was able to tell her all sorts of personal information about herself."

"That's crazy."

"It's the truth, and she was in tears by the time I finished reading her."

"Reading her?"

"Yeah, I gave her a psychic reading."

Brick scoffed. "You're not psychic."

"Apparently, I am. The nurse is in her late forties, and I was able to see scenes from her childhood and teen years."

Brick shook his head doubtfully.

"And get this…I even saw her future."

"You shouldn't have messed with that nurse's head like that."

"I'm telling the truth! In my mind, I saw the nurse getting out of a dark SUV and walking toward this cute little house with white siding and blue shutters. There were shrubs and big, yellow sunflowers in front of the house."

"You were imagining things."

"No, I saw that nurse's future. She had on white pants and an orange and white striped top. There were keys dangling in her hand. I knew the house couldn't have been in Philly because I saw a wooden walkway leading to sand and water."

With his eyebrows drawn together tightly, Brick asked, "What else did you see?"

"That's it. But when I told her details about the house, she got excited. She said she'd been looking at property at the shore, and the house I described sounded like a house she fell in love with, but it was out of her price range. She'd tried to get the owners to lower the cost, but she wasn't successful."

"So, what does that prove?"

"It proves that she's going to move into the house of her dreams. She said she doesn't own an outfit like the one I saw in my vision, but that's only a minor glitch in my story."

"I think it proves that you're not actually seeing the future," Brick reasoned.

Misty rolled her eyes. "Why are you being so negative? I know what I saw, Brick; I'm not making this up. Anyway, the nurse said she's read about people coming out of comas with newfound psychic abilities. She was so excited, she called a journalist friend of hers. She asked her to interview me, and as you already know, the reporter I introduced you to is going to write a feature story about me. It's gonna begin with the tragic night that a hater brutally attacked me and left me for dead, and it'll end with me waking up from the coma with the ability to prophesize the future."

Brick shook his head apprehensively. "Are you seriously going to allow people to believe you can predict the future?"

"Yes, because it's true. The reporter said I'll probably start getting a lot of donations when people read about my misfortune. I'm hoping to turn this into something much bigger than mere donations."

"So, the old Misty is back with a brand-new hustle," Brick said sarcastically.

"You're making it sound like I'm going to be scamming people. I came out of that coma with a gift and there's nothing wrong with profiting from it."

"Are you planning to set up shop with a crystal ball and a deck of tarot cards?"

"Think bigger, Brick! First, I need to get my appearance up to par. Get some cosmetic surgery on my face so I can look good—you know, for my clients and also for you."

"I'm not worried about how you look. I told you you're beautiful to me exactly the way you are."

"That's sweet, but I want cosmetic surgery. When I look in the mirror, I want to smile at my reflection, not cringe."

"When you were staying at your mom's house, you told me you didn't care about your appearance anymore. You said you were through with material things and uninterested in earthly pleasures."

"That's because I was planning on killing myself, but if I have to live in this world, then I don't want to look like a monster."

"You don't look like a monster, babe."

"Yes, I do. It's bad enough that I'll never be able to walk again, but having to live with a hideous face is too much for anyone to deal with and not lose their mind."

Brick squeezed her hand reassuringly. "I accept you. Why can't you accept yourself?"

"You didn't turn down cosmetic surgery when my mother offered to get the scar removed from your face, so stop being a hypocrite."

Brick laughed. "Wow, like old times, you're still running off at the mouth. I get that you want to look like your old self, but I'm skeptical about this psychic thing."

"Why do you think I'm lying about being psychic?" Misty asked.

"I'm not saying you're lying, but maybe your mind was playing tricks on you."

"Remember what I told you about being with Shane…around the time I convinced you to help me kill myself?"

A shadow fell across Brick's face. "I don't want to think about that. Those were dark days. At first I thought I had killed you, and after your mom revived you, she wanted me locked up for attempted murder. If you hadn't pulled through, I'd be spending the rest of my life in jail."

"Well, I did pull through, and I'll tell anybody who thinks about accusing you of anything that I took those pills on my own."

"We both know that I helped you try to end your life, Misty," Brick said with a grave expression.

"And no one needs to know. That's between you and me."

"Getting back to this psychic stuff, do you really want the spotlight on you when you should be focused on recovering?"

"I need to focus on something other than lying in bed for the rest of my life."

"You're not going to be confined to bed. I'm going to get you one of those motorized wheelchairs."

"Am I supposed to be happy at the prospect of getting around in a wheelchair? My life is fucked and we both know it; give me some credit for trying to be self-reliant."

"You don't have anything to worry about; I'm gonna take care of you."

"I don't want to have to rely on anyone other than myself. This is a chance for me to lead a productive life and be useful; I don't want to miss the opportunity. So, stop being negative and support me in what I'm trying to do."

"What exactly are you trying to do?"

"With the media coverage, I'll be able to attract clients. Eventually, I'd like to do seminars and group readings. I want to write books…maybe get a TV show. Psychics make a lot of money."

Brick looked at Misty with pity in his eyes. "I don't want you to set yourself up for disappointment. Suppose last night was only a fluke?"

"It wasn't a fluke. Like I was saying, before I came out of the coma, the last thing Shane told me was that I had to come back here so I could touch people's lives."

"Shane is dead; I'm never gonna believe you were actually with him."

"Believe what you want. I know we were together, and I know what he told me."

Brick glanced down at his hand, which was resting gently on hers. "Our hands are touching; do you see my life flashing in your mind?"

"No, but that's probably because I already know everything about you."